345

GLORY HOLE

William MacLeod Raine

GLORY HOLE

Thorndike Press · Thorndike, Maine

Library of Congress Cataloging-in-Publication Data:

Raine, William MacLeod, 1871–1954.
   Glory Hole / William MacLeod Raine.
     p.   cm.
   In large print..
   ISBN 0-89621-829-5 (lg. print : alk. paper)
   1. Large type books. I. Title.
[PS3535.A385G55   1987]
813'.52—dc 19   87-15635
                                                                        CIP

Copyright © 1951 by William MacLeod Raine.
All rights reserved.

Large Print edition available in North America by arrangement with Houghton Mifflin Company, Boston.

Cover design by James B. Murray.

To Claire Raine
"While the Sands o' Life Shall Run."

1

A big rangy man in the late forties with the weatherbeaten look of one who has lived long on the frontier turned in at the Windsor Hotel and walked to the office counter. The spruce clerk stopped picking his gold-sprinkled teeth with a quill and swung the register around. Before signing as a guest the new arrival let his eye travel down the page to check on recent entries. The point of the pen came to a halt opposite a name.

"Henry Page still here?" he asked.

The clerk checked the record. "Third floor. Room Three-eighteen."

"I'll be moving in with him," the stranger said, and wrote on the register, John Taggart, Leadville.

The man back of the counter was not so sure about that. "I'll have to ask Mr. Page whether that is agreeable to him," he replied.

"It will be agreeable," Taggart answered with quiet assurance.

The room clerk was a little annoyed. Henry Page might be a tenderfoot, but he was well dressd, neat, a man apparently used to the best and willing to pay for it. This person who called himself Taggart wore scuffed boots with the dried mud still on them, stained jean trousers, and a wide-brimmed black hat the worse for wear. His upper lip was clean-shaven, but a grizzled beard covered the lower part of his face. From the corners of keen gray eyes tiny wrinkles spread, etched into the strong tanned face by the untempered sun of the high lands. The man looked self-reliant and there was a certain note of authority in him. The mining camps and the ranches of Colorado held many enough like him to be his own blood brothers. But though the clerk would not have admitted it, he felt superior to those close to the soil. Men like Page, suggesting wealth and family, were much more his dish.

"I could send up and let Mr. Page know you are here," he demurred.

Taggart picked up his valise. "I won't trouble you. I'll let him know myself. Have a boy show me up."

A bellhop in a bright new uniform took him to the elevator. As yet there were only a few elevators in Denver, but the Windsor had three of them. The hotel was new, advertised as the finest hostelry between Chicago and San Francisco. Already its cuisine was celebrated. The best wines and delicacies were brought from New York and the variety of game offered was unequaled in the country. Taggart followed the boy along a corridor, his feet sinking into an Axminster carpet.

At 318 the boy knocked on the door. A pleasant voice called "Come in." Taggart dismissed the boy, opened the door, and closed it behind him. A young man in his shirt sleeves was rising from the bed upon which he had been lying. The sun slanting through the west window lit up his blond wavy hair and gave the tips a golden hue. He was a slender man, perhaps twenty-three, and the good fit of his tweeds showed the well-knit light figure to advantage. The eyes were brown and the bone structure of the face finely modeled. If there was any weakness it lay in the mouth, which gave Taggart an impression of self-indulgence, though the sheriff was not sure this feeling did not arise partly from the luxury of the room furnishings. For the sardonic gaze of the officer had taken in the Wilton carpet, the handsomely carved walnut bed and dressing table, and the satin curtains trimmed with old gold brocade that draped the long windows. It occurred to him that this young man was likely to spend the next fifteen or twenty years of his life in surroundings very different.

Page guessed the reaction of the sheriff. "A bit elaborate," he agreed, "but the only vacant room when I arrived. Don't blame me because the silver mines are booming Denver."

Taggart flung his hat on the dresser, put down the valise, and lit a cigar. He guessed that the hint of defiance in his prisoner did not go very deep. Page was probably feeling pretty sorry for himself. The sheriff did not blame him for that. Through poor judgment he had got himself in a bad jam, and his fiber was too soft to take this stoically.

"Haven't had a bite to eat since breakfast," the sheriff said. "What say we go down and see how the grub assays in this shebang? Then I can brag all the rest of my life that I once was one of the Windsor Hotel crowd."

He smiled, to mitigate the criticism, and offered a cigar to his companion. Page declined, quite courteously. He smoked expensive cigars or none at all. Until recently he had been in a position to disregard cost and his taste was for the best. He still found it hard to realize, in a world which had handed him some hard knocks, that he was no longer a favored child of Providence. This ought not to have happened to him.

It was Taggart's opinion that Page was a bit of a fool. After the shooting when he had escaped to Denver he could have jumped a train for the East. The law would not have pursued him, since Leadville was a hotbed of crime where the officers were too busy to hunt down criminals who had got away. Instead of keeping on the move he had sent word to the sheriff to come and get him, though he must have known how strong the feeling in the cloud city was against lot and claim jumpers.

"What was the idea in lighting out and then giving yoreself up?" Taggart asked.

"I decided I didn't want to be a fugitive all the rest of my life," Page said curtly. He did not care to discuss his motives with the man who would presently put the handcuffs on him.

"There are a dozen killings in the camp every month," Taggart remarked. "And even more holdups. As I walked uptown to take the stage for Denver I met three men out on bail for murder. None of them will be convicted. But you had to pick out Bert Vining to kill. You'll probably be sent to Cañon City for ten years. It don't make sense to pull yore freight and not keep going."

"Nothing I have done makes sense," Page said bitterly.

"I didn't more than half expect to find you here. Thought likely you might change yore mind." Taggart wished he had. The setup was one he did not like. In Leadville claim-jumping was a more serious crime than murder and young Page was guilty of both. Recently two men had been hanged by a mob, one of them a holdup and the other a claim jumper. If the scalawags around Tiger Alley became excited they might break into the ramshackle jail and put a rope around this tenderfoot's neck. In the town were hundreds of worse men than Page, but that would have no weight. The factors that in his home town might have counted in his favor — education, class, personality and speech — would tell against him with the riff-raff. To them his alien superiority, the touch of unconscious insolence that marked him, would be like a red rag to an infuriated bull. They would not see him as just a boy in trouble.

Taggart brushed aside his sympathies. He was sheriff of the county and his duty came first with him.

"Are you likely to panic again and try a bolt?" he asked his prisoner.

"I'm going to see it through," the young man answered doggedly. "What I did was in self-defense."

"I hope you can prove that. The point I am getting at is that if you will give me yore word not to try to escape I won't put the cuffs on you in public."

"Much obliged, Sheriff," Page said. "I won't make you any trouble."

"You would only be making trouble for yoreself," Taggart differed. "I would cut you down before you had got a dozen yards. That's not a threat. I'm not expecting you to try anything foolish."

Page smiled bitterly. "Not a threat, only a promise."

"I'd better wash up for supper," Taggart suggested.

He removed his coat and unfastened the scabbard that held the revolver under his arm. This he put on a chair close to the washstand. From the ewer he poured water into the bowl. In spite of his worn, soiled clothes he was a cleanly man and gave neck, face, and hands a thorough scrubbing. With a comb taken from his vest pocket he combed his hair carefully, the wet firelock plastered in a quarter-moon on his forehead in the prevailing barbershop fashion.

The headwaiter ushered him and his prisoner to a small table halfway down the dining room and handed each of them a menu in a silver frame. If Taggart was impressed he did not show it. He did not look at the food list.

"I want a good steak smothered in onions and hash-brown potatoes," he said. "And plenty of coffee."

Page was not interested in food. The troubled future lay too heavily on his mind. He ordered mountain trout, the first item his eyes met, and with it a small bottle of Barsac.

The gaze of Taggart roamed around the overdecorated room. "It's sure a tony hotel," he commented. "I don't know as I ever was in a more elegant one. Must eat and sleep three or four hundred."

His roving eyes fastened on one of two women seated at a table to the left and back of them. "I'll be doggoned if it ain't Erma Roberts." The sheriff rose. "Stay right where you're at," he told his companion, and moved across the floor to greet the woman he had recognized.

Erma Roberts was the favorite variety actress of Leadville. Though she was well into her thirties and had begun to take on a double chin and the middle-aged spread, she was still a good-looking woman. Both kind and shrewd, she had acquired some of the blunt roughness of surface necessary to make her popular in the mining camps of the West.

She said, "Hello, John. Meet Miss Joan Regal. She's starting up tomorrow to get a touch of high life at Leadville. Don't get me wrong. I'm meaning only the altitude. Miss Regal, meet Sheriff Taggart."

The sheriff did not need Erma's modifying explanation to know that this young woman was not the dance-hall type. She was young, not over eighteen he judged, and her lovely violet eyes looked up at him shyly from under thick long lashes. The planes of her face and the bone conformation were very attractive, framed in dark hair parted in the middle and gathered into a chignon at the back. A blue print dress fitted snugly the trim figure with the small high breasts. She looked well in it, though the costume was neither new nor expensive. A tear in the waist had been beautifully mended with neat small stitches.

The sheriff said he was glad to meet Miss Regal and he hoped she would like Leadville, the greatest mining town under God's green footstool. Joan murmured in a low voice, a little husky, that she was sure she would.

Henry Page was used to the incongruities of the West, but in spite of his preoccupation with his own troubles a curiosity stirred in him about the relationship of these two women who looked so unlike. The rather flamboyant appearance of the older one was saved from an overstress of sex by the friendly warmth of her honest face, but she seemed a strange companion for the virginal young creature who might have just emerged from a sheltered existence in a small eastern town.

After Taggart returned to eat his smothered steak and hash-browned potatoes he explained that Miss Roberts was returning from a tour of the Montana and Nevada mining camps to join the company at the Grand Central Theater, which had recently been built on the site of Billy Nuttall's Théâtre Comique. She had scored a big hit at Billy's place and was sure to do as well at the more elaborate Grand Central. Erma had what it took to pack them in the aisles. The young lady with her was going up to the silver camp to join a brother living there. She and Erma had met a few hours earlier at the hotel for the first time. Miss Regal had not heard from her brother for several months and was worried about him.

"Wanted to know if I had met him," Taggart said. "I had to explain there are five thousand young fellows milling around in the camp and I hadn't met but a few of them."

Page hoped she would find him. Her lovely youth was not fit to cope with the raw, rough life of this riproaring mining town.

★

Taggart locked the door and put the key in his pocket. He frowned in uncertainty at his prisoner. "I ought to fasten yore wrist to mine with the cuffs while we sleep."

"Suit yourself," Page answered shortly. He knew there was no sense in being ungracious. The sheriff was making the situation as easy for him as he could, yet it was always in the undercurrent of the young man's thoughts that he was being dragged back to the penitentiary or the gallows. He had to be brusque to keep from voicing self-pity.

"It would be mighty uncomfortable for both of us," Taggart commented. "You would be right foolish to pull any shenanigan now. I sleep light. Now, if you'll give me yore word not to try to escape I won't shackle you."

"I've already given you my word," Page said, an edge of resentment in his voice. "Take it or leave it. I could have been in Chicago by this time if I hadn't made up my mind to go back."

Taggart shrugged his shoulders. He turned out the light and got into bed beside his prisoner. Within five minutes he was snoring. It was well on toward morning before his bed mate fell into troubled sleep. The tangled web of his life, what he had done and its consequences, raced in pictures unhappily through his mind. At best he was going to be shut up from the world like a dangerous animal unsafe to leave at large. His thoughts had become a treadmill that wore him out.

Two of the six hotel guests who got into the depot coach after breakfast were the women Taggart had met the evening before. The coach rolled down Larimer Street over the cobblestones to the lower Cherry Creek bridge and to the station in West Denver from which the narrow-gauge train started for the mountains.

Already the cars of the train were pretty well filled but from the two seats facing each other at the rear of the last car a brakeman tossed out a dozen pieces of baggage to make room for the sheriff, his prisoner, and the two women. Taggart put Page next the window opposite Joan Regal. He himself chatted with Miss Roberts about her Montana trip. Occasionally he joined in the talk of the four men seated across the aisle. One of them had his arm in splints. He had broken it and three ribs in a fall down a fourteen-foot upraise. Cheerfully he admitted that he had not a dollar to fly with and that the shaft of his mine was down only forty feet, but he was buoyantly sure that he was on his way to carbonates or China. The words they used had no meaning for Joan. She did not know that carbonates meant wealth; and apex, lode, drift, cross-cut, and float were terms that conveyed no more to her than Greek.

The conductor shouted "A-ll aboard," and the wheels began to turn. Miss Roberts reminded the sheriff that he had not introduced his friend. She smiled at the morose young man. "Is he deaf and dumb — or just shy?"

The shaven upper lip of the officer was grim. "His name is Henry Page. You couldn't rightly call us friends. He is my prisoner."

Erma was not shocked. She had spent a year in Leadville. "Goodness, me!" she exclaimed. "What's he done? It can't be very bad, or you wouldn't have arrested him."

"Now looky here, Miss Roberts," Taggart protested, grinning at her dig. "That's no way to talk. Leadville is skittish you might say, because it is young and full of pep, but one of these days we are going to make it a nice quiet city. Answering yore question, this young man is accused of claim-jumping and murder."

Page watched the eyes of the young woman opposite him grow big with startled dismay. He thought bitterly, *All good women are going to look at me like that from now, as if I were a dangerous wild beast.*

The actress said promptly, "He doesn't look bad to me. I'll bet it was some scoundrel he got. Your town is full of people that need killing, Sheriff. Don't tell me it isn't."

Henry Page needed cheering more than at any time before in his easy life. The words touched him deeply. He said, his voice a little ragged, "Miss Roberts, I'll always remember your kindness."

"According to an old hymn we used to sing, we are all vile sinners," Erma replied lightly. "Fact is, most of us have a big streak of good in the bad. You too, young man. Let's hear your story."

Page felt bitterly that he was the victim of injustice. He had not meant to talk, but to his surprise he found himself telling the tale of his undoing. A month earlier he had come to the camp, a mining engineer looking for an opportunity in this fabulous silver district. From a squatter he had bought a claim on Fryer Hill. A gang of thugs had contested his right of possession and had given him twenty-four hours to vacate peaceably. They were employed by the Vining brothers, gamblers who owned a notorious place called the Silver Palace. He had gone to them and been told that he had jumped their claim. They had bought the property six weeks earlier from

Jeff Reed, the original owner. His explanation had been brushed aside coldly. They had given him an ultimatum and if he wanted to live he had better get off the Sally McGee. Young Page had made the mistake of thinking the gamblers were bluffing. Armed with a Colt .45, he had slept in his blankets on the claim. During the night he was attacked by five or six men. His answering fire had killed one of them, young Bert Vining. Without friends in the town, Page found himself faced with a charge of murder he had no evidence to refute. His enemies were powerful and ruthless. He had hidden in a prospect hole and left town after dark with a freight outfit. Later he had decided to return and face the charge. To run away would leave his reputation clouded for life.

Erma turned to the sheriff. "Sounds like a straight story, John," she said.

Taggart agreed with her but did not say so. He did not care to line up against him enemies as powerful as the Vinings. Yet he was an honest man. "I don't know the facts," he said. "The Vinings have recorded a quit-claim deed from Jeff Reed. They claim Page was the attacker. They will show evidence to that effect true or false."

"It will be false," Erma decided promptly.

"You know the Vining crowd, a bunch of crooks. We'll get the best lawyer in town and he will clear Mr. Page. We'll get Ted Downing."

The sheriff did not think it would be that easy, but he did not say so. Nor did the prisoner share the optimism of the actress. There were political undercurrents involved that would run against him. Just now he was preoccupied with another angle of his case. His unhappy eyes were fixed on Joan Regal. She had not spoken a word since Taggart had explained their relationship but she had listened intently. He wondered what judgment she was passing on him. For the moment she represented all the young girls with whom he had danced and played tennis, all the gay careless friendships wiped out when he put the brand of Cain on himself. Did she think he was beyond the pale, an outcast whose life could not possibly touch hers?

The train was moving through the foothills toward the front range that rose sharp and clear before them. It left open country and entered Platte Cañon, a narrow defile where the track twisted and turned like a snake. From the window Joan could see the engine puffing its way along the stream that paralleled the railroad. Here and there the gorge widened to small green parks filled with autumn color, the scrub oaks a blaze of red and the aspens in the draw a golden glow.

In one of these the train slowed to a halt. After a short wait a brakeman announced that the engine had a hotbox and they would be delayed half an hour. Men poured out of the stuffy car into the open air. A big red-shirted bearded miner pulled up with a whoop at sight of the actress. His face was flushed from drink.

"It's Erma Roberts, boys," he shouted. "We'll have her do a turn right damn now." He drew from his pocket four or five gold pieces and jingled them in front of her.

She waved him aside good-naturedly. "Put up your money, Jack Ferguson. You can hear me for a dollar at the Grand Central tomorrow night."

He dumped the gold pieces on her lap. "I want to hear 'The Bogie Man' now. You've been away six months and we've missed you. Come on, Erma, and be a good fellow."

The actress was used to the open-handed vagaries of the mining camps. Seventy golden dollars were not to be scorned.

"All right, Jock, if you want it that way. Pass the word around so that the boys will be quiet and listen." After he had plowed his way out of the car, Erma explained to Joan. "He made a big strike a few months ago and has money to throw at the birds. I might as well help him get rid of it."

A clerk employed in one of the Leadville smelters was called into service to play an accompaniment on a mouth organ. When Erma appeared on the rear platform the crowd greeted her with cheers and applause. Joan stood on the lower step, the sheriff and his prisoner close at hand.

"What will it be, boys?" Erma asked.

" 'The Bogie Man' first," Ferguson shouted.

Like all the top variety actresses Erma put into her turn verve and plenty of action. The mining camps did not want nuances but heartiness. She did little dance steps between the verses and combined with her singing a lot of facial expression and illustrative gestures. When she came to the chorus she walked up and down the platform leading her audience in the words.

> "*Oh, whist, whist, whist, here comes the bogie man;*
> *Now go to bed, you baby — you Tommy, Nell, and Dan;*
> *Oh, whist, whist, whist, he'll catch you if he can,*

*And all the popseys, wopseys, wop run
from the bogie man."*

They made her sing the whole song again, then began calling for their favorites. Erma did not forget who was paying for the entertainment and took pains to catch Ferguson's nod of approval before she began each selection.

She gave them "Biddy Doyle," using an umbrella for a shillelagh, imitating cleverly the Irish brogue.

*"What will you do at all
When the snows begin to fall,
With your back agin the wall,
Biddy Doyle?"*

Her audience clamored for more songs. She gave encores generously and was relieved when at last the engineer blew the whistle as a signal the train was about to start.

The engine puffed laboriously up Kenesaw Mountain and from the summit dropped down a sharp grade into South Park. At Red Hill the passengers transferred to wagons and stages. They met fifty outfits engaged in returning from Leadville to which they had been hauling supplies. By the roadside lay the bodies of scores of horses and mules from which a strong stench arose. Taggart explained that these animals had been brought from the Middle States to haul the heavy wagons containing supplies for the silver camp. Unaccustomed to the altitude the horses broke down under the work, had hemorrhages, and died quickly.

Joan pointed to a mound with a wooden cross over it. "Isn't that a grave?" she asked.

"Yes, miss," Taggart replied. "Humans break down too. Between Denver and Leadville there are a heap of those graves, mostly of tenderfeet who tried to pack big loads on foot or else got caught in blizzards. This is a he-man's country with the bark on, Miss Regal. It's no place for softies. They curl up and wither. But you don't need to be scared. A good woman is as safe here as if she was in God's pocket."

At Fair Play they stopped while the driver put on an extra brake shoe before beginning the stiff ascent to Mosquito Pass. The passengers got out to stretch their legs. A slender, graceful man wearing a white broad-brimmed hat and a Prince Albert coat of broadcloth stepped forward from the station, nodded coldly to the prisoner, and drew the sheriff to one side. He evidently had something important to say, for the two men had a low-voiced conversation that lasted for several minutes.

Erma noted them with some curiosity. "I wonder what brought Cape Wallace down here," she said.

"Who is he?" Joan asked. She had noticed how lightly and with what smooth-muscled co-ordination the man walked.

"A gambler," the actress answered. "Probably the best dressed man in Leadville. He works at the Texas House. Everybody knows him — and nobody knows him. He goes his own way, a lone wolf. Of course his profession bars him from meeting any good women."

At the end of the platform the women turned and passed the two men again.

"He has a cold face without any expression in it," Joan commented.

"That may be his professional mask," Erma guessed. "His eyes have life in them. They are reckless and devil-may-care."

When the driver called "All aboard" the gambler took the seat on the box next him. Joan observed that though Wallace had stood beside them while some packages were being lashed on top of the stage the sheriff had not introduced him.

A frisky near-wheeler cut a few didoes as they started. Joan was nervous.

"If the road is as dangerous as they say, do you think it is quite safe to use a wild horse?" she asked the sheriff.

"It will be tame enough before we have gone a quarter of a mile," Taggart told her.

"I heard a man at the station say the stage was robbed night before last," she mentioned.

"Passengers don't get hurt in holdups," the officer explained. "Road agents would be very polite to you. They don't rob women."

The girl did not enjoy the trip over the pass. Her imagination had built up this journey to a perilous adventure. As they got higher it grew colder and the wind blew in fierce, shrill gusts. The angles of the ledge turns were sharp and the lead horses seemed to be walking off the precipice into space. She dared not look down at the gulf of darkness that dropped from the edge of the narrow road. Each new stretch appeared more hazardous. The worst moments were when they met freighters coming down and had to take the outside of the shelf.

A six-mule wagon outfit came face to face with the stage near the head of the pass. The boss of the freighters consulted with the driver of the Concord. All the passengers were ordered out. The bed of the road was a rock slope coated with ice and there was scant room to pass. If the wheels of the stage slipped a few inches it would go over the edge. Ropes were attached to the springs and all the men including Page hung on to them while the driver of the mules negotiated the lane close to the overhanging wall. To add to Joan's fears a sixty-mile gale was screaming down from the summit.

The gambler was standing near Joan while the stage was being moved back from the edge to the middle of the road. Her frightened eyes met his. He said casually to Taggart, "We're past the worst of it now." Joan was grateful. She knew it had been a message of comfort for her.

From the head of the pass they drove across the flats and stopped at a ranch house. The sheriff, his prisoner, and the gambler left the stage.

Miss Roberts was surprised. "Aren't you going to town?" she asked the sheriff.

Taggart said curtly, "Not tonight."

Erma had a farewell word for Page. "Don't get downhearted. We'll get Ted Downing for your lawyer and he will pull you through."

Joan murmured in her low husky voice, "We'll pray for you."

It was the first time she had spoken to Page. A lump swelled up in his throat. This was the last time he would hear friendly words or see a sympathetic face. From this hour he would be under lock and key, herded with criminals and felons, until the day they brought him out to meet the judgment awaiting him.

2

It was nearly midnight when the stage topped the hill from which they could look down on the lights of Leadville. Out of dance halls and theaters the blare of music beat out into the night. The smelters were belching flames and below them ran refuse slag like rivers of fire. Chestnut Street was crowded with ore wagons, freight outfits, and burro trains loaded with supplies for outlying camps, and the sidewalks were jammed with men going in and out of saloons and gaming places. Kerosene flares advertised in front of each establishment its entertainment. A night shift of carpenters was working on the skeleton of a new bank building, and the sound of the saws and hammers blended with the shouts of drunken miners, the rattle of chips, and the occasional boom of a shot racketing down the street.

The scene appalled Joan. "What are so many men doing out so late at night?" she asked.

"This is only the shank of the evening in Leadville," Erma told her. "There is no night in this town, especially on Saturdays. The miners are all here blowing in their wages."

"Don't they ever sleep?" the girl said, puzzled.

"Tomorrow is Sunday," the actress explained. "They can sleep all day then, if they can find beds. Hundreds of them are rented three shifts every twenty-four hours. One man tumbles in when the preceding one is roused. Newcomers sleep on the floors of saloons or freeze in packing boxes."

The stage made a path through the traffic and drew up at its station. A crowd had gathered to wait for its arrival. About a dozen of them pushed to the front. Angry shouts filled the air.

"Bring the bastard out, Sheriff," a raucous voice cried. "We'll take care of him right now."

Joan shrank against the shoulder of the actress as the door was wrenched open.

"Where's he at, Hank?" demanded the leader of the group, a big bearded heavy-set man with a face, as Erma put it later, ugly as galvanized sin.

The driver, Hank Foley, set the brake and came down from his seat. "If it's Page you're lookin' for, why Taggart got off with him a dozen miles back, Mr. Vining."

"Got off," Ben Vining repeated. "God-almighty, what for?"

"I dunno. He didn't tell me why. When they got far as the Baxter ranch Taggart said they weren't going any farther."

Vining ripped out a furious oath. A man back of him shook a lifted fist and cried, "We'll git him yet."

Erma spoke tartly. "If you'll kindly let us out, Mr. Vining."

The big man stepped aside. "Sure, Miss Roberts. We don't aim to bother you any. It's that killer Page we want."

Joan followed the actress out of the stage. A panic fear choked her throat. In the placid world she had left men like these did not exist. She asked in a small voice, her teeth chattering, "What shall I do? I wrote my brother to meet me and he isn't here."

"Don't worry about that," Erma told her cheerfully. "We'll find him tomorrow. Tonight we'll put up at the Grand. Tom Walsh has a room reserved for me." Her gaze searched the outskirts of the crowd and chose two men. "Bob, if you and Mose aren't too busy playing you are the law maybe you could find time to escort two ladies to their hotel."

The men pushed forward and picked up the valises Erma pointed out. "Glad to see you back, Miss Roberts," one of them said. "Me and Mose aren't in this welcome party of Mr. Vining."

Joan clung to Erma's arm as they moved down the sidewalk crowded with drifting men. Her companion comforted the girl. "Don't be afraid, dearie. Any one of them would fight at the drop of the hat to keep you from being insulted."

Except for the Clarendon the Grand was the leading hotel in town. The room reserved for Erma was on the third floor, a dormer apartment facing Chestnut Street. It was clean and the double bed comfortable.

The actress threw off her coat. "You're dead tired after the long day," she said. "What you need is sleep."

Fear still stared out of Joan's eyes. "They were waiting there to — to kill Henry Page," she cried softly.

"Yes. But they didn't get him — and they won't. Trust John Taggart for that. Cape Wallace must have found out what they meant to do and took the stage for Fair Play to warn John."

"It's a terrible place," Joan wailed.

"There are nine good citizens here for every

bad one," Erma replied staunchly. "Now go to bed, girlie, and forget about Page. He'll come through all right."

Joan fell asleep as soon as her head sank into the pillow. Once during the small hours she was awakened by the sound of group singing. Startled, she sat up. The voices were so near she thought for a moment they were at her bedside.

Snatched from sleep, Erma said drowsily, "What's the matter?"

"I dreamed they were singing at the bedside."

The actress listened. She recognized the song, "Men of Harlech." "Welsh miners — probably drunk," she explained.

Joan went to the window and looked out. The first faint streaks of day were sifting into the sky. Though the song had died down, the music of the bands from the honky-tonks on State Street beat across to her. Nearer was another sound, the steady thump-thump of feet on the sidewalk. The pack of men shifting to and fro was almost as dense as when the stage had arrived.

Joan crept back into the warm bed and dropped back into sleep. When she opened her eyes again the sun was sending its warm rays across the room into them.

The dining room was closed before they reached it, but the proprietor waved to them to come in and eat. Tom Walsh was a pleasant, unassuming man, and in his wildest dreams it could never have occurred to him that he was soon to become a multimillionaire, the friend and partner of the King of Belgium, and that his daughter would be the owner of the Hope diamond.

While they ate breakfast the women consulted as to the best way to find Jim Regal. Erma suggested they go to the post office and find if the letters Joan had written her brother had ever been called for.

"But they would have been sent to the dead-letter office," Joan said.

"Not from a town like Leadville where the population shifts so much. A man might be here one month and at Redcliff or Aspen the next, then back here again. The office would probably hold the mail unless asked to forward it."

Erma offered to go with Joan to the office. There would be a long line waiting in front of the windows. She knew Eric Johnson, the postmaster, and could get quick service. In her mind was another reason. It would distress Joan to walk the crowded streets alone with the eyes of dozens of men following her.

The actress had long lost her shyness. She had learned the knack of using men to wait on her needs.

Erma walked directly to the door marked private, knocked on it and said, "Let me in, Eric. It's Erma Roberts."

The door was opened at once. Johnson was a blond young Scandinavian. He held out both his hands to shake those of the actress. "Heard you were in town," he said. "We're tickled pink to see you back."

Erma introduced Joan and explained what she wanted. Inside of three minutes the girl had in her hands the letters she had written her brother.

"He never got them," Joan said unhappily. "Where can he be?"

The eyes of the postmaster and the older woman met. There were several possibilities. The most likely one was that Jim Regal had drifted out of town. But there were also more sinister ones. A good many men had come to the silver city, been around for a few days, and then disappeared. Most of these had moved to other camps or become discouraged and returned to their homes in the East. But a small percentage of them had met death for their money in Tiger or Stillborn Alleys and others had been murdered and their bodies dropped into abandoned prospect holes. Within the month the *Herald-Democrat* had come out with a front-page headline HELL LET LOOSE to call attention to four killings and one suicide on the same day.

"We'll find Jim for you," Erma promised Joan as they walked back to the hotel.

A crowd jamming the street in front of Pap Wyman's gambling house blocked the sidewalk. The air was full of angry threats focused on three horsemen facing the mob, their mounts backed against the wall. The rage of those on foot beat upon them with an impact almost physical. Cape Wallace and the sheriff flanked the rider in the center, Henry Page, from whose cheeks and lips fear had driven all color. He sat erect, motionless, but it was plain a cold icy claw had tied a knot in his stomach.

Erma's frightened eyes swept across the crowd. Some of them, she guessed, had been drawn here by curiosity to share in the excitement, but a score or more intent on a lynching were clamoring for the prisoner to be turned over to them. She recognized Ben Vining and one Sam Ukena, a ruffian in his employ.

Neither Taggart nor Wallace had drawn a weapon but the thumb of the sheriff's right hand was hitched in his belt close to the butt of the .44 resting in its holster.

"Take it easy, boys," he advised coolly. "This man is my prisoner and nobody is going to take him from me. He will be tried and if found guilty will be punished."

"Now you have said yore piece, Sheriff, nice and proper, you can turn the fellow over to us and you won't get hurt," Vining jeered.

As a law officer Taggart had played a part in the long battle for order that was still being waged on the frontier. He had faced mobs before and knew that to show weakness would be fatal. "Don't get ideas, Ben. Start anything and I'll put a slug in your belly."

The color in Vining's beefy face deepened to purple. "You're talkin' too big for your breeches to the folks who elected you. This fellow is a killer and we aim to stop his clock right damn now."

A ripple of movement flowed through the crowd, the preliminary warning of a forward surge.

"Hold it, Ben," Taggart called sharply. "I'll cut you down sure as you are a foot high."

His revolver came out and covered the leader. As if this had been a signal Wallace drew too.

Ukena shouted, "What chips you got in this game, Cape?"

"I'm sitting in as John's deputy — holding a six-full," Wallace retorted contemptuously. "Don't call it unless you have a better hand."

The women stood frozen in their tracks a few yards back from the outskirts of the pack. Without lifting his gaze from the furious upturned faces the Texas House croupier flung an order at them.

"You and your friend get out of here, Miss Roberts, before the massacre begins."

Men in the rear began to edge away. Erma drew Joan into the recess of an entrance to a building.

Vining modified his arrogance. He realized that neither the sheriff nor Wallace was bluffing. They would fight to protect the prisoner. "You're not showing a lick of sense, John," the mob leader snarled. "That's no way to talk to yore friends. We'll remember this, come election." He turned, raging, to Ukena. "Let's go, Sam. We'll take care of this murderer later."

The strain in the street lifted. Men began to talk of the affair as they moved away. In a few seconds the crowd had broken up and gone about the business of the day.

Joan said, the fear not yet lifted from her, "I didn't know men could be like that — so like wild beasts. It's terrible."

"Look at it the other way, dear," Erma advised. "You didn't know two brave men could face down the wild beasts. Henry Page will be safe now until the trial."

Erma set inquiries afoot. She was hail-fellow-well-met with many men in town. All classes of men liked her from the millionaire to the mine mucker, and they respected her for the barrier she set to her friendliness. Some of the rich and well-to-do had mistresses and others patronized women on the line. But in this wild camp where license prevailed it was understood that Erma Roberts was as untouchable as the good women who attended the Assembly Balls and served tea in the afternoons to their friends on delicate china.

She picked up her first lead from Cape Wallace. He sent her a formal note saying he had some information about Jim Regal she might like to hear. They met by appointment at the Ditch Walk just before noon. Erma watched him as he moved toward her with such easy grace. No man in the town was more sure of his manners. She wondered how many good women, barred from knowing him because of his profession, had been disturbed by the remoteness of his fine inscrutable eyes. Perhaps she was more drawn to him because an actress too was outside the conventional social circle, especially if she worked in a variety house.

Wallace had first become aware of young Regal as a patron at the roulette table over which he presided as croupier. The boy's dark good looks, combined with his recklessness and discontent, had attracted his attention. They had become acquainted at odd moments when business at the wheel was slack. Regal was an ore weigher and did not like the job. The croupier remembered the boy particularly because he had made a pun about the young fellow's job by misquoting a line of Milton's sonnet on his blindness, *They also serve who only stand and weigh it.* Next time Jim had come into the Texas House he had either lost or quit the position. He began to look hungry and shabby, then had spruced up remarkably in new clothes. At that time he was running with a man named Soapy Sills, a fellow of bad repute. Wallace had seen neither of them for six weeks.

This report on Jim distressed Erma. The inference was that he had gone bad. It was very likely. Scores of parasites in the district lived outside the law. She did not tell Joan what she had learned. It would do no good to frighten the girl with unproved suspicions.

Joan had other worries. She had brought with her only enough money for the journey and in a place like Leadville no work could be found suitable for a young woman well brought up and carefully chaperoned. Already she was living on money lent her by Erma.

A variety actor doing a jugglery turn at the Grand Central mentioned to Miss Roberts that since his assistant was getting married he needed a girl to take her place. All she was required to do was to hand him his props and join the patter of the act. Pierre Renaud was a very decent man, married and the father of two children. Erma did not think Joan would accept the position, since she would have to wear a boy's page suit of green velvet and would of course be blacklisted socially in the town. Since nobody knew her and she did not expect to stay long the loss of prestige seemed unimportant to the actress, but she knew Joan lived in another tradition. She would probably feel disgraced.

Joan's first reaction was shock. "Oh, I couldn't," she cried. "I just couldn't." At night she lay awake for hours worrying over her problem. Erma was generosity itself, but the girl's pride would not let her live off her friend. She knew now that her impression of all actresses being immoral was absurd. Next morning she told Erma that she would accept Renaud's offer. Yet her heart quaked at the thought.

Miss Roberts taught her how to walk across the stage and how to use her voice to make it carry to the audience. But Joan was so excited and shaky the first night that her words scarcely reached the first rows. In the page suit, though covered from head to foot, she felt naked. But she was so young, so pretty, so manifestly shy, that she took the fancy of the rough audience at once. Nobody heckled her and the applause was long and spontaneous. From the boxes a shower of silver was tossed to the stage.

As it turned out, Erma was the one badgered. She was singing "Biddy Doyle" and stood facing the house as if seeking an answer after putting the question.

> *"What will you do at all*
> *When the snows begin to fall,*
> *With your back agin the wall.*
> *Biddy Doyle?"*

A miner half-seas over leaned forward from a box and mimicked the actress. "Sure, there's room for the poor colleen in Peter Clancy's heart and under the roof of his shanty till the summer sun melts the snows."

Erma sang the next verse without paying any attention to him, but Clancy did not intend to be ignored.

"Tell her there's a spalpeen up Stray Horse Gulch just wasting away for little Biddy Doyle," he urged.

Not in the least embarrassed, Erma stepped over to the side of the stage nearest the box. She put her hands on her hips, arms akimbo, and still in character retorted in the Irish brogue, "I'll be tellin' her to waste no time on a drunken oaf like Peter Clancy after she has bounced a rolling pin off his thick skull."

This was the sort of repartee that Leadville understood. The house responded with a gale of laughter and cheers in which Peter himself joined boisterously.

As they were undressing in the room they had rented on the third floor of the Grand Central building Erma congratulated the girl on her debut. "They are going to like you and treat you well," she said. "They know you are a lady. Just keep your head high and proud, dearie."

"I was awf'ly frightened," she confessed, "and so embarrassed when they flung those dollars to me from the boxes."

Miss Roberts was sitting in front of a glass

removing the grease paint from her face. "How much was in the shower?" she asked.

"I don't know. I didn't count it. Of course I can't take their money. So I gave it to Pierre. He was so pleased."

Erma swung round on her stool. "But they didn't give it to Pierre. They gave it to you. With them it's hard come and easy go. It's their way of telling you they like you."

"I know," Joan said. "But I don't want to keep it. I wouldn't feel right about it."

Her friend understood the girl's reluctance. These same men showered their money on the harlots who lived on the line. Joan did not want in any way to be classed with them.

As Erma looked at Joan, this girl seemed to her the loveliest thing she had known. Erma had been married once and had longed greatly for the child that never came. In her mind she had adopted Joan. She herself had fought her way up and had toughened in the process, though in spirit she was still generous and kind. But Joan was just emerging from girlhood, eager to run forward and embrace life like a lover, unaware of the devastating blows the years must deal her.

All Erma's frustrated love went out to the girl transplanted from a protected home to this raw, bawdy town. She did not want Joan to have to fight and grow hard. She wanted her to stay gentle and fine and lovable. Yet she did not intend to let anybody impose on her. She would have a talk with Pierre. He was a decent little fellow, and he would realize it was not fair for him to garner all the harvest of Joan's popularity. As soon as Erma pressed the point he would agree to increase her salary.

3

Henry Page had come to Leadville against the advice of his father, a tight-lipped arrogant banker in Akron, Ohio, and now that he was caught in the net of a conspiracy he was stubbornly resolved to keep his plight a secret from his family at home. He would ask for no help, even though he was despondent and full of fear as to the issue. His heart was bitter, for his life was ruined by what he felt to be no fault of his own.

To Sheriff Taggart, who had dropped in for a friendly visit, he poured out his perplexity and his anger. What kind of a place was this, where an honest man standing up for his right could be trapped by scoundrels and destroyed?

Taggart sat on his cot and talked. He sketched the history of the camp from the old days when placer miners had washed gold in California Gulch and been hampered by the blackish-gray sand which clogged the riffles.

In time the placer diggings had played out and the ten thousand gold seekers had scattered over the earth. Now twice as many had returned to take their place, for it had been discovered that the heavy sand was rich with silver. From California Gulch the prospectors had pushed north across Stray Horse Gulch to Carbonate and Fryer hills where beneath the strata of silicified dolomite they found pay veins that already had made a dozen millionaires.

"The difficulty is, son, that a camp like this comes to life so quick that for a while the law can't catch up with it," the sheriff explained. "There are plenty of good people here, but there are also a lot of thugs, gamblers, prostitutes, and gunmen who come like buzzards to share in the rich pickings. Trouble is, the better citizens don't consider this their home. They are here to get rich in a hurry and then get out. So they don't stand up to the scalawags and face them down. They haven't time to waste in making the camp a good town. One of these days the bandits living in the gulches and the riffraff in Tiger and Stillborn Alleys will be cleaned out."

"And meanwhile they let me be sent to the penitentiary or be hanged," Page protested bitterly. "I paid Jeff Reed eleven thousand five hundred dollars for the Sally McGee. Along with two hired men I worked on an armstrong at the shaft. Not a word from the Vinings. They weren't interested until the Sonny Boy, the next claim to mine, struck a big vein of pay ore. Then they moved quick, because I was a tenderfoot with no influence. Was it my fault Bert Vining was killed while trying to jump my mine?"

Taggart knew this young man was not to blame. But the Vinings were a vindictive clan, closely knit together, and they would exact vengeance in full from the young engineer. Unfortunately they wielded a power few would care to challenge.

"Don't get too downhearted," the sheriff comforted. "You have a good friend in Erma Roberts. She has been working on Ted Downing to take your case. He is a good lawyer, sincere, knows how to talk to a jury. Ted is hanging back some, but I'll bet she gets him."

"Why doesn't he want the case?" Page asked.

"Probably busy." Taggart knew that was not the real answer. Anybody who defended Page effectively would make an enemy of the Vinings, since the only chance of an acquittal was to attack and discredit the gamblers. This would take courage, and a young lawyer establishing himself could not be blamed for side-stepping the anger of men supported by the whole lawless element of the town.

With the sheriff's permission Erma called at the jail next day, bringing with her a good supper from the Clarendon. Her friendly good cheer warmed the prisoner like fine wine. She brought good wishes from Joan and presently mentioned that Downing was outside and would talk with him if he wished.

Page liked Downing. The lawyer had heard the story from Erma and was in complete sympathy with the young man. There did not seem to be a great deal on which to hang a defense, but they talked the situation over at length. Erma felt sure Henry would be acquitted and assumed that if so he would at once leave the district before the Vinings could harm him.

Page did not correct her, but there was a core of stubbornness in him. He did not mean to let fear of them drive him out. He would stay and fight to regain his property. That, however, was wishful thinking since there was small chance of a favorable verdict. The Vinings were building a strong prejudice against him. Except his own word he had no proof that he had not led an attack on the gangsters.

Downing paced the floor of the cell, searching for a way out.

"If you had any powerful friends here to help," he suggested.

Page looked up from the cot where he was sitting. "I haven't any," he said. "The only man who knew me before I came is a cousin of mine, Cape Wallace. He was the black sheep of the family. Already he has saved my life after my father practically drove him out of town."

"Are you and he personally on good terms?"

The answer of the prisoner was bitter. "He doesn't want to have a thing to do with me. Can you blame him?"

Downing filed the information away for reference, though he did not see what good it would do them. The lawyer was a wiry red-headed man still under thirty. He was half-Irish and intolerant of injustice. Depression rode his shoulders as he walked downtown from the jail. In this topsy-turvy place no indignation could be aroused over the fate of a man nobody knew. It was every man for himself here. There could not be another spot in the world, he thought, so full of crazy inconsistencies. He passed the skeleton framework of a Presbyterian church rising next door to a *bagnio.* The evening lights were just coming on and a barker in front of the latter was shouting the charms of the "fallen doves" within. Through the window Downing could see the "herder" in a dirty white shirt emblazoned with a big diamond passing out pasteboard checks to girls entitled to them for drinks bought by their partners. The Little Church on the Corner, a saloon so named from its stained-glass windows, advertised Denver prices, two drinks for twenty-five cents. In one block he passed twelve gambling and drinking places, not counting two faro layouts in cigar stores.

He turned in at Pap Wyman's establishment. Three musicians were in the front window playing a violin, a harp, and a cornet. About a dozen games were going, including roulette, faro, chuck-a-luck, dice, stud and draw poker. Pap himself was in circulation, a short, powerfully built, florid man with a jovial manner. Pap boasted frequently that he employed none but pretty girls and that he ran a straight house. On a clock a sign was printed. "Please do not swear," and fastened to a stand by a chain was a large well-worn Bible. Another sign requested customers not to shoot the musicians as they were doing their damnedest.

The place was already filling rapidly. One of the customers at the bar was Quint Vining, a small neatly packed man with a white, impassive gambler's face. The light blue, shifting eyes were quick with life. He stood, apparently at negligent ease, a forearm resting on the bar and a foot on the rail. But his indifference was a pretext. He saw Downing the moment he came through the swing doors and though he did not shift his position his gaze followed the lawyer through the crowd. A thick-set man with immensely broad shoulders and arms so long they gave him an ape-like appearance stood beside Vining. In his heavy dull eyes there was a completely deceptive sleepy look. Actually his reactions were fast as chain lightning.

Quint Vining said softly out of the corner of his mouth, "Mort, tell Downing I'll see him in Pap's office in five minutes."

Mort Heisman made his way through the pack of people slowly. One watching him might have got the impression of logyness, but those who knew him well were aware that in an emergency he moved with great swiftness.

He touched Downing on the shoulder and murmured in his ear the message. The lawyer nodded. "I'll be there," he said.

Vining was chatting with Pap Wyman

when Downing entered the office. Pap rose and waved the lawyer to his chair. "If you gentlemen are talking business I know you will excuse me," he said.

"No business that you or anybody else can't hear, Pap," Downing replied promptly.

Quint Vining said nothing, but his silence suggested that what he had to say was private. Wyman left them, offering to send in drinks if they wished.

"No drinks," the lawyer answered.

The gambler took two cigars from a vest pocket, and when Downing shook his head lit one for himself. He did not hurry. When he spoke it was in the friendly voice of an older man giving advice to a younger.

"You've done well here, Ted, and you can go a long way — if you keep your feet on the ground and don't make mistakes. There are twenty lawyers in this town who never earn more than bread and butter. They know law, but they haven't what it takes to get along. I've been watching you, and I'm impressed. I need a smart young lawyer and I'm prepared to pay him a good retaining fee."

Downing knew that Vining was offering to set his feet on the road to fortune. As the gambler's attorney he would be a busy man and some of the litigation would be very important. Quint and his brother Ben were getting a foothold on both Fryer and Carbonate hills by piratical devices that a shrewd unscrupulous lawyer might make secure. Implicit in the overture of course was the understanding that Downing would abandon the defense of Henry Page. Moreover, he would be the mouthpiece of that element in the community which stood not only for a wide open town but lawlessness. If he accepted, he could escape the long struggle of a young attorney to advance himself, but at the expense of surrendering his self-respect.

"You ought to be able to find a man here who will meet the specifications," Downing said dryly.

The gambler jabbed a forefinger at the younger man. "I'm talking to you, Ted. If you've got the sense of a louse you'll jump at the offer. Within five years you will be a rich man."

Downing shook his head. "I can't take it, Mr. Vining. By the time the trial of Page is ended you wouldn't want me, anyhow."

"Why waste your time defending a man who is certain to be convicted?" Vining demanded impatiently. "All you will get out of it is injury to your reputation. Unless he is a fool a man looks after himself first."

"Let's say I'm a fool then." The redheaded lawyer looked straight at the gambler, challenge in his eyes. "I'm going to defend Henry Page, and by God I'm going to get him acquitted."

The cold eyes of Vining narrowed. "I'll make it my personal business to see that you don't," the owner of the Silver Palace retorted, his voice icily gentle. "And it will be a pleasure to fix it so that you will be disgraced and disbarred."

Heisman's big body filled the doorway. His sleepy eyes rested on the lawyer and after a moment shifted to his boss. "Did you want me, Quint?" he asked.

Vining blew a fat smoke wreath lazily. His answer was a silken murmur. "Not just now, Mort. I'll let you know when."

The lawyer turned and walked out of the room, his shoulder brushing against the body guard. He knew he had made an enemy. For the moment he was glad he had. His eyes were hot with anger.

About this time Erma Roberts would be coming down stairs to go to her dressing room. Downing decided to have a talk with her, since she had been working with him in behalf of Henry Page. One pleasant angle in consulting Erma was that her starry-eyed roommate was usually present. When the lawyer's mind was not occupied with business it often drifted to Joan Regal. During the past week he had been at the Grand Central four times to see her act. It was so simple that a child could have done it, but to him there was sheer glamour in her gracious loveliness.

Downing met them as they came down the stairs and turned in to their dressing room after them. He told the women of his encounter with Quint Vining. Though he had boasted that he would free his client, he admitted that he did not see a chance of winning an acquittal for Page. The cards would be stacked against him.

"I know Page is telling a straight story, but I can't prove it," he said. "And Vining will have half a dozen witnesses with stories all pat to show Page jumped his men with a gang of thugs."

"The men Vining puts on the stand will have to be scoundrels and riffraff," Erma replied. "Nobody else would swear to a pack of lies."

"You think that I could discredit them." Downing shook his head. "One or two of them maybe. I won't have enough information about the rest."

Joan looked at the lawyer, dismay in her

eyes. "You mean that they will send Mr. Page to the penitentiary for just defending himself and his property. But they can't do that."

"They will unless we can find a way to show up their game so that public opinion will back us," Downing answered.

He could claim that this case involved a great deal more than the fate of Henry Page, though the bitterness of the Vinings toward the prisoner was the main factor in forcing it as the test of the power of the vicious element. Hitherto lawlessness had reigned because the better element in the town had been too busy and too careless to make a fight. Unless backed by organized support no single citizen could stand up against the criminal depravity of the underworld without great personal danger. Downing had been warned. He could probably still make a perfunctory defense of Page and save himself, but if he went beyond that his reputation would be attacked and his life imperiled.

He did not like the alternatives. By temperament he was not a crusader. But he was an honest man, and after he had made his choice he had to live with his critical judgment of himself. He could not defend Page honorably without attacking the Vinings and all they represented. No matter how much he shrank from it he had to do his job.

Erma looked thoughtfully at the lawyer, a worried frown on her face. Downing had touched lightly on his meeting with Quint Vining, without mentioning the man's threat. But she knew the gambler and guessed at what had been omitted.

"I wish I hadn't involved you in this case, Ted," she said.

Joan spoke quickly. "I don't see why. I think Mr. Downing is the best lawyer we could have got to help Mr. Page."

"I wasn't thinking of Henry Page," Erma answered dryly. "He made his own bed, and I don't see why Ted should lie in it."

"I'm not offering myself as a sacrifice in his place," Downing reminded her with a smile.

"You are making an enemy of the Vinings," the actress flung back at him.

He shrugged lightly. "I wouldn't want them as friends."

"Of course not," Joan agreed, a touch of warmer color in her face.

Erma started to say more, but Downing shook his head slightly. What Joan did not know would not worry her.

When Downing walked into the Texas House the business of the day was still light.

Cape Wallace had just come on shift and was lounging against the roulette table smoking a cigar. He had not yet skinned the cover from the wheel. His white shirt was immaculate, his Prince Albert broadcloth coat well pressed, and his custom made boots polished to a looking-glass shine. The lawyer knew him by sight but not by name. Until he had asked a question of a bartender he was not sure this good-looking man with the impassive face and reckless eyes was the one he wanted.

The croupier met his "Mr. Wallace?" with one clipped word, "Right."

Downing gave his name and mentioned that he was going to represent Henry Page at his trial. "I understand he is your cousin," the attorney added.

"Was he bragging of it?" Wallace asked dryly.

The lawyer ignored that. "He is in a pretty bad jam and he pledged me not to write his people about it, but I thought I had better talk it over with you."

"Why?" Wallace brushed the ash from the end of his cigar. His voice was courteous but indifferent. One leg was thrown over a corner of the table, a hand still in his trousers pocket. "I'm no longer connected with the Page family. This boy's righteous old father made that clear to me when he decided I was a bad egg and drove me from my home town." A sardonic smile touched his lips. "I wonder how Mr. God will enjoy having his son sent to the penitentiary."

"Henry isn't going to the penitentiary," Downing said.

Wallace looked at the lean strong-jawed face, a little surprised. It occurred to him that there was a lot of man behind it. He had noticed the light confident step and the easy muscular co-ordination, but these do not carry far unless there is will back of them.

"You expect to get him off?" the gambler asked.

"The chances are against it." Downing's eyes held fast to those of the other man. "I'm thinking of Quint Vining," he answered. "Quint won't be satisfied with a prison sentence."

"What makes you think that?" Wallace had come out of his cynical coolness. He flung the cigar into a spittoon.

"Quint didn't exactly tell me that but he took pains to let me guess it. I suppose you know the true story."

"I know the Vinings. That is enough. They made a sucker out of the kid and trapped him. Get me right. I've got nothing against Henry.

I'm not cutting in. That's all."

"You've cut in already when you saved his life," Downing said.

"Did he send you to me?"

"No. He said he couldn't ask you to do any more. But I thought I ought to give you the chance."

"Fine. Now you are in the clear." An ironic smile touched the face of the gambler. "I would advise you to write to his father. Maybe he will guarantee your fee."

"Don't worry about my fee," Downing suggested.

"On second thought I'm willing to pay part of it — say up to a couple of hundred dollars — if you'll write to old moneybags and tell him I'm doing it."

"No, thanks. I'm not interested in paying off your grudges, only in getting an acquittal for my client. I don't see much chance of that, since perjured evidence will be stacked against him. The Vinings want a conviction as a justification for a lynching or a killing from ambush. In any case I think they mean to rub out young Page. But for you he would have been dead already."

"If it's that way why bother about an acquittal?"

"I take first things first. After being freed

he could start for the East before they got a chance at him."

"What do you think I can do about it?"

"I don't know. There may be witnesses who saw what happened at the Sally McGee that night, men who are afraid to come forward but who might testify if we could build up a sentiment to protect them. So far everybody seems willing to let the Vining version of what took place go by default. If we can't get good people interested to help him your cousin is lost. I think he was right all the way, but I run up against a wall when I look for evidence. The men who worked for him at the mine have left the district, bought off by Quint Vining in my opinion. The deed they have filed is a forgery, but unless I can find the man who sold to Page I can't prove it. The story of the fight the Vinings build up at the trial will be false." Downing slammed his fist down on the corner of the roulette table. "I'm not going to let them get away with it."

Cape Wallace slanted a long look at the lawyer. He did not think this fighting redheaded Irishman would get anywhere against the Vining gang but he liked the fellow's spirit. It was time somebody stood up to the horde of *banditti* who had come like locusts to feed on the rich pickings at the silver camp.

The better-class gambling houses, such as Pap Wyman's and the Texas House, considered themselves business establishments. The games were on the level with the usual percentage in favor of the house. No hangers-on in their employ rolled customers or waited in alleys to rob them when they won. The owners and employees of such places realized that Leadville would not long remain an open town if lawlessness was permitted to run wild and as a matter of self-interest resented the carnival of crime that infested the city.

"When I was a kid I read in the Bible of a young fellow named David who went out to fight the champ Philistine, a terrible giant called Goliath, taking with him only a sling and some pebbles. It turned out fine." There was a note of friendly derision in the conclusion of Wallace. "Maybe you too can pull a miracle out of the hat."

"While you sit in the grandstand and look on," Downing answered, and left him to think that over.

Wallace watched him go, not very well satisfied with himself.

A parade was coming down Harrison Avenue and turned into Chestnut. It was led by two strutting pipers blowing pibrochs. Back of them marched a troop of sixty men, all dressed in the kilts of the Royal Stuart pattern — tartan stockings, sporrans of white goats' hair, corded velvet vests, plumed Prince Charlie bonnets, and shoulder plaids with silver buckles and cairngorm jewels. Each man carried a *skean-dhu* thrust into his stocking. Behind these rode two men in a barouche drawn by four white horses. One of them was Paddy Ryan, champion pugilist of the country. He was the guest of the man beside him, H. A. W. Tabor, the leading carbonate king of the camp. Eighteen months before this Tabor had grubstaked with supplies from his store two miners who had struck it rich. Formerly a prospector himself, he had tossed his winnings into claims right and left. Nearly all of them had proved bonanzas. With the Little Pittsburgh, the Chrysolite, the Matchless, and a dozen other rich mines back of him he had risen from a storekeeper always in debt to a multimillionaire. Already he was lieutenant governor of the state and was reaching for a seat in the United States Senate. The Tabor Highland Guards had been formed ostensibly to protect the camp from the Utes but really to keep claim jumpers from the mines of their sponsor. The expensive and spectacular uniforms were to gratify the man's vanity. He was a simple soul and loved display. At the moment he was bowing right and left, a silk hat waving in his hand.

It was a ridiculous performance, but from it Downing plucked an idea, to mobilize public opinion on behalf of Page through the influence of the big companies. He had been invited to a dinner Tabor was giving for Paddy Ryan at the Clarendon. While the champagne corks were popping fast the mine owner introduced him to the thick-set young Irishman with the reddish hair and blue eyes.

"Paddy is going to polish off next a young fellow named Sullivan," Tabor said.

"I've heard the Boston strong boy is pretty good," Downing replied.

"I like 'em good," the champion answered complacently.

"When does that fellow Page's trial come up?" Tabor asked the lawyer. "I hear he has no chance." He explained the case to the pugilist.

"I want to see you about that," the lawyer said. "Can you give me ten minutes tomorrow? I think I see a way to help your chance for the Senate."

"All right, Ted. Tomorrow morning — say about ten."

In the miner's office next day Downing put

his case briefly and forcibly. Armed men had jumped the O'Donovan Rossa and a dozen other mines. This had to be stopped unless the owners were willing to let the desperadoes take whatever they wanted. A score of lawsuits were pending in the courts, several of them against Tabor and his associates. The Page case was attracting a good deal of attention. There was no doubt the Vinings were wholly to blame. Now was the time to show the claim grabbers they could not get hold of rich properties by violence, guns, and perjury.

Tabor pulled at his long handle-bar mustache. In spite of the childish streak in him he was an honest, public-spirited citizen. "I've heard all that before, Ted," he said. "Git down to hardpan. What you want me to do?"

"Throw your weight on our side. You will get credit for cleaning up the camp. It will help you a lot politically. I won't be here myself for the next two weeks. I've got to go back to Wisconsin and find Jeff Reed. We need his testimony and I can't reach him by mail."

"You'll need money." Tabor wrote a check for a thousand dollars. He was generous and he gave money freely. "I'm not ready yet to come out publicly against the Vinings — not with this political campaign coming on. They control a lot of votes. Sure they are a bad influence, but they are not treading on my toes too much yet. I think Quint will play with me in this campaign. Soon as it is over I'll help you smash them."

"Right now they are running a shaft in that little triangle they claim above your Tom Boy to rob you of your ore," Downing suggested.

"I'll take care of my ore, son, and you take care of yore client." Tabor chuckled reminiscently. "A thief has to get up early in the morning to beat me. Keep in mind Chicken Bill."

Chicken Bill had sunk a shaft not far from the Little Pittsburgh and he found the digging hard work. He salted the prospect with some sacks of ore borrowed at night from Tabor's Little Pittsburgh and next day sold it to Tabor for forty thousand dollars. While the camp was still roaring with laughter the new owner sank the shaft ten feet deeper and struck a rich vein that netted him millions.

"I know you have the Midas touch," Downing admitted.

"I don't know him," Tabor denied indignantly. "But I never borrowed from anybody yet I didn't pay him back."

Downing explained the literary allusion.

"Some of our leading men are having a

meeting tonight about the railroad situation," Tabor said. "I'll bring up this matter of Page, but I don't think they will do anything now. We don't want to stir things up too much until we're sure of both railroads. Why don't you go see the *Chronicle* and the *Herald-Democrat*? They are always hollering about good government."

"I've seen them both," the lawyer explained. "Like you, they don't want to tie up their policies with a campaign for Page. They can't throw overboard all this false evidence the Vinings are piling up." But he did feel that the newspapers would report the trial fairly.

4

The trial of Henry Page was three days old. A procession of witnesses for the state had been taking the stand to testify that the Vinings had bought the Sally McGee from Jeff Reed a week before Page had reached Leadville, though they had failed by an oversight to record their purchase till later, and that the defendant had twice jumped the claim to take possession from the lawful owners. Downing had been unable to shake their evidence in cross-examination but had made it clear to the jury that some of them were a bad lot.

A huge fellow with heavy rounded shoulders took the chair and was sworn. His name, he said, was Sam Ukena, and he was employed as a guard by the Vinings. His story varied only in slight details from the others who had preceded him. He had been on the day shift and had gone home for supper, after which he had returned to the mine and was there when the Page gang attacked. He identified the defendant as the leader of the jumpers and as the man who had shot Bert Vining. The prosecuting attorney, a large middle-aged man in a Prince Albert coat, with a head of fine silky white hair and the manner of an old-fashioned statesman, waved his hand toward Downing.

"Your witness, sir," he said with a slight bow.

"You worked all day at the Sally McGee on the twenty-eighth with no interruption from the defendant?" Downing asked.

"That's right. He wasn't around. Not till after it was dark."

"You said your shift ended at six and you left for supper. Why did you go back to the mine?"

"I went back to see the fun."

"What fun?"

"Why, the trouble with this fellow Page."

"Had he sent you word he was going to attack?" Downing asked smoothly.

"I didn't say that," Ukena growled.

"But you felt sure there was going to be fun, as you call it?"

"I knew he was a bad egg and would try some shenanigan."

"And that he would try it on this particular night. Are you a mind reader, Mr. Ukena?"

"Don't get funny with me," the big man snarled. "It ain't safe."

The judge brought down his gavel sharply. "The witness will confine his remarks to answering questions."

Downing asked how far away Page had been when he killed young Vining and was told that it might have been about sixty yards.

"You mentioned that it was dark," the lawyer suggested.

"Not so dark but what I could see him."

"Was he carrying a rifle or a pistol?"

"A rifle. Seems to me he had a six-shooter too."

"You examined his pistol and saw that it was a revolver carrying six bullets?"

"How could I examine it when he was sixty yards away?"

"Oh, you just thought it might be a revolver. Are you sure about the rifle?"

"Bet yore boots I am."

The lawyer shifted the attack. "Where were you, Mr. Ukena, between September eleventh, eighteen-seventy-seven, and August thirtieth, eighteen-seventy-nine?"

Mabry, the prosecuting attorney, jumped to his feet. "Objection, your Honor. I submit that for the purpose of this trial it does not matter where the witness was some time in the past."

The judge asked Downing the object of the question.

"To show the character of the witness, that he has been a criminal," the lawyer replied.

"I think the question is material," the judge decided. "You may proceed." He turned to the clerk. "Read the question."

"I was knockin' around the country somewhere," Ukena answered sulkily. "I wouldn't know just where I was."

Downing smiled blandly. "Would it refresh your memory if I read an affidavit from the warden of the Missouri state penitentiary that you were doing your knockin' around in prison, serving a term for robbing the passengers of the riverboat *Jefferson Davis*?" The lawyer stepped forward and handed the paper to the judge. "Your Honor, I wish this to go on the record as evidence."

"They framed me," Ukena shouted, his face purple with anger.

The judge glanced over the paper and passed it on to the jury. "It is so ordered," he said.

The next witness answered to the name of Amos Scudder. He was a shifty-eyed fellow from Tiger Alley with a head almost as fleshless as the skull of a skeleton. In cross-examination Downing asked only one question.

"Are you the same Amos Scudder against whom there is an indictment for wounding with a knife John Pelly who is at present in a hospital recovering from five slashes on the face and body?"

Mabry rose angrily. "I object, your Honor, to this continuous smearing of my witnesses. Mr. Scudder is out on bond. There is evidence he struck in self-defense. Is it fair to prejudge before his trial the case of a man presumably innocent?"

The low amused laughter of a woman reached the judge. He looked sternly at Erma Roberts who was seated with Joan Regal on a bench near the front.

"No levity will be permitted in this courtroom," he announced. To the clerk he said curtly, "Strike the question from the record. In the form the attorney put it a prejudice is raised that is entirely improper."

Downing was satisfied. The question could not be erased from the minds of the jurors.

The smelter twelve o'clock whistle blew and Judge Lamson adjourned court for dinner. Among those who filed out of the room was Cape Wallace. He had been a constant attendant ever since the jury had been chosen.

Henry Page had been keenly aware of Joan Regal's presence from the moment she walked into the room with Erma. As she sat leaning forward a little, snatched into an intent interest, a breathing color in her cheeks, it seemed to him that her loveliness lit the drab courtroom like a torch. The state's evidence had been piling up against him, but the sympathy in her soft eyes warmed his desolate heart. If they had met in other circumstances he might perhaps have thought only that she was a charming girl and forgotten her soon. He would not have needed to cling so desperately to her interest in him. She was a symbol of all the pleasant days he had known before this tragedy engulfed him, a light of hope in a storm to a shipwrecked sailor.

Erma said, "Let's go and say a word of cheer to the poor boy."

"Yes, let's," Joan agreed. "He must feel awful."

They edged forward along the aisle while the crowd pushed past them in the opposite direction.

"How is it going?" Erma asked.

"All for the prosecution so far," Downing replied. "We'll have our innings late this afternoon and tomorrow."

His eyes were on Joan. She had offered her hand to Page and he was holding it as if he could not let go.

"I'm sure it is going to be all right," the girl was saying. "Nobody could believe those men after Mr. Downing showed what scoundrels they were."

"None of the witnesses told the truth, but Ted could not get anything against several of them," Page told her. "I don't know what the jury will think."

Several of the jurymen were looking across the room at the group as they filed out of the room.

"You girls didn't do any harm coming forward to speak with Henry," Downing said. "The jury will count it in his favor that nice women are his friends and believe in him."

The jailor said to his prisoner gruffly, "We'll be going now."

Joan watched the two men leave, then turned impulsively to the lawyer. "You'll get him off, won't you?"

"I don't know," he hedged. "I think we have a good jury. We can thank Sheriff Taggart for that. He hand-picked the panel to get decent citizens. I'm hoping the jury will decide a lot of the testimony is perjured. The trouble is that our defense is negative. We have no witnesses to show the Vining gang were the attackers." He added hopefully, "But we have two brothers named Gail who are working the Minerva farther up the hill. Going up to their claim in the morning and coming down about six o'clock they saw Page and his two men at work on the Sally McGee."

"The day of the fight?" Erma asked.

"Yes. They stopped to talk with Page a few minutes on the way down. Their testimony is at complete variance with all the witnesses the Vinings have put on the stand to show they were in possession during the day."

"If Mr. Page was already there working he couldn't have been the attacker," Joan said.

"He couldn't have been — and he wasn't," Downing agreed. "But the jury will have to balance against seven prosecution witnesses the word of our three, the Gails and Henry himself."

"What about the men he had working for him?" Erma inquired.

"I can't find them. They have gone — vamoosed. Of course Quint Vining bought them off to leave the camp."

"But that's terrible," Joan cried, the color running hot in her cheeks. "They can't do that to an innocent man. Isn't there any justice here?"

"The camp is young yet — and wild," Downing explained, and told a story to illustrate his point. "A few months ago a lawyer went to Judge Binner and suggested he not be too hard on one of his clients. Binner promised to be just to him. The lawyer grew alarmed. 'My God, Judge, don't do that,' he begged. 'You'd have to send him to Cañon City for the rest of his life.' A good many people think that justice should be dealt out discreetly with one eye on its political implications."

Erma nodded. She knew her Leadville. "You have built up quite a sentiment in favor of Henry Page, and that ought to have some effect. The mine owners are for him."

"In a very timid way," Downing agreed. "They are careful not to say much for fear of starting trouble."

"Joan and I wrote a little song about Henry to sing on the stage for an encore, but the management heard of it and nearly had a fit," Erma said. "I had to give up the idea."

"I'm glad they stopped you." Downing looked gravely from Erma to Joan. "Don't get mixed up in this. It's no business for a lady. There is dynamite in it."

"You be careful yourself, Ted," the older woman warned.

The girl's eyes grew wide with alarm. "You don't mean — you can't mean that Mr. Downing — "

The lawyer laughed. "Erma doesn't know what she means. It's just that we are all too much keyed up about this. If you'll excuse me I'll be going. I have a lot of work to do before court opens this afternoon."

Quint Vining had been present since the first day of the trial. He sat in the second row, relaxed and at ease, apparently only an interested spectator. But the cold eyes in his bloodless rock-hard face missed nothing of what was taking place. Downing was sure there was an understanding between him and Mabry. The prosecutor was going through the routine of the trial with dramatic fervor, the image of a good man determined to enforce law for the people he represented. Yet it was all a pretense. He was Vining's man, and though the boss never lifted a hand he was pulling the strings that made his puppets move.

The first witness called by Downing was a surprise and a shock to the prosecution. They had felt sure that Jeff Reed had disappeared in the Middle West and could not be found. When his name was called a small wrinkled man past middle age walked spryly down the aisle to the witness chair. He sat there easily with fingers laced and chewed tobacco while the questions were asked. Yes, he knew the

Vinings, but he had never done any business with them. None of them had even talked with him about buying the Sally McGee. He had not written the signature on the agreement that was supposed to be his. The only sale of the mine he had made was to Henry Page, who had paid him for it eleven thousand five hundred dollars. That was the sum and substance of his testimony, and though Mabry stormed at him and threatened the penalties of perjury the little man stood to his story and continued to chew his cud imperturbably.

The prosecutor asked for a fifteen-minute recess, during which period he retired to his office and had a talk with Quint Vining. At the expiration of that time he announced that he intended to indict Reed for perjury. This was for the benefit of the jury. Downing smiled and said audibly, "If you can prove he wasn't telling the truth I'll quit the practice of law."

The judge silenced them and gave both a sharp reprimand. "Bring on your next witness," he ordered Downing.

The Gail brothers told their story. Downing put several others on the stand to show that Page had been working without apparent interruption at the mine for several weeks. He offered the canceled check to the court as evidence of ownership, and he was about to call on Page as his last witness when a man rose from one of the spectators' benches and said, "I have important evidence, your Honor, that I feel I ought to give." The man was Cape Wallace.

Judge Lamson glanced at the paper in front of him on which was written the list witnesses. "I don't find your name here, Mr. Wallace." He turned to Mabry and Downing. "Do either of you know anything about this man? Is he your witness?"

Both disclaimed having had any contact with him. The judge spoke to the croupier, censure in his voice. "If you have evidence, as you claim to have, why have you waited till this late moment to let the court know?"

Wallace stood in the aisle, at graceful, almost insolent ease. "I didn't want to get mixed up in this if I could help it," he explained.

"You were willing to withhold important evidence to save yourself a little trouble?" Lamson said severely.

The gambler lifted his shoulders in a little shrug. "Unless I thought it necessary. Looks to me now that I had better give it."

The judge called him up and had a whispered conversation with the man, after which he said aloud, "Take the stand." When Wallace had been sworn, Judge Lamson addressed the attorneys. "This is entirely irregular but seems necessary. I shall ask the witness to tell what he knows about this. The defense and the prosecution may then examine him. But I wish to say here that the witness has erred grossly in concealing what he claims to have seen."

The story Wallace told was that on the evening of the twenty-eighth he had got through work about nine o'clock, having been on the day shift at the wheel. He had eaten supper at the Tontine. The evening was pleasantly cool and he decided to take a walk. Since he had a small interest in the Rainbow's End he strolled up Fryer Hill to see how far the men at work had sunk the shaft. The night was dark, with neither moon nor stars showing. He had never been up to the mine and was not able to find it. Giving up the idea, he turned back toward town. By sheer chance he blundered onto the territory of the Sally McGee. A man's voice challenged him. He moved forward with his hands up. The defendant was there alone, in his hand a pistol. Page explained that he was spending the night there to prevent anybody from jumping the claim, though he was not really expecting any trouble. After a minute or two of talk Wallace parted with the man. He was in a clump of spruce not twenty yards away when he heard a voice order Page to come out of there or get shot. "I heard Page call back that he intended to protect his property. Then the shooting began. One or two of the attackers were using rifles, the rest pistols." Wallace spoke almost indifferently, without the least sign of bias. He might have been telling about a fishing excursion from the tone of his voice. "They began to work closer. I could see their shadowy figures, but it was too dark to recognize anybody. Somebody yelled, 'Oh God, I'm hit.' That ended the firing. I could hear men scuttling away in the darkness. So I lit out too."

Downing rose to examine, filled with the fear that he was about to step into a trap. He was sure that the glib story of Wallace was a lie cut out of whole cloth. If the man had been at the Sally McGee and talked with Page just before the shooting the prisoner certainly would have told his counsel. What Downing did not know yet was the object of this perjured evidence. Cape Wallace was a bold and audacious scamp. It might be that he was trying to save his cousin by meeting the false testimony of the prosecution with the same weapon. Or he might be a tool of the enemy.

Quint Vining had threatened to have the defense lawyer disbarred. Perhaps he intended to use this man's perjury as the basis for proceedings against him. Yet it did not seem likely that Vining would bolster the case of Page to get at Downing, for it stood out like a sore thumb bandaged that if the story of Wallace was accepted by the jury Page must be acquitted.

"Do you often walk in the evening, Mr. Wallace?" Downing asked.

"Not often."

"Did you ever before go up Fryer Hill after night?"

"No."

"Wasn't it strange that you chose the night of the twenty-eighth to tramp up there?"

"I felt restless — wanted to get the smoke of the Texas House out of my lungs."

"And by sheer chance — I think that was your expression — you were at the Sally McGee at the exact time of the battle?"

"Correct," Wallace answered. He was quite cool and undisturbed, and he wasted no words explaining the improbable chance.

"Have you any evidence to prove you were there except your own word?"

"Only your client's memory," the gambler said, with a faint derisive smile.

"You said Henry Page carried a revolver. Did he have any other weapon as far as you know?"

"No."

"If there had been a rifle there would you have seen it?"

"I think so."

"Were you armed?"

Wallace hesitated an instant. "I had a pistol," he said.

"Did you take any part in the fighting?"

"Not any."

"Even though there were five or six against one?"

"It was none of my affair."

"And after it was over you did not wait to find out who was dead or injured?"

"I had no chips in the game."

"Since that night have you ever spoken of this to anybody until today?"

"No."

"Why not? Don't you know that as a good citizen it was your duty to come forward and tell what you saw and heard?"

"A dozen men are killed every month in and around this town. I don't intend to get mixed up in any of these quarrels if I can help it. But it looked to me as if this guy was being framed."

Mabry was up instantly sputtering wrath. "Objection, your Honor. There has been no evidence whatever to support such a charge."

"Objection sustained. Confine yourself to what you know, Mr. Wallace. What you think is not evidence." The voice of the judge had the sting of a small whip lash.

"Did you recognize any of the attackers?" Downing inquired.

"No. Too dark. And they were too far away."

"Do you know which side fired the first shot?"

"No."

"Or who killed Bert Vining?"

"I don't *know*." The gambler added, drawling slightly, "And the judge does not like me to guess."

Judge Lamson hammered on the desk and leaned forward, anger on his face. "One more remark like that and you'll go to prison for contempt of court," he snapped.

"You have not forgotten that you are under oath to tell nothing but the truth?" Downing said.

"I haven't forgotten."

Downing waved the witness over to Mabry. He was not satisfied. Very likely there was already a suspicion in the courtroom that he had bribed Wallace. But what could he do about it? He wanted very much to keep clear of any charge of collusion, but his primary business just now was to clear his client and he could not do that by wholly discrediting this heaven-sent witness.

While Mabry was putting Wallace through a scathing cross-examination, Downing had to make up his mind whether to put Page on the stand or not. Assuming that a client was innocent, it was nearly always better to have him tell his side to the jury. By not doing so he gave weight to the presumption that he dared not risk a cross-examination. But to let Mabry get at Page now might be fatal. Henry would either have to deny the story of Wallace and lose the chance of probable acquittal or endorse it and so perjure himself. It would be to the personal advantage of Downing for Page to break down the gambler's testimony, but that would be asking too much of a man whose life was at stake. Bad though it would look, he decided not to let Page give evidence.

Mabry was doing his best to entangle the witness. He was a hit-or-miss attorney who prepared his cases badly but made a good show in the courtroom. He was a favorite with juries because he was a tub thumper and put on a good act. But in Wallace he had met his match. The gambler watched his dramatics with a sardonic amusement almost insulting. Though the prosecutor worked for an hour, perspiration beading his florid face and pouring in a rivulet down his back, he did not succeed in shaking the gambler's story. When he gave up at last he was a weary man.

Downing asked for a ten-minute recess. He took Page into the office of the clerk.

"Listen to me and don't say a word — not one word until I ask you a question," the lawyer warned. "Since you did not mention to me that you saw Wallace at the mine just before the battle I don't know whether he is lying or telling the truth. But if you go on the stand Mabry is going to find out. And he'll get it out of you that Wallace is your cousin. As it stands now the man's testimony will acquit you — if the jury believes him. If Mabry gets a lick at you they won't be in doubt, they will know. The point is that if the story Wallace told is shaken you are sunk. The jury will think we tried to rig up perjured evidence and flubbed it. He was a first-class witness and he sounded sincere. At the very worst for us he has raised a big doubt they can't escape. Now here is the nub of it. Go on the stand and you'll have to back him up or say he was lying. Think before you answer this question. Do you want to go up there and face Mabry's cross-examination or don't you?"

Henry Page realized the dilemma in which he was caught. For a long minute he marshaled the arguments in his mind before he answered. All through the trial it had been clear that he must tell his story and face the lies that had been told. But Cape Wallace had cut the ground from under his feet. His cousin had lied to save him. To tell the truth would be to send both of them to the penitentiary.

"I don't like it," he told his lawyer. "I want to fling their lies back at them. But I don't see how I can now. I shall have to stay off the stand."

After the judge had called the court to order five minutes later Downing said quietly, "Your Honor, the defense rests."

It was almost as if the defendant had admitted guilt.

There was still one more highlight in the trial, Ted Downing's speech for the defense before a jammed courtroom. He began quietly by analyzing the evidence bit by bit — the forged bill of sale, the character of the prosecution witnesses as brought out in their own testimony, the fact that a large part of their testimony had been proved false by good men with no personal interest in the case and the deduction from this that the rest of it was not dependable. Without mentioning the Vinings by name he made a bitter attack on the audacity of lawbreakers who dared come into court to make a mock of justice by putting their own guilt on the shoulders of the man they had tried to destroy. It was true that Henry Page was on trial for his life, but there was a deeper truth involved. The city of Leadville was on trial to determine whether it was the home of honest fearless citizens or the prey of the debauched and vicious element which had so long and so flagrantly scoffed at and insulted the decency of all good men and women. The clock was striking the hour of solemn decision. There were men in this courtroom now — he swung 'round and his steady eyes looked at Quint Vining — who were leaders of all the corruption and crime and vice that was making the name of this fine city a stench throughout the land. If they succeeded in destroying Henry Page they would realize that the conscience of Leadville was drugged and that no evil deed was outlawed. He sat down in a tense silence.

The charge of the judge was fair and unbiased. It was noon when the jury retired to consider the case. The six o'clock whistle was blowing at the smelter when it returned with a verdict of Not Guilty.

As Downing and Page walked along Chestnut Street after the trial, a battery of eyes followed them. For a week there had been heavy betting as to the verdict, with the odds three to one against acquittal.

A miner watching them said to John Taggart: "You've lost a boarder, Sheriff, but it ain't going to do him any good. He's jumped outa the frying pan into the fire, as you might say. The Vinings will get him sure. And that lawyer of his too. Downing had better light out sudden, after the way he went for Quint."

Taggart shook his head. "Ever look in that redhead's eyes? He'll stay here and take it. That guy's legs couldn't run away."

Downing had succeeded in making the trial significant and dramatic, but nobody believed the fight had ended. If a poll had been taken of those who saw the two young men turn in to Pap Wyman's for a drink a majority vote would have shown the opinion that at least one of them and perhaps both were marked for death.

Four or five men were lined up at the bar when the lawyer and his client stepped up to it. They offered friendly congratulations, but one of them, Jock Ferguson, murmured advice in the ear of Downing.

"None of my business, but if I was you I'd get my client hustled outa town and headed for the East right soon," he said.

"Henry says he is staying here," Downing answered.

Page overheard and leaned forward, an elbow on the bar, to speak to Ferguson across his friend's body. "Why should I let a bunch of criminals drive me away? I own a mine here, and I'm going to protect my rights."

"For how long?" Ferguson asked bluntly.

The answer of the young man was edged with sharpness. "I don't know. After all, Quint Vining isn't God."

Ferguson rasped the palm of his hand over an unshaven jaw. "If you look at it that way. Still an' all, God has a right smart bit of business to transact here and there. Seems like he has kinda let Leadville slide, wouldn't you say? Of course it's your funeral, not mine. But a spry young fellow like you has a heap of living to do yet if he's let alone."

"You think I won't be?" Page asked.

"I'm not thinking out loud," the miner replied with a cautious glance around.

"Your advice is good medicine," Downing agreed. "I wish I could get Henry to take it. He could get somebody to handle his mine."

"I meant my advice for you too. There are parties in this town don't like you any better than they do him."

The lawyer put out a feeler. "Don't you think there has been a sort of crystallizing of sentiment lately, a determination to have decency and enforce the law?"

"Don't bank on that, Ted," warned Ferguson. "Those skunks haven't near reached the end of their rope yet."

A boy pushed open the swing doors and came into the room. Pap Wyman pounced on him. "What you want?" he demanded. "No kids allowed in here."

"I brought a note from Miss Roberts for Mr. Downing," he explained. "Someone said he was in here."

Wyman pointed out the lawyer. "Give it to him and beat it, son," he ordered.

Downing read the note and passed it to Page. It was an invitation to join her and Joan for dinner at the Clarendon. Henry nodded. The lawyer wrote an acceptance beneath Erma's signature.

They met the women in the parlor of the hotel and with them adjourned to the table reserved for them in the restaurant. The dining room was filled almost entirely with men, and the noise of their talk beat like a wave on the newcomers as they entered. The clatter of voices died down momentarily at sight of them. The two men had been on the front-page spreads of the newspapers for several days and the women were popular characters.

Joan had not much to say, though she was very happy at the result of the trial. She murmured to Downing, "You were wonderful."

He was much pleased at her praise but shrugged it off. "Cape Wallace saved the day," he said.

"Wasn't it providential he was up at the Sally McGee at the time of the attack?" the girl replied.

Downing agreed dryly. "Very fortunate."

They were halfway through supper when the Vinings and Mort Heisman came into the restaurant. Quint bowed stiffly to the women as he passed their table. His brother glared at them in silence. He was distinctly not a lady's man, if one excepted the attention he gave a blonde, Mamie Stull, whom he had put into her furniture. More blunt and impulsive than Quint, he usually pushed directly to his end with no finesse. The sleepy eyes of Heisman rested on the seated men with no expression.

In passing Quint stopped at a table to talk with Buck Harrigan the city marshal. The officer was a medium-sized powerfully built man of forty, a notorious character chosen for his position in the hope that his reputation as a killer would overawe other bad men. It was known that he and Heisman were as wary and jealous of each other as two strange dogs.

Downing's gaze shuttled from Quint to his brother. Ben and Mort Heisman had their heads close together in whispered talk. More than once their glances slid to those at Miss Roberts' table. When Quint turned to join them their heads drew apart swiftly. The lawyer had the impression that they were discussing some plan in which Quint had no part. This was strange unless the Vinings disagreed on some course of action, possibly one that involved Downing and his client.

These men were dangerous enemies. They could bide their time and strike unexpectedly. Against assassins there is no sure defense.

Heisman ate fast and rose to go before his companions. He lit a cigar, answered a question asked by Quint, and walked out of the restaurant.

The girl's eyes followed him to the door. "Is he a friend of Mr. Vining?" she inquired.

"He works for him," Downing answered.

"I wouldn't think he would be a good workman," Joan said. "He looks half asleep."

"Heisman has the reputation of being thorough," the lawyer commented grimly.

"You boys stay away from him," Erma admonished sharply. "While I was here before he killed a man."

In Joan's eyes was a startled look. "You don't think — " she began, and did not finish the sentence.

"*I'll* not tread on his toes," Page promised.

"You ought to leave here at once," the actress scolded. "You are pigheaded, like a little boy afraid someone will say he is scared."

"If anybody said that about me it would be true," Page admitted with a wry smile. "I'll go as soon as I can sell the Sally McGee."

"Stay home at night, both of you."

Joan opened her eyes wide. "But Mr. Page has been acquitted. The Vinings can't do anything now, can they? They wouldn't dare."

"Their brother is dead. They won't forget that."

While Page was helping Joan into her coat Downing told Miss Roberts not to worry, both of them intended to be very careful.

"Are you armed?" the actress asked in a whisper.

"Yes — for what that's worth. I don't think Quint will do anything for some time. He can't afford to stir up public opinion against him."

The young men left the women at the stage door of the Grand Central and went around to the front to buy tickets to the show. Champagne corks were already popping in the boxes. The curtain had not yet gone up and a drunken man in the pit was singing "Clementine." A boy selling newspapers passed down the aisle shouting, "Page acquitted of Vining killing."

As was customary in variety shows the curtain went up to show all the actors and actresses sitting on the stage in a crescent with the blackface dancers at the ends. The eyes of both Page and Downing picked up at once the girl in the green velvet boy's suit. She was to Downing a sheer delight. As he watched her later helping Pierre Renaud with his props no feeling of anything cheap or sordid came to him. She was no trained actress, had never learned the artifice of putting her personality beyond the footlights, but she had that quality which cannot be acquired by effort, a pristine glamour more touching than art. These hard, tough miners sensed something exquisite in the girl, a note of sweet and fragile youth unconsciously appealing to their chivalry. She had that most elusive charm — wistfulness. It might be accidental and have nothing to do with her inner life, but it gave her a distinction that set her apart.

All of this Henry Page realized, but back of the attraction he had a shocked disapproval at seeing her in a male costume displaying her fresh loveliness for pay to the miners. He was filled with the prejudices of the period. With the exception of a dozen or so topnotchers on the legitimate stage, such as Irving, Booth, Clara Morris, and Mary Anderson, members of the acting profession were a class apart. In Joan's act there was no emphasis on sex, nothing suggestive, but Henry felt she ought not to be on the stage at all. It was a violation of all the proprieties. One could not touch pitch without being defiled. From such contacts she ought to be protected. His rationalization did not carry far enough to consider the circumstances that had driven her to accept the work.

While the stage was being reset after the juggler's act a man dressed as a comic character with a false red beard and shaggy wig above which was perched a very small low-crowned derby came out before the curtain to sing a song.

"This is going to be dreadful," Page suggested. "What say we go?"

Downing nodded. He was not interested in the rest of the program.

The booming voice of the comedian pursued them down the aisle:

> *"I used to love a gal there, they called her Sally Black;*
> *I axed her for to marry me, she said she was a whack.*
> *'But,' says she to me, 'Joe Bowers, before we hitch for life*
> *You'd ought to have a little home to keep your little wife.'"*

The thumping and whistling applause followed the departing two into the street.

"There's no accounting for tastes," Page said.

As they walked along the sidewalk their talk was casual. It did not touch on the two subjects uppermost in both their minds — the danger of attack and their feeling for the girl who so charmed them. They had come together through a hard and grilling experience. A common peril menaced them both. Since they liked and respected each other, they had been moving toward friendship. But the tie that bound them was still slight. The fire a girl had lit in their hearts could snap it.

At Harrison Street they stopped in front of the saloon The Little Church on the Corner.

Their ways parted here. Behind them lay the lights and noises of the places of amusement. At this point Chestnut Street was almost deserted, though there was a rumor of somebody stirring across the road.

"Keep a sharp lookout as you go down the street," Downing warned. "You ought not to be out at all so late."

"That goes double," Page answered. "Remember what Jock Ferguson told you."

"I don't think we'll have trouble soon," the lawyer said. "Quint is too smart. You've had luck today. I hope it holds up. 'Night."

He turned to go. The blast of a gun roared across the street. A bullet tore between them and crashed through the stained-glass window that gave the saloon its name.

5

His shift ended, Cape Wallace turned over the wheel to his relief. In the washroom he took off his working jacket, cleaned up, and donned street clothes, after which he helped himself to the elaborate free lunch set out at the lower end of the bar. He ate leisurely, his lean flat-muscled body loose and easy, watching cynically the variant life that flowed in and out between the tables.

The Texas House was furnished without regard to expense. In the main hall the gambling equipment was of the best and the fine chandeliers were decorated with a hundred crystal pendants. Upstairs the private rooms were all carpeted and in most of them was a piano. On a raised platform an orchestra of violin, cornet, trombone and piano was now playing "Madame Angot." Yet the clientele was a rough-and-ready mixture ranging in dress from soiled miners' slops to broadcloth and silk hats.

After his fashion Wallace was a philosopher and he found the absurd contrasts of Leadville amusing. On his shift just ended a man known as Scotty had played the roulette wheel for four hours using twenty-dollar gold pieces for chips. A week before the man had been working an armstrong in Stray Horse Gulch, so broke that he did not have the price of a dinner. Yesterday he had sold his claim for thirty thousand dollars and tomorrow he was going back without a dime to work for three dollars a day on the same shaft.

Snatches of talk drifted to Wallace. "... say he's sloped for Texas" ... "... hand caught between the bonnet of the cage and the collar of the shaft" ... "Soiled dove bumped herself off by swallowing carbolic acid an hour ago in Tiger Alley, third in a month" ... "... ran into a wash formation" ... "No, I quit the Come-and-Get It hash house because the grub didn't assay high enough" ... "Expect to be in bonanza next week."

That was Leadville — high-spirited hope brushing shoulders with icy despair.

Wallace moved toward the door, shouldering a way through the increasing crowd. At the table he had just left a man in a ragged shirt and coat was having a run of luck. He was playing two corners and the number 17.

His winnings he scooped into a shapeless hat already half filled with chips of assorted colors and values.

Flares in front of the gambling houses and saloons lit up the packed sidewalks. There had been a day of melting snow and the churned streets were slushy with mud. A milkman was making his route driving two burros with barrels balanced on each side of them. Splashing down the street came a belated stage. Two covered wagons lumbered heavily past.

Wallace lit a cigar and watched the night life ebb to and fro. It was a night of stars, not too cold for comfort. This was the best hour of the day for him. His work was done and he could get away from the press of people around his table either playing or eyeballing.

Ben Vining passed and pulled up to accost him angrily.

"We're not forgetting what you did today, Wallace," he said, a threat in his voice. "I don't believe you were up at the Sally McGee at all."

The croupier looked him over, his eyes coldly contemptuous.

"You'll never know," he retorted, and sauntered down the sidewalk.

Cape Wallace was not expecting trouble but

he kept his eyes open. The Vinings had not liked his testimony and some day they would try to get even. But they would probably not move too fast, since they could not be sure his story was a fabrication. That hour on the witness stand while he had been perjuring himself still gave him a chuckle. Quint Vining had been hoisted by his own petard. The troop of liars he had sent to the witness stand had brought to the jury no conviction of truth, but he had put his tale across nicely. The members of the jury could understand why a man might hang back as long as possible before volunteering evidence that would put him in bad with the vicious element and yet eventually be driven by his conscience to save one who was innocent. Of course Henry Page and his counsel had known that his testimony was false and dared not deny it for fear it might boomerang against the defendant. Cape Wallace did not admit to himself that he had run the risk of the penitentiary because young Page was his cousin. He preferred to put it on the ground that he had no use for the Vinings and believed in fair play.

He was drawing near to Harrison when he recognized Downing and Page at the corner on the opposite side of the street. The flares of the night-life center were back of him and there were no lights here except the one that came dimly through the Gothic window of The Little Church on the Corner. Since he did not care to meet either of these men he drew back into the semi-darkness and waited for them to go. Evidently they were about to separate for the night. Downing lifted a hand in farewell and turned to head north.

The crash of a revolver boomed along the street canyon. Before the echo of it died the roar of other guns cascaded into the night. Flashes stabbed the gloom. The shuffle of moving boots on the sidewalk made an undertone. A voice inside the saloon yelped, "God-almighty, I've been shot."

Instantly the pattern of the scene set itself for Wallace. This was an ambush arranged to destroy Page and his lawyer. Vaguely bulked in front of him were the figures of men, one in the shadow of a doorway, another back of a corner, a third behind a parked wagon.

The attacked men were answering the fire as they backed away from the light of the saloon. Swift messengers of death were lancing back and forth across the road. The sound of them went rocketing up the street.

Wallace moved forward close to the wall, swift and cat-like, his revolver out. The fellow in the doorway, a huge muscle-bound man as graceless as a rhinoceros, lumbered flatfooted along the sidewalk to keep pace with the ambushed pair backing away. His .44 belched flame. One of the figures in the shadows opposite reeled.

"Got one," he cried.

The man was Sam Ukena, and at the instant of his triumphant shout he caught sight of Wallace scarcely twenty feet away. Startled, he fired too fast. The bullet tore through a sign suspended over the sidewalk above the head of the gambler. It was the ruffian's last chance. A slug from Wallace's weapon tore into his stomach, a second reached his heart. His great body swayed and his feet spread to steady him. He teetered on his feet, then the knees buckled under him and he plunged down. As he struck the sidewalk his fingers convulsively jerked at the trigger again and the lead ripped a groove along the planks. A shudder ran through his body, the last sign of life in it.

The man back of the wagon snarled a question, "Get him, Sam?"

Sharp in the mind of Wallace was the realization that in a moment the attention of the killers, all of them within a dozen steps of him, would be diverted to the stranger who had stumbled into the ambuscade. He ran forward over the sprawled body of Ukena to take shelter in an arch leading to a meat market. The impact of his rush jolted him against the hard heavy-set frame of a man crouched there.

"Dammit, Sam, look where you are going," the earlier occupant complained.

The man was Mort Heisman. Wallace did not wait for him to find out his mistake but with the heavy barrel of his .45 pistol-whipped him on the side of the head. Staggered, Heisman relaxed his hold on the gambler. At the second blow his body sagged along the wall to the ground.

The fellow huddled back of the wagon had discovered that the body on the sidewalk was that of Ukena. Close to panic, he called, "Let's get outa here."

A few seconds later he was racing down Harrison at the heels of another of the ambushers. The sound of their footfalls died away.

During the battle there had been no sign of anybody on the street except those engaged in it, but in an incredibly short time the sidewalk and road were packed by men emerging from the Little Church and others pouring down from the lighted district.

Wallace pushed his revolver back into its

scabbard and took the gun from the unconscious hand of Heisman. As he crossed the street he dropped the weapon of Vining's guard into the bed of the wagon. Through the skirt of the gathering crowd he moved toward its center. Nobody knew that he had participated in the fight.

Page was on his feet but leaning against the wall for support.

"Badly hurt, Henry?" Downing asked.

The wounded man drew a hand covered with blood from under his waistcoat. "I'm hit. In the shoulder — or maybe my lung," he said.

"We'd better get him into the saloon and send for a doctor," Wallace said.

While they were helping Page through the swing doors somebody on the other side of the street gave a shout.

"There's a dead man here." He added a moment later, "Holy smoke, two of them."

The crowd surged across the road. One of the alleged dead men was coming to life, conscious of a thumping headache, a bloody head, and a tiptilted world full of staring eyes.

"It's Mort Heisman," a man said. "He needs a doctor too."

Heisman got to his feet unsteadily and glowered at the circle of curious and excited bystanders. "Where's my pistol?" he demanded harshly.

It was not on the ground and nobody had seen it. The gunman flung out a bitter curse, pushed through those about him, and weaved groggily down Harrison Avenue. He did not know exactly what had occurred, but somebody had thrown a monkey wrench into their ambuscade. As soon as he found out who it was he would rub him off the map.

After giving Page first aid the doctor said the bullet had just missed the lung. If there were no complications the patient ought to recover. A door was taken from its hinges and on it Page was carried to his rooming house half a block away. Downing and Wallace helped to carry him.

"I don't understand exactly what happened," the lawyer said. "They were lying in wait for us — four or five of them at least. All of them were firing and Henry was hit. Then the firing stopped and those that could ran away. Who killed Ukena? I'm sure we didn't."

"Likely one of his gang got excited and shot him by accident," Wallace suggested.

"And then got more excited and pistol-whipped Heisman," Downing commented. "That doesn't make sense."

"Thank your lucky stars and let it ride at that," the gambler suggested. "With a lot of guns going off you can't tell what will happen. Somebody is bound to lose his head."

Downing dropped the subject. He had to arrange for a nurse and see that his friend was made as comfortable as possible.

With the help of another man Wallace carried the door back to the Little Church. The saloon was crowded with patrons eager to talk over the difficulty that had just taken place. The proprietor grumbled at his luck while he helped the bartender serve drinks. His Gothic window was ruined, spoiled by the hole made by the bullet that had crashed through and broken a glass of beer a miner was lifting to his lips.

"Eighty-seven saloons in this town," he complained. "And when a guy wants to pull off a fight he has to come down here for it. All I get is grief."

Four men sat around a poker table in an upstairs room of the Silver Palace. Ben Vining reached for the bottle of whisky and poured himself a second big drink.

"Did you tell Heisman eight o'clock?" he asked irritably.

Quint looked at his brother, a faint contempt in his opaque eyes. "I said eight. He'll be along presently. Mort is a little sore, because he didn't pull off that damn-fool play you and he cooked up."

Ben glared at his brother angrily. "You would have said it was fine if it had worked. How could we tell some outsider would come buttin' in and gum the works?"

"I told you to let me handle it, but you had to try and slip over a fast one on me. Result is we're in bad when there was no need of it. I've been busy all day trying to fix the thing up. I went to the newspapers and explained how you boys were attacked. They were pretty cool to me — wanted to know how it happened that the first bullet fired, the one that went through the Little Church window, came from across the street, the side where my boys were. Fact is, the town has made up its mind I fixed a trap to get Page and Downing as they were going home. That is bad."

The door opened and Mort Heisman walked into the room. A white patch covered a wound on the side of his head. His dull eyes swept the room sourly. Amos Scudder pulled out a chair for him.

"Sit down and have a drink, Mort," he said.

Heisman slid into a seat, drew the bottle to him, and poured a water glass nearly half full.

He downed the whisky at a gulp. "This a post mortem?" he demanded, his challenging gaze on Quint.

"You might call it that — over the wrong corpse," Quint answered coldly, his hard chill eyes resting steadily on his bodyguard. "These fellows are troublemakers and ought to be bumped off. I grant you that. But I told you it was my job to handle."

"You bet." Heisman laughed insolently without mirth. "To take care of by proxy. They're in yore way, so they got no business to live."

Quint said softly, his face drained of expression, "There's a right way and a wrong way to do a job, Mort."

"Sure," the gunman retorted irritably. "And yore way is always the right one."

"We're not here to quarrel, Mort. You and Ben went ahead on your own and beefed this. Point is, to figure what's the best thing to do now."

"I've got that figured already, soon as I find out who butted in." Heisman's voice was hard and flat, his mouth an ugly tight line.

The fifth man present was Buck Harrigan, the city marshal. His splenetic laughter was a jeer. "Some hellamiler he must have been, to rub out Ukena, pistol-whip you, and send the other bully-buss boys skedaddlin' away from there."

The bleak gaze of Heisman fastened on the marshal. "I don't get it what Mr. Harrigan is doing here, Quint," he said. "You bringing the law into this?"

"I invited Buck here," Ben Vining explained hurriedly. "Thought we might decide to arrest Page and Downing for waylaying you boys."

"You've tried the law once," Heisman snarled. "A lot it got you."

"Not much," Quint agreed. "No more than your crazy play last night."

The marshal put both his forearms on the table and let his narrowed eyes rest on Heisman. He was a medium-sized powerfully built man of forty, a swaggering bully with plenty of courage back of his raffish front.

"Like Ben says I was invited here," he said, his words dripping challenge. "Any objections, Mort?"

Long seconds ticked away in the heavy silence while Heisman made his choice. His sleepy eyes met unwaveringly those of the officer. There was bad feeling between the men. Both were "bad men." Each felt a distrust of the other, a premonition that some day there might come a moment of decision between them. It was born partly of wariness and partly of the jealousy notorious gunfighters had toward a rival. Vining's guard was not afraid of Harrigan, but there was no sense in forcing the issue against one who was known to have killed seven.

He smiled thinly, with a surface politeness that obviously had no sincerity back of it. "No offense meant, Buck," he said. "I was only asking for information. Seeing as I am in this, I like to know where we stand."

"I'll tell you where we stand, Mort," Quint told him. "After last night we have to move carefully. We'll let Page and Downing alone for a while. Those are orders. If anyone disobeys them I won't back him up."

"You're going to let this fellow Page get away with killing Bert?" his brother asked angrily, color flooding his red-veined face.

"Not on yore life." Quint's voice was cold as a wind blowing over a glacier. "But from now on I'll say how and when we take care of these fellows."

"You don't want them arrested then," the marshal said.

"No. That might kick back on us." He hammered softly with his fist on the green table. "Get this right, all of you. We're coming near to a time in this town when the rough stuff won't go. It isn't a camp any longer, but a town of twenty thousand people. Railroads are coming in, as you know. If the big boys here get what they want this will be the state capital instead of Denver. They think this place is too wild. It has to be tamed down. All right. We'll throw in with them. Tiger Alley and the worst of the houses of ill repute will have to go. We'll ride the reform wave."

Ben stared at him in blank astonishment. "You going to throw down all the boys who have backed yore play?" he wanted to know.

"Not unless they get too raw. We'll have an open town, but it will be organized. The houses, the gambling places, the honky-tonks will keep right on doing a land-office business, but they will work more quietly and smoothly than they have been doing. We'll whoop it up for civic improvements and we'll support all the churches. But we'll thumbs-down on holdups and stage robbers. Most of them have played a lone hand anyhow."

"You going to run for mayor?" Ben inquired tartly.

"No, but I expect to be riding on the bandwagon of the fellow who is elected and to contribute liberally to the campaign expenses." Quint let his cold arrogant eyes sweep over them. They did not like this change of front.

Lawlessness was the condition on which they throve and they could not understand why Quint Vining, all of whose holdings were originally based on rapine and violence, should make a sudden about-face. Like it or not, he meant to drive them to his will. If they could not see the handwriting on the wall, he could. A dozen times today he had faced sullen looks and muttering about the attack on his enemies. "I'm going to look after you as I have always done. But we'll trot along nice and friendly with Mr. Law."

"I don't get yore idea," Ben blurted sullenly. "You expectin' to give up our claims on Fryer Hill?"

"Not an inch of one of them — except the Sally McGee. But claim-jumping is out from now on. The tide of feeling against it is too strong. Slick lawyers are a better investment. Wear out the prospectors with litigation and then buy them out for a song. Don't worry, boys. There will still be plenty of pickings, more than ever if we drive out the lone wolves who give us a bad name by robbing and killing."

"Just where does Henry Page fit into your Sunday school program — and Edward Downing, Esquire?" Heisman purred gently. "Or do you aim to settle their hash before you turn pious?"

"Respectable not pious is the word, Mort," corrected Quint. "We'll still be doing business at the old stand but in a little different way. And for the present you may forget about the gents you named. *You can be sure I won't.*"

"If I get you right, Quint, you are to do the deciding who is to be killed and when," Scudder said, a satiric grin on his skeleton face. "A guy doesn't get gunned till you press the button. Kinda Mr. God you aim to be, don't you?"

"Use your brains, Scudder, if any," Quint retorted sharply. "This town is due for a clean-up. It's coming, sure as Christmas. Point is, do we jump in and guide it, getting rid of a lot of riffraff that does us harm instead of good? Or do we sit around like bumps on a log and get rubbed off the map too?"

"Maybe I am blind, Quint," Heisman said. "But I haven't noticed this wave of moral indignation. There is as much hell-raising now as there was a month ago. Sure this ain't a case of cold feet?"

Quint ignored the jeer. "The best people in town are bringing their families up from Denver and from the East. They are building nice houses on the other side of Sixth Street for their women and children, and they are sleeping in walnut beds and eating off mahogany tables. They are not drinking coffee out of tin cups but from china their parents used in New England and Ohio. Ladies go calling on one another in the afternoon and are served tea with little sandwiches. The dresses at the Assembly balls were made in New York or in Paris. Everywhere I hear talk that the town is too rough. This isn't a camp any longer but a city. I've seen this change before in other places. After people of that sort bring their kids to a place they won't stand for a hurdy-gurdy town. They clean it up."

"I'll put in my nickel's worth," the marshal said, spilling tobacco into his pipe and lighting it. "Quint is right. From where I sit in this game I'm in a position to see a storm coming when you can't. And boys, it's going to be a hell of a big one if it gets going. You'd better get under cover while there is time."

Ben Vining was the first to fall into line. He knew his brother was shrewd as well as ruthless. "Well, it's no skin off my nose if they clean up Tiger Alley and Stillborn," he agreed sullenly. "Same with the holdups and stage robbers. They don't bring a dollar in to us. Point is, will these reformers quit when you tell 'em that's enough?"

"They will if we are helping to guide the reform," Quint answered. "Most people want this to be a wide-open town but under control. We'll play along with the churches to a reasonable extent."

Heisman said, "All right, Quint, play it your way."

Harrigan looked at his watch and rose. "After Quint has made this a Sunday school town I won't have a thing to do but loaf, boys. Now I have to make a bluff of riding herd on Tiger Alley and State Street." His cold derisive eyes drifted over the others in the room, a thin smile mocking them. "I hear Parson Tom is having a revival next week. It will be nice to see you boys going down the sawdust trail to the amen corner. I read in the good book that the righteous prosper and the wicked come to grief. Let us now all sing, 'Ring the Bells of Heaven.' Put yourselves into the singing hearty, brethren." At the door he lifted his hands in blessing, then went out of the room shaking with laughter.

He left behind him a man whose dislikes had crystallized into hatred. A suspicion too had filtered into Heisman's mind, the thought that Harrigan might be the man who had upset their ambush last night.

In a complimentary reference to Erma Roberts the *Chronicle* had once dubbed her the Little Mother of the Camp. She had a heart that went out to those in trouble and more than once from the stage had made appeals for the needy that brought them aid. So it was natural for her to appoint herself visiting nurse in chief for Henry Page. After the patient had reached the convalescent stage Joan Regal became one of her assistants and took a two hour turn at his bedside in the afternoon. For the sake of propriety the door of the room was left open.

Henry was no longer in danger. With those who had attended him during the first days while he had been in pain and distress he had been a petulant and rather exacting patient, but when Joan was in the room he was deeply contented. Her presence ministered to the weakness that reached out for comfort. He loved the feel of her cool soft fingers on his forehead and he contrived to get as many of those gentle personal contacts as possible.

She was reading to him Dickens' *Great Expectations* one afternoon and he watched her with eyes that could not get enough of her gracious loveliness. He interrupted her low, sweet, throaty voice to ask for a drink of water. After taking a sip or two he handed back the glass and caught her by the wrist. Joan knew he had tricked her, but as she looked down into his long-lashed imploring eyes she did not resent it. A pulse of excitement beat in her throat.

"I can't put the glass down until you let me," she murmured.

"You have two hands," he reminded her.

The smoldering fire in his eyes lit a flame in her blood. With her free hand she put the glass down on the bedside table.

"How long am I to be a prisoner?" she asked, trying to keep her voice light.

"You know I love you, Joan," he said.

The words released a dammed reservoir of emotion pent up in her. He drew her down and she knelt beside the bed. She put an arm beneath his head and he kissed her eyes, her throat, her lips.

"Someone may see us," she whispered.

"Who cares?" he asked, his smile warm and gay.

Not Joan at that high moment. His kisses sent a heat running through her lithe young body. She returned them, passionately and eagerly.

Footsteps passed down the hall. Joan raised her head and listened. "Someone must have seen us," she said, snatched back to earth.

"If so, someone thought what a lucky man I am," Henry answered. "Don't worry, dear.

Men and women have kissed ever since Adam and Eve in the garden."

"Yes, but — he'll think I am — a light woman. He may talk."

"He probably did not even look in as he passed."

Joan was not quite happy about it, in part because she was shocked at what she had done. Her aunt had taught her the social convention that a girl before marriage must withdraw from the advances of a man even though engaged to him. If she is a lady she keeps her lover cool and respectful. Joan had not only failed to keep him at arm's length; she had encouraged him with kisses ardent as his own.

Ted Downing and Erma Roberts dropped in as they usually did about this hour in the afternoon. Downing got more pain than pleasure from his visits. For it was plain that Joan was falling in love with Page. Ted had felt sure she would. Henry had the Byronic appearance that young women of the period found romantic — superlative good looks, an eager gaiety, the mercurial temperament that could be merry or appealingly unhappy. When Downing looked in the glass he saw a redheaded Irishman with a well-boned rugged face that just missed homeliness. Nothing there to excite a girl. He was a man's man, about as romantic as a ham sandwich, he reflected.

Even the strain of weakness that ran through Henry was attractive to women. In it was a touch of wistfulness, of the grown-up child demanding a maternal sympathy. It was not that Page lacked courage. Throughout the trial and the battle afterward he had carried himself well. But there had been times when his lawyer had walked into his cell and found him on the verge of despair. What he lacked was fortitude, the stiffness that will stand up to any adversity.

Erma sensed in Joan embarrassment and was much interested in the differences in character of Henry and Ted Downing. Page had been brought up in a smug respectable environment, and appearances meant a great deal to him. Deeply interested though he was in Joan, he was ashamed that she was working for a living, especially as a variety hall actress. If he married her, his wife's past would be something to conceal after he took her back to the Midwest. It would not occur to Downing to have such a feeling. Joan's accidental environment did not at all affect what she was.

That there had been some lovemaking before she and Downing arrived, Erma felt sure.

With intent to draw information from Joan she mentioned that evening in their room the impression she had gathered of the difference between the men.

The girl flared up at once. "I don't think you are right at all," she differed. "Henry was brought up among nice gentle people and he went to a good school. After the way he has been treated here you would not expect him to care for these barbarians. At least I wouldn't."

"He ought to feel friendly toward some of them," Erma pointed out. "Several rough miners came forward and testified for him. A jury of them found him not guilty. Look what Ted Downing did for him and at what risk. I sometimes wonder if Henry is grateful enough to him."

"Of course he is," Joan answered. "He told me how much he owes Mr. Downing."

"It's easy to say that." Erma lifted her shoulders in a shrug. "Henry expects to have things handed to him on a silver platter. I like him. But I wish he weren't so smug and satisfied with himself."

Joan flushed angrily. "You are talking about the man I am going to marry," she said.

"Oh, my dear, I didn't know." Erma took Joan in her arms and held the girl tight. "I hope you will be as happy as you deserve —

and I am sure you will be."

But it was in her mind that her friend had fallen in love with the lesser man of her two suitors.

6

Ted Downing strolled down Chestnut Street, a deceptive picture of a young man at ease. In his being there was no evidence of the wary sense of fear that was now a part of his daily life. After a wild night Leadville was just beginning to yawn and stretch itself before coming awake from sodden slumber. A hundred men in the Mammoth Sleeping Palace were still dead to the world. Movers in covered wagons close to the curb lay lax on shuck mattresses, their teams tied to the rear. A Sunday quiet brooded over this canyon of false fronts, log cabins, and more pretentious frame buildings shouldering one another indiscriminately. As yet the tramp of moving feet did not echo from wall to wall. The rattle of chips and the click of billiard balls, the blare of bands, the patter of the spielers had not begun. Except for a swamper or two sweeping out the saloons and gambling halls the street showed no sign of life. Cards and empty bottles littered the sidewalks. In front of Casey's Place a miner peacefully snored, still unaware that somebody during the night had emptied his pockets. Downing stepped over his body and walked past the deserted business establishments to his office.

He stopped in the doorway to lift his eyes from the higgledy-piggledy rabbit warren of a town which haste and chance had flung up so swiftly to gaze at the snow-clad ranges towering above it. Back of Fryer Hill, scarred with hundreds of gopher holes and the dirt from them clawed out by human rodents, lay the Mosquitos bare and stark; and to the west the Continental Divide with Mount Elbert and Mount Massive rising above the long range, the highest peaks in the country, their ribs seamed with snow-filled gulches. The air that whipped down from them was fresh and clean, and the rising sun was painting their crests with a pink glow. Downing wondered what the Maker of all this beauty thought of the welter of crazed humanity drawn here by the lust for gold. Yet he felt that back of the greed was something heroic in the high hope that drove men through grime and hardship and defeat toward that rainbow's end that beckoned.

Ted closed the door and brought his mind

back to his own plight. It might be that he was still under a sentence of death set for the near future, unless the Vinings had modified their plans on account of the public resentment and would concentrate on punishing Page alone. There were few precautions he could take, since the initiative lay with the enemy. He went armed. He was very careful about going out after dark. But no matter how wary he was he had to expose himself to the chance of assassination. It was his philosophy that when danger could not be avoided the safest way was to ignore it as if it did not exist. Downing knew he was no hero, but he had been brought up in the school of hard knocks and he was tough. Moreover, he did not believe they would get him.

Page was in much greater danger, both because he was the one the Vinings most wanted to destroy and because he was less able to look after himself. He ought to leave the camp as soon as he could travel. Maybe he would now that he had had a taste of the punishment laid up for him. If he did he would probably send for Joan Regal to join him in the East. That could not be helped.

Quint Vining's change of front, as announced in the *Chronicle*, was surprising and perplexing. He had come out in a strong interview with a demand that Leadville clean house. The vice alleys must be purged and the road agents and footpads suppressed. The silver city would never be voted the capital of the state as long as murderers roamed its streets. This was the richest and most vital mining camp on earth and nobody with good judgment would ask that it be anything but a wide open town. But that need not mean crime. The law must be strengthened to make the city a desirable spot in which to bring up children, one in which good women would not fear for the lives of their husbands. Vining urged that a committee of fifteen, chosen from the best citizens, be appointed by the mayor to devise ways and means to bring about the necessary reforms. He would be very glad to serve on such a body.

And make sure it did not interfere with any of his interests, Downing thought. The lawyer knew there had been a rising tide of resentment against conditions, but it must be stronger than he had estimated it or Vining would not be so ready to give way before it. He must have weighed the prospects carefully before he decided to throw overboard the worst of the riffraff whose captain he had been. Though Quint had been a bad citizen, reputable people would probably forgive him his past if he threw his influence now in support of a clean-up campaign, even though they might be suspicious of the reasons that moved him. In a frontier camp, as Leadville still was in spirit, one did not inquire too closely into a man's record. He was judged by his present conduct rather than by his past.

But it was fixed in Downing's mind that a man like Quint Vining did not change. He was a virile scoundrel who worshiped money and power, a man ruthless and cruel, moved by an appalling malignity. His hatreds would endure, and so would his inordinate appetite for success. He was not given to gratifying swift impulses. He knew when to wait and when to strike.

Downing buckled down to work on a case he had coming up in the district court. He spent hours looking up citations that might be applicable. Then he was hungry, and to save time he decided to eat at the French Coffee House on the other side of the street.

Three men were walking abreast on the plank sidewalk as Downing came out of his office. The oldest of the three the lawyer knew, a man in his forties named Soapy Sills, heavyset and bowlegged, with light restless eyes set deep in a weathered face, the lines in it sharp and haggard. It had not been proved, but he was under suspicion of being a member of the Hayden band of stage robbers. His companion on the right was a showy, raffish fellow with rusty hair and a nose that had been broken. He had flinty shallow eyes and a steeltrap mouth straight as the slit in a watermelon.

Downing nodded at Sills. "Been away, Soapy?" he asked casually. "Haven't seen you around lately."

"Jest moseyin' here and there," Sills answered. "Meet Red Mosely and Jim Wesley. Gentlemen, Mr. Downing."

The lawyer's glance shuttled to the young man on the outside — and held fast. Jim Wesley was lithe as a cat, a blackhaired youth well dressed and graceful. The eyes in his reckless devil-may-care face were dark and long-lashed. The lips below the small neat mustache suggested self-willed petulance. It occurred to Downing later that he was too good-looking for character. Life had written nothing on that handsome face but self-indulgence. But for the moment there registered but one impression — the likeness of this boy to Joan Regal. He stared at the lad.

Wesley's laugh covered annoyance. "You'll know me again, Mr. Downing," he said.

The lawyer apologized. "Sorry I was rude.

I — the fact is you reminded me of somebody I know."

"I'm always reminding somebody of his dead brother," the young man sneered.

"Not in this case," Downing replied. "My thought was that you resembled somebody very charming. Have you been in Leadville long, Mr. Wesley?"

A shutter seemed to drop over the dark eyes of the youth. "I'm no tenderfoot," he answered sulkily, and pushed past his questioner.

Downing followed the men with his eyes. The incident depressed him. This boy's likeness to Joan was remarkable. His name was Jim. He even had mannerisms resembling hers — a certain light lift of the hand, a quick turn of the head. But Jim Regal ought not to be a companion of men like Sills and Mosely. It was written on both of them that they were evil.

While Ted was eating dinner he pondered what was best to do. Very likely the boy did not know his sister was in town. He ought to be told. Yet if the youngster was tied up with outlaws it might be better for Joan not to know. He knew she was devoted to her brother. To find out the truth might break her heart. He decided to put the problem up to Erma Roberts.

She was shopping at Daniels & Fisher's store when he found her fitting a pair of elbow-length six-button kids.

Erma brushed aside his doubts at once. "Of course we'll tell Joan. Her heart can't be so easily broken. If Jim has strayed into bad ways she will want to save him from his evil companions."

"If we tell her she will be hurt," Downing objected. "You know how fond she is of her brother. It is bound to make her unhappy to find out he has gone bad."

"Unhappy, of course, but we can't keep her in a glass cage away from trouble. For all her dainty ways she is as tough as you are. She'll take whatever she must." Erma slid a friendly derisive look at him. "You don't know much about women, do you? Your friend Hal Page could tell you that Joan isn't a Dresden doll. He doesn't wrap her up with courtesy but teases and scolds and sometimes bullies her — and she likes it."

"I never had a sister and my mother died when I was seven," he explained.

"Other men have sisters you could meet," she suggested.

"I've been too busy to know any of them," he said. "Now what about this Jim Wesley, as he calls himself? Do you want me to find him and let him know his sister is in Leadville? He cut me off sharply when I asked him if he had been here long."

Erma drummed her fingertips on the counter, silent for a moment as she considered the situation. "He knows you are a lawyer, and if he is in trouble he may think you are trying to trap him. If so, he would very likely just disappear again. I think I had better get in touch with him."

"But how?"

She smiled. "By woman's wiles. Find out where he is staying, so that I can send a messenger to him with two tickets to the show. I'll put in a note to come back to the dressing room and see me after my act. He'll meet Joan there before she goes on."

"Will he come?"

"He'll come, if only out of curiosity. He won't be sure why I asked him, and he'll want to find out."

Downing nodded. "He'll be flattered. It will stick in his mind that you may have seen him and been attracted by his good looks. And since you are a prominent actress he will like to think that. I can't help wishing he wouldn't come. He can't bring anything but unhappiness to Joan. My judgment is that he is unstable as well as weak and wilful."

"Maybe we can get him to turn to a better way of life," Erma said. "A lot of boys wobble wrong for a while and yet turn out good citizens."

That was true of hundreds of young men in the West, Downing knew. No longer bound by the restraints of home, by a local public opinion that imposed upon them a standard of decent living, they cut loose and ran a wild course until their sense of right and wrong pulled them up. If there was character in them they made a right about face and settled down before it was too late.

Downing looked up a former client of his who had affiliations with the underworld and asked him to make inquiries. The man, known as Short Dick, was a harmless ne'er-do-well skillful at mooching drinks from those hospitably inclined. He had a wide acquaintance in the town. A few hours later he reported that Dan Hayden and several of his gang were staying at a cabin on a ledge above Sourbelly Gulch but at the moment three or four of the outfit were drinking at the Never Say Die saloon, among them the young fellow who called himself Jim Wesley.

Jim was surprised and his vanity gratified when a messenger brought him two tickets for that evening's performance at the Grand Central with the compliments of Erma Roberts and an invitation to come back to her dressing room after her act. He showed the note to Mosely, who read the invitation and leered at his younger companion.

"Shows what a pretty baby face will do," he said. "She picks you when she might have had a he-man, meaning me. You'd better go. Erma has the rep of being choosy. A dozen guys have made a try at her and got nowhere — and she makes eyes at a kid not dry behind the ears."

The clapping hands and stamping feet brought Erma back for a third encore. She sang a verse of "The Blue Alsatian Mountains":

"Adé, Adé, Adé,
Such songs will pass away,
Though the Blue Alsatian mountains,
Seem to watch and wait alway."

The audience would not let her go. She returned to the front of the stage, smiling at the friendly house. "Positively my last appearance tonight," she said, and told a story of Paddy Burke, who was sitting in a box to the right applauding vigorously. The point of it was that he had met her on the street earlier in the day and after some repartee, in which she had called him a mick, agreed proudly that he was Irish, "but not clay-pipe Irish." There was a roar of laughter as she disappeared in the wings.

When Erma reached her dressing room Joan said, over her shoulder, "They liked you tonight."

"I've completely run out of new stories to tell," Erma replied. "The one I gave them tonight was pretty thin."

A pulse of excitement was beating in her throat. She had not told Joan that her brother was in town, since she was not at all sure that he would accept her invitation and if he did that the reunion would be a happy one.

Joan turned. "Will I do?" she asked. She had learned that without grease paint her face appeared to the audience too pallid, but she used it very sparingly.

There was a knock on the door. Erma said, "Come in." A young man she had never seen walked into the room, but she knew at once he must be Jim Regal. He looked at her, then at the girl on the chair.

"What are you doing here?" he demanded.

"Jim!" Joan cried, her eyes bright with joy.

She flew at him and flung her arms around his neck.

He kissed her, held her close, then pushed her back, his fingers circling her wrists. The young man's gaze swept her costume. "Why are you wearing that disgraceful get-up?" he snapped.

"Is it so bad?" Joan asked, a flag of color flying in her cheeks. "I have to wear it — in my act."

"What act?"

"On the stage. I help a juggler."

"God's sake! What's got into you? How come Aunt Mary let you leave Hillcrest for this hell hole anyhow? Has she gone crazy too?"

"Aunt Mary died two months ago. I wrote you all about it, but you never called at the post office for the letter. When I didn't hear from you I got worried. So I came out to find you."

"I wasn't lost. I've been — away." He added irritably: "At Redcliff and Ten Mile. I didn't know about Aunt Mary."

"If you had written just a line to me, Jim," the girl said, close to tears. "I read the articles in *Leslie's* and *Harper's* about this camp — how wild it was — and when no word came from you I couldn't stand it."

"So you disgraced us by becoming an actress — in a variety hall," he flung out.

"No disgrace at all," Erma differed sharply. "What else could she do while she was looking for you, her money all gone? You ought to be proud of her, earning her living honestly."

He said loftily, "The Regal women do not go on the stage."

"The Regal men prefer that they starve," Erma retorted. "Young man, get off your high horse. You walked out on your sister and she had to look out for herself. This town respects her. Every miner who comes to the Grand Central knows she is a lady and treats her as such."

He flushed angrily. "I didn't walk out on her. I left her in the care of her aunt, perfectly safe. She ought never to have come here. It's no place for a young girl. And since you believe in plain speaking, I'll say that this is between me and Joan and is none of your business."

"Jim — Jim," his sister pleaded. "Erma is my best friend. She has done everything for me. You don't know how much. I just couldn't have got along without her. I was so unhappy — about Aunt Mary and you."

"She got you into this play-acting," he charged.

"Erma found me work, and I am grateful to her," she said. "Don't be stuffy, Jim. I'm no actress. All I do is hand Mr. Renaud his props and sort of feed up to his patter. He's quite nice."

"I don't care how nice he is," her brother answered arrogantly. "You'll quit tonight. I'll tell him you are through."

Joan's answer surprised her as much as it did him. "When I decide to stop I'll let him know," she said quietly.

It was a declaration of independence. She felt a queer sense of exultation, as if she had escaped conventional shackles that had bound her. She had moved all her life in a tight atmosphere where it was not proper for ladies to work.

Surprised, he stared at her. His sister had always been docile and gentle, accepting decisions made for her. This was not the girl he had left at Hillcrest. "You'll do as I say," he told her sulkily.

"No, Jim." Her eyes met his directly. "You can't live my life for me. I like earning my living. It does something for me."

"A woman's place is in the home," he said, much annoyed.

"When she has one," Joan amended. "I haven't."

She was amazed at her own assurance, and at the critical judgment she was passing on her brother. All her life she had joined her aunt in spoiling him. They had minimized his wildness and explained it away. Her love for him had swayed her opinion. But during the past weeks she had been on her own and had met life at first hand. She had gained confidence in herself and was looking at him objectively. He had just heard of the death of the aunt who had brought them up with unfailing devotion after the loss of their parents and he had been so full of his own selfish resentment that he had not yet expressed even perfunctory sorrow.

A boy knocked on the door and called, "Your turn, Miss Regal."

"Don't be angry, Jim," the girl said gently. "We're not at Hillcrest now. This is another world."

She walked past him out of the room.

Young Regal had a low boiling point and anger simmered in him now. "You did this to her," he fumed, glaring at Erma.

"Oh no," she corrected. "You did it as much as anybody. By leaving her alone. She came out to a freer environment and found herself. Joan is a lovely girl, dear and unspoiled. This hasn't hurt her at all. She is human, and it pleases her to be popular. But, as she says, she isn't an actress. It's up to you now. You can take her home, if you can persuade her that you will stay there and behave."

"You're one of those managing women who like to run other people's lives," he accused. "I don't need any woman telling me what to do."

"Maybe I am." Erma smiled. "I was just about to suggest you go and see Joan's act. There is nothing objectionable about it."

"All right. I'll go. But I won't change my mind. She has no right to be parading on a stage in a man's clothes."

He found a seat near the back of the house, and, though he was already well primed with liquor, ordered another shot of whisky. Renaud was busy keeping four balls in the air and at the same time carrying on a patter in which Joan joined. In spite of the prejudice he entertained Jim Regal could not fail to see that his sister was not only popular but respected. The audience reponded to the charm of her shy and lovely youth by refraining entirely from catcalls or comments during the act and after it was finished they called her back several times by continued applause.

After the performance Jim met Soapy Sills

at the Silver Palace and was introduced to Quint Vining. Presently Soapy drifted to a roulette table and the owner of the gambling house invited Regal into his office. He motioned his guest to a chair and from a cupboard drew a bottle and two glasses.

"Not the stuff I serve my customers," he said with a smile.

Jim could not guess why his host had brought him here. Quint chattered pleasantly for a few minutes before enlightening him.

"It must have been a surprise for you to find your sister here, Mr. Regal," he said presently.

"So you know my name," the young man replied.

"It's my business to know a lot about a good many people in this town. I don't care whether you call yourself Regal or Wesley. That isn't the point."

"Just what is the point?" Regal asked.

Vining lit a cigar, leaned back in his chair, and sent a fat smoke wreath drifting across the room. "It's rather a delicate business and perhaps no affair of mine, but I am a good deal older than you and I don't like to see young people making a mistake."

Regal was startled. He was implicated in a project that was to be pulled off very soon and he wondered if word of it had come to the ears of Quint Vining. "Am I making a mistake?" he asked.

"I hadn't you in mind," Quint said, and left that cryptic suggestion for the young man to think over.

Jim's body relaxed. He did not see why he should worry if somebody else was making a mistake. "If it is another man why not speak to him instead of to me," he suggested.

"It isn't a 'him.' It's a young lady."

"I am acquainted with several girls in town but no young ladies," Regal answered. "So I still don't see where I come in."

"You know this young lady. She is a very fine young woman, superior in every way, one for whom I have great respect, an opinion shared by the whole town."

"Are you by any chance referring to my sister, sir?" Regal asked stiffly.

Vining raised a protesting hand. "Don't misunderstand me. A young lady's innocence sometimes betrays her into an indiscretion that is unwise."

"You are talking, I suppose, about my sister being on the stage."

"Certainly not." Quint hesitated, apparently considering whether he was making a mistake. "You may consider this an impertinence. But I think somebody ought to warn you. A young libertine, a scoundrel who killed my brother a few weeks since and immediately after his release shot down another man, has wormed himself into Miss Regal's — shall I say, friendship? — and has, I am afraid, completely fascinated her. He is a handsome devil, suave and sophisticated, the kind to ingratiate himself into the affections of a young girl with romantic ideas. He was wounded in his latest shooting scrape. With the kindest intentions in the world Miss Erma Roberts took over the nursing of the scamp. Your sister has been helping her. Sometimes together, more often singly, they have spent much time at his room looking after him. This has caused a good deal of comment."

Jim Regal rose abruptly, pushing the chair back with his knees. "Who is this fellow?" he demanded.

"His name is Henry Page. He is a claim-jumper and a troublemaker. To look at him you would never guess what a villain he is. As I have said, your sister is above reproach. But she is young and impulsively generous. Since you are her natural protector it is better to put you on your guard. When a young lady's feelings are involved there is no use talking with her. She can see no wrong in the man. She trusts him, and — " He shrugged his shoulders, leaving the sentence uncompleted.

"You are keeping back something," Regal cried, his eyes stormy. "What is it?"

"I've said enough," Vining answered, and immediately reversed himself. "If you must have it, a man passing the room on his way downstairs saw them embracing ardently."

"Where does this Page live?" the young man demanded angrily.

"I don't know exactly — somewhere on Chestnut, I think. You can find out easily. He is a bold ruffian, but if you stand up to him firmly it may make a difference. Since the fellow is a killer you will go armed of course and watch every motion he makes while you are with him. We don't know how he'll take this. Don't let him get the drop on you."

The bleak eyes of the older man bored into those of Regal. A cold wind blew through the young fellow. For a moment he felt the shadow of death brushing him. He was getting into something he did not like. Though he was furious at Page and at his sister, the anger in him had not reached the intensity suggested by Vining's advice. He had no wish to kill Page or be killed by him. The prospect opened was disturbing.

"I'm going to have to leave town in a day or

two," he said hesitantly.

"That is too bad. I think you are needed here now. Is the business that takes you away imperative?"

Regal's eyes went blank of expression. "It is important," he said sharply.

"Perhaps it may be sufficient to warn Page," Vining said. His tone carried a serious doubt of this.

"I'll serve notice on him to keep away from my sister," the boy promised.

"Don't forget that he is dangerous," Vining warned. "Maybe you won't have any trouble with him, but if you do — *make sure to strike first.*"

"You don't think he'll start shooting right away, do you?" Regal asked.

"I don't know what he will do. You never can tell how a bad man of his stripe will react. But I don't want a nice lad like you killed. If he makes a move that is suspicious pour lead into him. Don't hesitate an instant or it will be too late."

"Perhaps if I talked to my sister," Regal suggested.

"Not a bit of use," Vining differed. "He is the aggressor. Stop this at its source."

"I can't let him smirch my sister's good name."

"No," agreed Vining decisively. "But watch him closely."

When Regal left the room he went to the bar and had another drink — and after that another. He postponed action until tomorrow.

7

Henry Page rebuilt his lost blood rapidly and within two weeks of the night he had been wounded was able to dress and sit on the gallery in front of the second story of the rooming house. There he could see the turbulent life of the city flow past him. During his convalescence he had listened day and night to the restless beat of the feet below and to the blare of the bands from the dance halls and the honky-tonks. Looking down on the shifting crowds now, he was impressed again by the tremendous energy and the amazing hope that inspired this town on the roof of the continent. Every man who tramped Chestnut Street was a potential millionaire. He had a stake in some shaft on the hillside that was bound to turn out a Glory Hole. Most of them were enduring discomfort if not actual hardship. They consoled themselves with the assurance that if their luck was bad it was bound to change. Almost any day some extravagant absurdity was likely to set the camp roaring with laughter. The latest one was the story of Dead Man's claim.

A miner had been killed by a rock fall at the breast of a drift. The owner of the mine had hired two laborers to dig a grave in the rapidly filling cemetery. They put the corpse in a snow bank, and while digging struck pay ore. They forgot the burial and located the claim, which turned out to have sixty-ounce silver. Two weeks later somebody stumbled on the body frozen in the snowbank.

The first walk Page took was to a barbershop. The blond wavy hair that contributed to his good looks had grown unkempt. While the owner of the place trimmed it he kept up a steady stream of conversation. As a side line he did tattooing and the day before this a girl from the line, a "humdinger," had been in to have a special job done in the back room. The name Billy Boy was tattooed on her thigh and she wanted it changed to Freddy. The operator was proud of the result. She too had been satisfied and had paid him twenty-five dollars.

"She is a right genteel girl and you would have an elegant time with her, you bet," the tattoo surgeon said. "She is partial to hair tonic and I can rub one in for you that will smell nice all day."

Page thought he could do without it and said so. The barber whipped the apron from him, shook the hair from it to the floor, and folded it for the next customer.

"She is at Minnie's Place if you would like to know. I'm sure she would suit you. Ask for Belle." The man had lowered his voice to a confidential whisper. A miner had come in for a shave.

Henry sauntered down Harrison and along Chestnut toward Downing's office. There had been a heavy snow the previous day and in the night, and the traffic had made the street a bog of slush. In the gutters parallel to the sidewalks a long rampart of snow was piled five feet high. Some wag had stuck up a sign in it, "Keep off the Grass."

The lawyer joined Page for dinner at the Tontine. Two days earlier a freighter had brought in from the Bayou Salado a wagonload of deer, and venison steak was on the menu. They found it good. Page had the appetite of a convalescent and cleaned his plate. Two ladies, a mother and daughter, came in and gushed over Henry. He had met them before his difficulty with the Vinings. They were so pleased to see him recovered from his wound and able to be around. Henry brightened at sight of them. In his world women were important.

They were newly rich from a carbonate strike. Mrs. Folsom bulged in the wrong places and was plainly fencing with the encroaching years, but the daughter Nancy was a dark-eyed pretty creature full of life. Over her headdress of braids and puffs she wore a fascinator that framed her charming face. A fur tippet was fastened around her neck above a black cashmere dress of the latest pannier fashion. She was perhaps a little overdressed for so early in the day, but her bright youth could afford a touch of flamboyance.

After a perfunctory greeting at the introduction they practically ignored Downing and devoted their interest to Page. They told him the latest chitchat of the fashionable set and hoped so much he would be able to attend the Assembly Ball next week. Henry did not have an invitation, but he did not tell them so. He felt sure he could wangle one somewhere, and he reserved a quadrille with Mrs. Folsom and with her daughter a waltz and a polka. Downing could see that he was delighted at the warmth of their manner toward him.

"I don't really want to go to the Ball," Page explained to his companion after they had left the restaurant, "but it may help me a lot to make as many friends as I can among important people."

Downing agreed with him, rather dryly.

"I'll have to find some nice girl to take." Henry named two or three, one of whom might be available. All of them belonged to the wealthy society set. He had a very slight acquaintance with them, but his good looks and pleasant manners very likely would get him past the scrutiny of their mothers.

The lawyer was annoyed but did not express his feeling. Though resentment stirred in him, this was none of his business. But Henry had been turning all the charm he had on Joan. If he was in love with her why was he playing up to a group from which she was excluded? He had no right to be on both sides of the fence. As an actress in a variety theater Joan was beyond the pale set by the false standards of the society group. It seemed to Ted Downing that by catering to them Page was insulting the girl to whom he had been making love. There might have been some excuse if Joan had not been so fine and lovely.

Ted realized that he was more critical because his feelings were so deeply involved. After all Henry was only being himself, an easygoing, self-indulgent youth who usually put his own desires first. No doubt he was as much in love with Joan as he could be with anyone. When in trouble he had reached eagerly for her sympathy. Now he did not need her so much and he probably would not object to a flirtation with some other pretty girl. There was, it flashed angrily through Downing's mind, a touch of condescension in his friend's attitude toward Joan, as if he were King Cophetua stepping down to say, "This beggar maid shall be my queen!"

Downing could not help making one dig at him. "If you want to go to the Assembly why not take Miss Regal?"

Henry smiled, not at all offended. "My dear boy, I can't do that. I'd love to take Joan, but you know how these cats are. Very likely she would be snubbed. A selected list of women are invited, and I can't go outside of that for a partner. Of course Joan is worth a dozen of them. I must be careful not to put her in a position where her feelings can be hurt."

That was true enough, Downing knew. It would not do to take Joan. It did not seem to occur to Henry that he did not have to go either.

Page walked back to his rooming house and slept through the afternoon. The exercise had tired him. He awoke when a waiter brought him his supper from a restaurant across the street. Even if he had been stronger he would not have ventured out after dark alone. In the event that he went to the Assembly Ball it would be in a closed hack with another couple. After the dance he would not come home but would arrange to spend the night with the other man in the foursome. Word had reached him that Vining had given up any thought of revenge, but he did not mean to take any chances with the intentions in Quint's sinister mind.

Supper over, he lay on the bed and read Wilkie Collins' *Woman in White.*

Tired of reading, he yawned and looked at his watch. The time was five minutes to twelve. He rose on his elbow to turn down and blow out the lamp. A knock sounded on the door. It brought him to startled attention. Callers did not usually come at this hour. It might be one of the Vining gunmen. He rose softly, took his revolver from the table drawer, and moved to the door. He was careful not to stand in front of it. A bullet might come crashing through at him.

"Who is there?" he asked.

"My name is Regal. I want to talk with you." The voice had in it a note of excitement.

This must be Jim Regal, Page guessed. Downing had told him Joan's brother was in town. He unlocked the door and let in his visitor.

At sight of the pistol in Page's hand, Regal's face tightened. He thought of Quint Vining's words, *Be sure to strike first.* But he could not do that. He was trapped. Before he could move, a slug would tear into his belly.

Page's smile held embarrassed apology. He tossed the revolver to the bed. "Sorry," he said. "Thought it might be a fellow out to get me. Glad to meet you, Mr. Regal. Your sister and I are friends."

Jim drew a long breath of relief. The reaction following fear was anger. He was afraid his eyes had showed the shock that had twisted his stomach into a cold hard knot. The hand held out to him he ignored.

"That's what I came to talk to you about," he answered, his voice high and shrill. "I won't have it. You can't ruin her because you think she is a variety-hall girl with nobody to protect her. Let her alone. I'm serving notice."

Page stared in astonishment at the excited boy. "You're talking foolishness," he snapped. "I wouldn't hurt her for the world."

"You've hurt her already. You've compromised her reputation. Folks are talking about you and her. She is a good girl. You keep away from her."

"That's absurd. Why would anybody talk?

What have I done?"

"She visited you here in this room. Don't try to deny it. You can't get away with a lie."

"Miss Regal came here with Miss Roberts when I was wounded and very sick," Page explained. "They were here to nurse me."

"What business had my sister nursing you?"

"You know this town," Page said. "There are no regular nurses here. When someone they know is sick the ladies have to take a hand."

"She came to see you alone — several times," Regal charged. "Don't tell me she didn't."

"Is there any harm in that, when I was lying helpless in bed from a wound? She read to me. The door of the room was always wide open. Ask Mrs. Apperson, the landlady."

"I won't ask anybody. My sister ought not to know you at all. You were tried for murder. You killed Bert Vining. Before you had been out of jail a dozen hours you killed another man. You have no right even to speak to a girl like my sister. But you think she is fair game because she is on the stage." He repeated himself violently. "I won't have it. Let her alone. Stay away from her. I'm serving notice."

Page thought the boy might be right when

he said there was talk about him and Joan. A chaperon more conventional than Erma Roberts would never have let her come here alone, even though any passer could see into the room. But Erma lived by the casual code of the theatrical profession and formal decorum meant little to her. Yet Joan's kindness to him had been entirely innocent. He could not let her brother believe anything else.

"Listen to me," Henry urged. "You have everything wrong. I am not a murderer. A gang of thugs forced me to kill. And I am not a seducer. I hate to use the word when we are talking of Miss Regal, for I have never met a finer young lady. I respect and honor her. All who know her in this town feel the same way. There is no least shadow cast on her reputation. If you will make inquiries — "

Regal interrupted, his eyes hot with anger. "You don't have to explain my sister to me. You can't talk yourself out of this. I'm telling you for the last time. Let her alone, or by God, I'll come smoking. This is a last warning. I won't have you making love to her."

He turned and strode out of the room.

Henry sat on the bed, annoyed at the quarrel thrust upon him. Somebody was always putting him in the wrong unjustly. He did not like to be forced into decisions. It was pleasanter to drift and let problems solve themselves. This young fool was thrusting himself in where he was not wanted. Joan and he were able to determine what their relationship would be without interference. They did not need Erma Roberts to watch her like a hen with one chick, nor Ted Downing with his stuffy old-fashioned ideas about women. She was in love with him and he was very fond of her. He did not know exactly where that was going to take them, but it was nobody's business but their own. The one thing he was sure of was that he had no intention of harming her. Yet he was not going to give her up. After he had sold the Sally McGee he might marry her and take her back East with him, though it would be awkward if anybody at home discovered she had been a variety actress in a house at Leadville. He could make up his mind about that later.

Sheriff Taggart was in his office figuring up the monthly expense statement for the county commissioners when an excited rider swung from a saddle and came in with the news that an outgoing stage had been robbed near Malta and the shotgun messenger killed.

Hurriedly Taggart organized a posse of five and left for the scene of the holdup. They rode across the flats past Stringtown, meeting the tide of travel for the silver city that never ceased except during the darkest hours of night. They heard the crack of bull whips, the creak of ungreased wheels, the cursing of mule skinners. Freight outfits and a burro train passed them. Three wagons of immigrants drawn by oxen lurched forward, the canvas covers bellying in the stiff wind blowing down from the Continental Divide. A storm was brewing around Mount Elbert. Its summit was already covered by clouds, the crown truncated as sharply as if a giant sword had sliced off the top.

The posse met the stage returning to Leadville, on top of it the dead body of the shotgun messenger roped to the roof rails. The driver, Hank Foley, pulled the horses to a halt. "They got Bud," he yelled to the sheriff.

Taggart dismounted and listened to the story the driver and the passengers had to tell. The road agents had stopped the stage in a rock cut the other side of Malta. There had been five of them, all masked by bandannas. Bud Tulk had been ordered to drop his sawed-off shotgun, and as he raised it to throw the weapon to the ground one of the bandits had shot him. His body lurched forward and tumbled across the back of the near wheeler to the sand.

The six passengers had been lined up against the bank and five of them had been searched. The sixth was a woman, a school-teacher on her way to take her first job. She was told curtly by the leader of the outlaws, a squat heavy-set man with heavy rounded shoulders, to put her purse back, that they were not robbing women. From the boot the gold box was taken, broken open, and the contents emptied into a gunny sack. The outlaws had ridden toward the Mosquitos when they left.

The male passengers were a bartender, two miners, a greenhorn from Cleveland, and an Idaho Springs preacher who was expecting to organize a Baptist church at Leadville. One of the robbers with a grin had tossed back to the minister ten dollars of his own money as a contribution to the building fund. Taggart's questions drew from the passengers no clear description of the road agents. One of them chewed tobacco steadily and said nothing. The leader was a short heavy man. Several of them were big fellows. Of those in the stage the young woman had used her eyes to the best advantage. The man who had killed Tulk had reddish hair and he acted as if he were drunk. When they were ready to leave a slim young fellow brought the horses from the brush where they had been concealed. The redhead had called him Jim. He was scarcely more than a boy, she thought, and he was dressed better than the others.

Hank Foley told the story of the holdup clearly, but he was very hazy as to the appearance of the outlaws.

"Would you know any of them again if you saw them?" Taggart asked.

Foley was spilling tobacco into his corncob pipe. He stopped to lift his faded blue eyes to those of the sheriff.

"Nary a one," he answered, drawling the words. "I was right busy keeping my horses quiet."

Taggart knew what was in the driver's mind. This was the second time he had been held up and it probably would not be the last. If the bandits were arrested there would not be enough evidence to convict them unless they were caught red-handed with the loot on their persons. After they were freed they would remember what Foley's testimony had been, and if he had pointed a finger in their direction he might be rubbed out next time his stage was stopped.

It was Taggart's opinion that the Hayden gang had done this. The description of the leader fitted Dan Hayden. Members of the gang had been hanging around Leadville for several days and some of them had been drinking heavily. There were other possible suspects. Jesse James and the Ford brothers were still holed up in one of the gulches near the town, but they were lying low after a bank robbery in the Midwest and it was not likely they would involve themselves in trouble here. Moreover, this looked like the work of a less disciplined outfit. Top-flight bandits never killed unless forced to it.

The tracks of horses were visible in the clay soil. After leaving the cut they turned sharply toward the Mosquitos. But that proved nothing. The riders might swing down the river toward Buena Vista or make a wide sweeping detour into the Twin Lakes country. Or they might return to their cabin above the gulch on the outskirts of Leadville. Already there was a flurry of snow in the air. Before the posse had traveled a mile it was falling so fast that all tracks were blotted out.

"Kicking up its heels for a stemwinder," Billy Mawson said. He was Taggart's deputy, a lank lean old-timer with a long-jawed bony face.

The sheriff nodded. "It will be quite a snow, but it won't last long this time of year. By morning the storm will be over. Point is, what to do now. We can't just quit and go back to town while there is any chance of running into these birds. Not that there's much chance. They have got too good a head start. My idea is that they will hole up somewhere tonight and in the morning clear out of this country for a while. What say we drift down to Baxter's ranch and sleep in his barn, and then be ready to take off after breakfast?"

"Might as well," Mawson agreed. He added with a wry grin, "Take off for where?"

The wind had died down somewhat, or the sound of it was deadened by the heavy driving snow. Taggart wheeled and faced into the storm, heading for the river. The temperature had fallen and the cold began to bite through the clothing of the riders. Early darkness was beginning to fall. The men rode closely bunched, for they were traveling in a white circular wall that reduced their visible world to a ten-foot space. It would be easy to get lost if they did not stay together and follow Taggart, who knew this country like the palm of his hand and could almost have ridden it blindfold. The terrain was rough and uneven. To some of the posse, unused to the saddle, it seemed many hours before they came to a barbwire fence.

Taggart cut the wires with his clippers and

they rode across a six-hundred-acre pasture before the buildings of the ranch headquarters loomed up dark and shadowy. At the barn they dismounted and unsaddled.

A cowboy entered leading a horse. He stopped in surprise at seeing the barn filled with men. "What the hell!" he exclaimed.

"Sheriff's posse," Taggart told him. "After a bunch of stage robbers. The storm caught us. Afraid Baxter will have to put us up for the night."

"Sure — sure," the range rider said. "The old man keeps open house." He met another surprise. "Well, I'll be doggoned if here ain't another bronc that has been rid hard."

The sheriff joined him in the stall, where a travel-worn sorrel was eating hay. A saddle and moist blankets had been hung on wooden pegs driven into the wall back of the box. They told no story except that they had recently been on the back of a sweating horse in a storm. The robbers might have separated, each to go his own way till the pursuit had died down. One of them might be in the ranch house now. If they had stopped to divide their spoils the share of one might be at this moment hidden in the stable within a dozen feet of him.

"We'd better mosey to the house where it is

warm," the cowboy suggested.

"That's right, boys," the sheriff agreed. "What you need is a good fire and some grub. I'll be with you in a minute."

Led by the cowboy, the men trooped to the house. Mawson lingered. "Got an idee about that horse, John?" he asked.

"Just a long shot, Billy. Baxter's rider didn't know the horse. Somebody rode him in here not twenty minutes ago — somebody who had ridden hard and long. Now who?"

"You guess," Mawson drawled.

Taggart did not answer. His eyes, narrowed, looked into space. Suppose a man had ridden in with money taken from the stage, what would he do with it? He would not carry it with him to the house. He would hide it somewhere here in the stable until he was ready to leave.

The sheriff moved back into the stall. He patted the sweat-stained shoulder of the horse. The crib had been filled with hay pressed down hard instead of forked in lightly. Taggart reached to the bottom of the rack and searched with his fingers. They closed on something hard. He drew up a small canvas sack. It was filled with gold and greenbacks.

"Well, I'll be jiggered!" Mawson cried softly. "How did you guess?"

"More hay jammed in than the horse could possibly eat."

They buried the sack at the bottom of a well-filled oat bin and walked to the house. Mose Baxter welcomed them with a shout when they came into the big living room. He was a huge hulk of a man, bull-necked and heavy shouldered, with a leathery brown face out of which small cold pig eyes peered. His surface manner was hearty and jovial, but though he laughed and back-slapped a good deal the little eyes never warmed. Taggart was of opinion that you could not trust Mose any farther than you could throw a two-year-old bull by the tail.

"Where you been all this year, John?" he demanded. "I'm sure doggoned pleased you dropped around at last. Come on up to the fire and warm yore frozen bones, old-timer."

The other members of the posse moved aside from in front of the great fireplace to let the sheriff and the deputy get a chance at the heat. Taggart turned his back to the fireplace, his cold hands spread behind him, and let his glance sweep the room. Except for Baxter and the young man who had met them at the barn the only other person in the room beside the posse was a lad sitting on a stool reading the *Chronicle*. The sheriff's eyes came back to him. He was a graceful, well-set-up youth in good but travel-stained clothes, extraordinarily handsome. What held the officer's gaze was his great likeness to Joan Regal.

Taggart had heard that young Regal had been seen more than once with Soapy Sills and other members of the Hayden gang. He had no doubt he was looking at the man who had ridden the sweat-stained horse in the stable and had hidden the sack of money. This distressed him, for he liked and respected Joan. It was a pity her brother was a scoundrel who had drifted into evil ways for which he must pay the penalty.

"You boys are just in time for supper," their host boomed. "Can you put up with venison steaks and a good mess of trout caught only two-three hours ago by my friend Jim Watson?" Baxter turned to the young man. "Jim, come and shake hands with Sheriff Taggart, the best officer in the Rockies."

So that was to be the story. Jim Watson, alias Wesley, alias Regal had spent the afternoon fishing on the Arkansas, and since one cannot be two places at the same time he could not have held up the stage.

The alleged fisherman moved across the room with reluctant feet to greet the sheriff. "Pleased to meet you," he said, and did not look it.

Taggart shook hands with him. "Stranger in this country, Mr. Watson?" he asked.

"Yes and no." Watson's eyes slid away from the direct gaze of the officer. "I been around two-three months, sorta drifting. Can't seem to get located right."

A Mexican with a towel around his waist came into the room. "Supper is ready," he announced.

They sat on benches parallel to the table, on which had been placed dishes of potatoes and beans, hot biscuits, and platters of venison and trout. The cook served coffee from the pot into the tin cups beside the plates. Conversation died down while the hungry men devoured the food. Supper was almost over when Taggart spoke to Watson, who was seated at the other end of the table.

"You got a fine mess of fish," he said. "The trout must have been hungry. I reckon you were on the river all day."

Baxter answered for his guest. "Jim was at the meadows. Down there you can haul 'em out fast when the fishing is right."

Jim agreed uneasily. "That's right." Feeling this to be inadequate, he added, "For a couple of hours they were sure eager."

"How far are the meadows?" the sheriff asked.

Watson was caught out. Plainly he did not know. He flashed an appealing look at Baxter, who spoke up smoothly. "Maybe a quarter of a mile. You want good fishing any time, Sheriff, come down and spend a few days here. I'll see you get it."

Taggart thanked him. He was thinking that since the fishing waters were so near, the owner of the sorrel horse could not claim its worn condition could be due to the trip to and from the meadows. The only point still to be determined was that Jim had been the rider of the horse. He assigned the job of finding that out to Mawson, who left for the stable after supper to take care of the mounts of the posse. The cowboy and another deputy went with him. Taggart stayed at the big house to chat with Baxter and his wife. Regal also remained, obviously uncomfortable, still in his role of innocent drifter.

When Mawson returned he handed his chief a paper. "While I think of it, John, this is my expense account for that trip to Ten Mile yesterday."

Taggart glanced at the paper. He read:

Talked with the stable boy and the Mex cook. Both of them say Watson rode in on the sorrel just before we did.

He put the paper in his pocket.

"I reckon you boys are tired from your long ride. You'll be comfortable in the bunkhouse. The only spare room here is the one Jim has." Baxter rose from his chair, a host exuding hospitality. "Sleep tight, boys. Before you leave in the morning I'll see you have a good breakfast."

"That's fine, Mose," Taggart said. "You're sure treating us right. Mind if I change the arrangements some? I'd like to have Jim sleep with us in the bunkhouse. I'm arresting him for helping to rob the stage today."

Mawson was standing beside Regal, ready to cover him if he made a move. The color faded out of the boy's cheeks.

Baxter was shocked. He sputtered protests. John must be wrong. The kid could not have done it. He had been around all day except while he was fishing.

"No use, Mose," Taggart told him. "We found his share of the loot where he hid it. I'm taking him to town. And I would advise you to mend your ways. You are too friendly with road agents. First thing you know you'll be in a tight spot yourself."

Baxter shook his head reproachfully. "You've got me wrong, John. I'm a law-abiding citizen. But I keep a kind of roadhouse for travelers. I think this boy is all right, but if he isn't don't blame me. When guests come I take them at face value."

"I hadn't a thing to do with any holdup," Regal said.

With only Mawson in the room except himself and the prisoner Taggart grilled the young man for an hour. Regal denied having any knowledge of the money sack found in the crib under the hay. He had not in the past twenty-four hours been anywhere near Malta. Since he was innocent of the robbery he could give no information about the plans of the road agents. No questioning could shake him from his position, though the sheriff could see that he was badly frightened. The only admission he made was that his name was Jim Regal.

When they started back to town next morning the sun was shining brightly. Probably there would be weeks of pleasant Indian summer before winter closed in on this two-mile-high country.

8

Cape Wallace was a late riser. It was one o'clock when he came out of the Tontine after breakfast. He lit a cheroot and sauntered toward the Texas House. Men were busy laying water mains, and a long trench had been dug down the street. The dirt from this and the snow had been churned by the traffic into a morass of mud. As usual Cape was immaculate in a white shirt and a well-pressed suit of broadcloth. He did not see how he was going to get across the road without muddying his polished boots.

The problem of getting across was also troubling a young woman, whom he knew by sight, Miss Joan Regal. Since he was a professional gambler they were not on speaking terms, but he had given her a good deal of attention from a distance. Gentle, shy, and well brought up, the kind of girl he had known before he had declassed himself, she was the last person he would have expected to find in a variety show. His interest in her was deeper because she too had stepped outside the pale, though in her case with no turpitude.

As he approached, the girl looked up helplessly. She did not want to wade ankle-deep in mud.

Wallace stopped, smiling at her. "May I be your Sir Walter Raleigh?" he asked. Without waiting for permission he picked her up and stepped into the slime. He crossed the trench on a plank and plowed through mud to the far sidewalk.

Joan brushed down her skirts. The girl's face was one deep blush. "Really, Sir Walter," she protested.

"It's a Leadville custom when the street is muddy," he explained.

She laughed breathlessly. "Anyhow, you didn't whirl me around your head as Pierre does," she said. "I ought to be very much obliged to you. I really am — but a little embarrassed."

"Consider me just a bridge," he suggested.

"Your poor boots," she said, looking down at them. "And they were so nice and shiny."

"The damage can be repaired," he told her.

"You are Mr. Wallace, aren't you?" she asked. "I saw you testifying at the trial of Henry Page. He says you are his cousin."

"Yes," he answered.

They were moving side by side down the sidewalk. At the Grand Central Theater she stopped. "I live upstairs," she told him. "There is something I want to say to you, Mr. Wallace. But not just here. Shall we step into the theater?"

The front door was open to air the place. A colored man could be seen sweeping the stage. Except for him the house was empty. Joan led Wallace to a box and he held a chair for her. His curiosity was aroused. His only guess as to what was in her mind was that it had to do with Henry, and in this case he was completely wrong.

"Erma was eating supper with a friend last night, a Mr. Edgar Faust," she began. "He told her something I think you ought to know. It was about that fight when some assassins tried to kill Henry and Mr. Downing. Somebody interfered and saved them. He knows who it was."

The gambler said nothing, but he was intensely interested. There had been a lot of guessing as to the identity of the man who had upset the plan of the killers.

"Mr. Faust was at The Little Church drinking with a friend," Joan continued. "As soon as the shooting was over he ran into the street."

"I see. An innocent bystander intent on being important."

"He must have been one of the first outsiders to reach the spot," Joan said. "He saw a man run across the road and on the way throw something into a wagon standing close to the sidewalk."

The dead-pan face of Wallace told nothing.

"Later a pistol belonging to Mort Heisman was found in that wagon." Joan hesitated, then carried on. "Mr. Faust says you were the man who crossed the street. It worried Erma. She told him he might have been mistaken, and anyhow not to say anything about it to anybody else. He promised, but she does not feel sure he won't."

"Mr. Faust drinks too much," Cape commented dryly.

"Yes, and then he talks. At least Erma says so."

"I'm going to vote the prohibition ticket next election," the gambler said, smiling at the girl. "If I'm still voting."

"I don't suppose the Vinings will hear this, but if they do it might not be very safe for you," Joan replied.

Cape thought that an understatement. If they heard he was the man who had literally crashed their party the word would be passed to Mort Heisman, and if Mort knew, he would do something about it. The man's vanity had been wounded more than his head. For such a man to lose face was bitter medicine.

"Perhaps you could see Mr. Faust," Joan proposed.

"And get him to take the pledge," Cape added.

"Erma was very firm with him. I don't really think he will say anything now."

"That's a fine thought." The smile of the gambler was sardonic.

Joan liked the devil-may-care look in his reckless eyes. A phrase she had read somewhere jumped to her mind. *Gentleman unafraid*. But of course he was not a gentleman any more than she was a lady. He was a gambler, one who took risks lightly. But he was a man. A warm glow filled her. He had walked into desperate danger when the quarrel was not his. He had saved Henry for her — and Ted Downing too of course.

She said impulsively, her throaty voice rich with feeling, "You don't hold your life too high, do you?"

He shrugged his broad shoulders lightly. "I don't throw down on myself, but when the cards are dealt you have to play out the hand."

"You weren't one of the players," she said. "You didn't have to get mixed up in it."

"I was right there holding a six-full," he differed. "I couldn't lay it down without calling."

It was strange, Joan thought, how a word or a look could light your understanding of a man. You might go to school with a boy for years, talk with him, dance with him, and know nothing at all about his character; yet in one flashing moment of insight you might discover the code by which a stranger lived.

"*You* couldn't," she said impulsively. "A lot of people could." A smile illumined the lovely face. "I like you, Mr. Wallace."

He shook his head reprovingly. "You should not, Miss Regal. I'm an undesirable character — a reprobate outside your social circle."

"Not outside mine," she told him. "Since I have become déclassée I have a fellow feeling for undesirables."

"That's nonsense. You are a lady, no matter what the snobs on the hill think. Someday you will marry a good man and leave. Or you will leave here and marry one later."

"Have you one in mind for me?" she asked demurely. "One that could put up with a puling whitefaced girl?"

"That is a strange description of you."

"I am quoting Mr. Cape Wallace, his comment at Fair Play to Sheriff Taggart."

"Did I say that? A man can change his mind. I apologize humbly."

"Apology accepted, if you answer the question I asked."

His smile was gayly impudent. "All right. Since you ask for it. I offered you Edward Downing. A girl could not do better."

She laughed. "Good of you. He hasn't offered himself. What would you think of your cousin Henry? He likes me."

"He likes a lot of girls," Wallace said dryly. "I saw him in a barouche today with three, all of them pretty."

If Joan was disturbed she did not show it. "Dear me — three," she answered cheerfully. "And all pretty. He'd better move across the Divide to Utah."

"He had better go back to Ohio before he is sent there in a box," the gambler said grimly.

The smile went out of Joan's eyes like the light from a blown candle. "You don't really think that, do you, Mr. Wallace?" she asked unhappily. "Mr. Vining has come out against crime and lawlessness."

"So I read in the paper. There wasn't a photograph with the article, so I couldn't see whether his tongue was in his cheek."

"He sent word to Henry that he was going to accept the verdict of the court as a law-abiding citizen must."

"Then Henry had better watch his step."

All the pretty color had been driven from the girl's face. It was clear she was in love with Page.

"I hope you are wrong," she cried softly. "I think you are. But — isn't there anything we can do to make sure? I might go and see Mr. Vining."

"He would be surprised and grieved that you could suspect him."

She beat one fist into the palm of the other hand. "Then what can we do?"

"Persuade Henry to leave if you have any influence over him."

"I can't. He thinks everything is all right now. Perhaps you could."

"No. He came to see me after the trial. But our talk was formal and stiff. We were both rather embarrassed. Maybe I'm entirely wrong and Vining is a reformed man. As a civic leader helping to clean up the town he may have given up his private feud."

He left Joan troubled in mind. Later in the day another worry had come to increase her woe. Erma brought her word that her brother had been arrested for helping to hold up the stage near Malta.

In Sheriff Taggart's box of an office were only two chairs. He gave one each to Erma Roberts and Joan Regal. Downing sat on one corner of the table that served as a desk, one foot resting on the floor.

"I'm glad you came," Taggart said. "The boy is in a bad fix. He needs friends right now — and a lawyer."

"Is the evidence against him strong?" Erma asked.

She was speaking for Joan. The older woman knew that back of the girl's tight frozen face panic was rising in her.

The sheriff outlined the evidence. Jim had not yet admitted guilt, but he had contradicted himself a dozen times. His best out, Taggart thought, was to give evidence against the older men who had drawn him into this that would lead to their arrest and conviction.

"We would like to talk with him," Downing said.

"Please." The word broke from Joan, low-pitched and husky, almost a sob.

"Of course," Taggart agreed promptly. "Whenever you like."

The prisoner's first words to his sister were

sharp. "It's time you got here. I've been looking for you all day."

"We just heard you were here," Joan answered. She moved forward swiftly and kissed him. "Oh Jim — Jim! Why did you do it?"

"What makes you think I did it?" he snarled. "That's a fine thing for a man's sister to say."

"If you didn't do it we ought to be able to prove it," Downing told him. "I'm a lawyer, a friend of your sister. If you would rather have another attorney represent you that will be all right with me."

Regal turned on him, almost angrily. "All right. You're my lawyer. Get me out of here. Right away."

"Afraid I can't do that, unless you can show a clear alibi for the time of the holdup. I suggest you tell me what you were doing and where you were from the early morning of that day until the sheriff saw you at the Baxter ranch."

Regal told a rambling story that carried no conviction. He had camped alone the previous night and had slept late. It had been nearly noon when he saddled. He had met nobody all day until he reached the ranch. As he rode into the yard Baxter walked down from the house. He saw nobody else on the place.

In the stable he had picked up a fishing rod and a box of flies. On horseback he had ridden down to the meadows and fished. Late in the afternoon he had returned. To Downing's questions he gave unsatisfactory answers. He did not know why the stable boy had not seen the rod and the fish, nor could he give any reason why the cook had said he had himself caught the fish in the forenoon. All of them felt sure he was lying.

The evidence against him was not conclusive, but a damning fact was that until the posse arrived only one horse had come to the ranch, the sorrel ridden by Regal. The sack found in the hay must have come on its back, and in the bottom of the sack there had been a watch belonging to the tenderfoot from Cleveland who had been on the stage. In the present state of public opinion a conviction would be almost certain, unless Jim turned state's evidence and the other bandits were captured, and though Downing talked with his client every day the boy refused flatly to incriminate his confederates.

Joan or Erma frequently carried dinners to the prisoner from the Tontine or the Clarendon. Before Erma he pretended an indifference to his plight, an attitude taken to save his pride, but when his sister was alone with him he unbared his increasing fear. A mob might storm the jail and hang him. Bud Tulk had a great many friends and the feeling in the town was bitter. Why didn't she get him out somehow before — before he was dragged out to death?

The girl shared his stark terror. She knew better than he did the heat of anger against him. Even though he had been one of the robbers, he was not guilty of killing Tulk. She felt that it was not fair that the rage should be concentrated on Jim, and in the night horrible pictures rose before her of the screaming mob wreaking vengeance on him. Not six months earlier a boy of nineteen had been lynched for attempting to hold up a barber. The words of comfort Erma offered did not help. It was while Joan was lying awake staring into the night that a plan came into her mind.

Next day she talked it over with her brother. When she left the jail she was shaken with sobs. A handkerchief dabbed at her swollen eyes.

"She's shore broke up about that scalawag brother of hers," Mawson told the sheriff. "A nice little lady like her hadn't ought to have kin like that fellow."

Taggart agreed that the ways of Providence were peculiar, but he did not know what they could do about it.

★

Just before noon a Negro boy delivered a sealed note to Cape Wallace. He wrote, "I'll be there," below the signature and gave it back to the boy with a quarter for return to the sender.

At noon he strolled down the street and turned in at the Grand Central Theater. As before, the doors and windows were wide open for ventilation. There was nobody in sight but Joan Regal.

"Do you think I am too bold in asking you to go to dinner with me?" she wanted to know.

"Not too bold but indiscreet," he replied. "You must not go to dinner with a professional gambler. But I am here. You want something of me. What is it?"

"Yes, I do. I don't know whether you will do it. But there is nobody else I can ask."

Her face was pale and showed the trace of tears. She was both nervous and anxious.

"Try me," he suggested.

"It might get you into trouble," she said.

"I've been in it before," he reminded her.

"I want you to buy me a horse."

"That doesn't seem very dangerous. A gentle riding cob for a lady."

"No. A strong horse that will travel fast and far. And a man's riding saddle. I want the horse left saddled at the rack in front of Randall's bookstore tomorrow afternoon at five o'clock."

Wallace thought in rapid flashes. Randall's bookstore was almost opposite the jail. The horse would accommodate a young man who had urgent business away from Leadville.

He said gently, "Don't you think this might get *you* into trouble?"

"It doesn't matter about me." There was a wildness in her low voice. "I know what I am doing. I have to do it. But we don't have to talk about what it is and involve you."

To help a prisoner to escape was against the law. If he supplied a horse the penalty might reach back to him. But he was thinking of her. He knew his Leadville well. If nobody was hurt in the escape there would be no transfer of hatred from young Regal to his sister. The town would be more likely to applaud her for loyalty.

"I don't know what you have in mind," he said, "but I would like to be sure that the man who is going to ride this horse won't be armed."

"He won't be. I promise that."

"Good. The horse will be in front of Randall's at five."

She took a roll of bills from her purse.

"There is eighty dollars. Will that be enough?"

"I think so."

Joan picked up a parcel at her feet. It was wrapped in a piece of a gunny sack. "Please tie this at the back of the saddle. And, Mr. Wallace, I'll remember this all my life."

The gambler smiled derisively at himself as he left. Even if he helped the girl in her harum-scarum scheme there was no sense in getting emotionally stirred up about her.

Joan changed to a plain black dress, a long one that reached the floor. Erma was a little surprised.

"You'll gather all the dust there is on the sidewalk," she said.

"I'll keep the skirt lifted a little," Joan answered.

"I think I'm gaining weight," Erma mentioned, studying her plump lines in the glass. "Don't let me get lazy. What say I go with you now to see Jim?"

"I'd like that, but not today, dear. I want to have a serious talk with him." Joan chose a big floppy hat that covered her hair. "You don't weigh an ounce more than when I first saw you."

"It's fatal for an actress to get fat," Erma sighed. "I wish I wasn't so fond of eating."

The sun had set before Joan started, but the sky behind the crests of the mountains was still a blaze of color. There were twenty men to one woman on the sidewalks, most of them drifting about aimlessly. The girl no longer felt any trepidation at going out alone. Even the roughest miner made way for her respectfully. Among them she was, as Taggart had once told her, safe as in God's pocket.

She noticed as she turned in at the jail that a bay horse, saddled, with a roll tied back of the seat, stood at the hitch rack in front of the bookstore. The jailor said as he let her in, "You're later than usual today, Miss Regal." He was a fat bald little man, and she knew as women do that she was often in his thoughts.

"I won't stay more than a few minutes," she promised.

He unlocked the room where her brother was kept. "Call me when you are ready to go," he told her, and locked the door behind her.

"Is everything fixed?" Jim whispered.

She was already unfastening her dress. "Yes. The horse is in front of Randall's at the rack. A bundle of men's clothes is tied behind the saddle with some sandwiches wrapped in them."

"Did you get me a revolver?"

"No, I didn't. You are better off without one."

He ripped out a petulant oath. "Do you have to decide everything for me? I know what I want." He was already out of his coat and vest. His shirt came next and then his trousers.

The dress dropped to the floor and after it the petticoats. She stood before him in her undergarments, a slim beautifully poised figure with a look of clean-cut pride in the lift of the small head. They were nearly the same height. Except that they were a little loose around the waist his trousers fitted her well enough. The coat was too large but it would have to do.

As she fastened the dress on him she gave instructions. To her surprise she was much less nervous than he. "Take short steps and don't hurry. Let the skirt hang to the floor so that your boots won't show. I ought to have brought a razor to shave your mustache, but we can't help that now. Keep this handkerchief over your mouth and most of your face. You are unhappy and your body is racked with sobs. If the jailor speaks to you just murmur something back of the handkerchief. Take it easy. Whatever you do don't get frightened and start to run. There isn't a chance in a hundred you will be stopped."

"If he sees my boots — "

"Keep them under the skirt." She arranged

the hat so that it drooped over the face. "Good-bye, dear. Get out of this country as soon as you can."

She kissed him, then called the jailor. When he arrived she was sitting on the bed in the shadowy backgound, her brother's hat on her head, the smoke of a cigarette curling up from her fingers.

The jailor locked the door behind Jim. She heard their retreating footsteps and the comforting voice of the guard. "Don't you take it so hard, Miss Regal. They ain't convicted him yet."

Joan moved swiftly to the window and looked out from behind the bars. She could see the horse at the rack. Two men had stopped to chat in front of the bookstore. They were evidently just parting, but taking a long time about it. One would back away, then stop to say something else. Her heart died under her ribs. Would they never get through? If they were still there when Jim came they might see his boots as he mounted and drag him from the saddle. Another fear hammered in her breast. It was time Jim showed in the street. Had he been detected and arrested? The moments dragged, each of them a torture of suspense.

The talkers broke away from each other at

last. She saw Jim hurrying across the street with long strides, his anxious eyes shuttling to right and left. His nerve was breaking under the strain, she knew. With freedom so close he could not hold down his pace. A man coming down the sidewalk had pulled up to watch the woman whose gait was so unladylike. Joan's lips tightened. Her brother's panic might still ruin everything.

Jim pulled the slip knot fastening the horse to the rack, jerked up his skirts, and swung astride the bay. Below the dress a foot of muddy boots showed. His heels gouged into the flanks of the animal. It jumped to a gallop and raced up the road. The gaping man stared at the horse breasting the hill. To the jailor, who had appeared on the opposite sidewalk, he flung a question. "Who is the crazy woman?"

The jailor, Erasmus Head, had a moment of heart failure before he turned and took the stairs two at a time. He unlocked the door of the prisoner's room and shouted an order. "Come into the light and lemme look at you."

Joan said in a small voice, "I had to help my brother get away, Mr. Head."

The man choked back a string of oaths. His anger and his disappointment struggled for words to express themselves. "Godalmighty!"

he cried. "What's got into you! I let you see him alone, and — and — "

"I abused your trust in me," the girl confessed. "After you had been so good to him and me — letting me see him at any time and bring him things. I expect I ought to be whipped, but — he is my only brother."

He was unhappy for himself, since he might lose his job, but he was distressed for her too. She might be sent to prison for what she had done. He was a widower, fat, bald, and forty. A dozen times he had been to watch her act. Though he knew there was not a chance in the world for him, he had fallen hopelessly in love with the girl. She had made a fool of him. That was bad enough, but it was much worse to think how much she might have to pay for what she had done. The emotion churning in him exploded in vexed resentment.

"Tell it to the judge when he sentences you," Head snapped, and slammed shut the door.

She heard him lock it and go down the stairs hurriedly. In spite of the plight she was in, Joan was sorry for the little man, both because of the blame he would incur and because she had shattered his faith in her. No doubt he thought it was a despicable thing for her to do. But how else could she save Jim —

if he was saved? The jailor was on the way to give the alarm. In half an hour or less a posse would be on the road. But Jim had a long start on a good horse. In the gathering darkness he would be hard to find. By morning he should be fifty miles away.

The night life of the town had begun before the door opened again. It let in Sheriff Taggart and Ted Downing. Head was just back of them carrying a lighted lamp.

"You've fried a pretty kettle of fish, young woman," Taggart said.

Joan was frightened, but she did not show it. "I'm sorry, Sheriff," she told him. "But of course you see I had to do it."

"I don't see anything of the kind. A young lady like you has no business breaking the law by assisting a prisoner to escape."

"But he is my brother."

"Half the prisoners in the country are somebody's brother. If Jim isn't caught you'll be in a bad jam."

"Do you think he will be?"

"Sure. Sooner or later. Mawson is out with a posse. It's not likely they'll get him tonight. Do you know that you can be sent to the penitentiary for this?"

She said to Downing, "You won't let me go there, will you, Ted?"

He answered quietly, "No."

"Why don't you scold me?"

"Why should I, if you had to do it?"

"I was afraid, Ted. I heard talk about a mob. Jim did not kill Bud Tulk. How could I just sit and fold my hands?"

Taggart interrupted. "How come a saddled horse was waiting outside so handy?"

"Aren't there always saddle horses on the street, Sheriff?"

"From what I hear he knew it was to be there and made straight for it."

"Wouldn't you expect him to take the nearest horse?"

"I'll find out whose horse it was. I think somebody else was in this jail break with you."

"No. Jim and I did it all by ourselves."

"The story of your part in Jim's escape is already all over town," Downing said. "On my way down the street three different men stopped me and offered to go bail for you."

"Will you thank them for me?"

"I did, and told them it wasn't necessary. I'll see Judge Lamson and get you out either tonight or tomorrow morning. You haven't any dress here, I suppose."

She shook her head. "And this suit is a dreadful fit."

"I'll get your clothes from Erma."

After they had left her Joan's thoughts drifted to a comparison between Henry Page and Ted Downing. She knew the lawyer was the better man and that his love was deeper and stronger. He was more faithful and more responsible. You could trust him and know that he would be true. But when she looked at Henry her heart beat faster. There was something frightening about his kisses. They swept her away as the undertow does a swimmer.

When Joan appeared on the stage the evening of her release there was a storm of applause that lasted five minutes. She had to step to the wings to avoid the shower of gold and silver tossed back of the footlights. These men had been angry at her brother for what he had done. They would have been glad to see him sent to the penitentiary for twenty years, but their animosity did not carry to the girl who had arranged his escape. She was already a favorite, and they warmed not only to her loyalty but to the wit and gallantry that had freed him under the eyes of the jailor. The members of the troupe, including Erma, were delighted at her exploit, and though Downing said no word to indicate it she knew he was in love with her as much as before.

This support cheered her greatly, but she waited with some apprehension to find out how Henry would take it.

It was not until the third day that he dropped in to see Joan. She met him with a touch of reserve. He had been in no hurry to declare himself on her side.

Joan discovered that he was very well pleased with himself but not so well pleased with her. He had been to the Assembly Ball and he told her all about it. Evidently he had enjoyed himself immensely. The matrons at the top had been very friendly. He had danced the whole evening, except for one polka that he had sat out with a dowager in an elaborate imported French dress. She had tapped his wrist playfully with her fan and given him a little lecture.

Since it seemed to be expected of her, Joan asked on what subject. He hesitated a moment, then decided to make a joke of it. He mimicked the dowager's manner and her speech. Young men would be young men of course, but they must avoid letting themselves get trapped by charming but designing young variety actresses.

Henry's laughter got no echo from Joan. She rose, arrowstraight, fire flashing from the eyes in the lifted head.

"I'm sure she is right," Joan said stiffly.

He saw he had made a mistake. "Can't you take a joke, dear?" he asked. "I was only making fun of her."

She thought, *He told me just to let me see how socially important he is, and how grateful I should be for his attention.*

"I'm not only designing, but I am a criminal and my brother is a bandit," she continued. "Perhaps I ought to wear a bell like a leper to warn young society men away."

"Don't be that way, Joan. You know you are twisting my meaning. I'm very fond of you. The only reason I went to the Assembly was because I want to sell the mine and it is important to know the right people."

"And not to know the wrong ones," she added, a small whiplash in her husky voice. It was in her mind to ask him if he expected to sell the Sally McGee to any of the girls he had been taking for a drive, but she stifled the question because she did not want him to find out she was jealous.

"Of course if you want to take everything I say the wrong way," he replied sulkily.

The coppery flecks in her eyes were bright with temper. "I'm not good enough for you, Henry. It was shameful enough to be a variety-hall girl without the disgrace of having a brother who is a criminal. You found it hard to swallow that bitter pill. You would have liked me to disown him — never to go and see him. When you were in trouble you were glad enough for a little friendship."

Anger flared up in him. "All I had done was to defend my rights. I hadn't been a stage robber. If you want to know why I don't like this precious brother of yours, it is because he came to my room and threatened my life if I didn't keep away from you. He accused me of being a murderer and a seducer. He was drunk and abusive. Then he gets involved in a robbery and a killing, after which you pull a melodramatic prison break that has set the whole town talking about you. Since you ask for it — no, I don't like any part of it. A lady does not make herself conspicuous."

Joan was shocked that Jim had made a scene with Page because she had paid too little heed to the conventions when he was ill, but the young man's blunt appraisal of her conduct drove that into the background.

"But then I'm not a lady," she retorted swiftly. "I'm just trash from a variety show. You couldn't possibly explain me to your dowager friend with the ice water in her veins. I won't embarrass you by forcing you to try."

Erma walked into the room and knew at once that she was interrupting a quarrel. "Oh,

I'm sorry," she said.

"Don't leave," Joan told her. "Mr. Page is just going. He has been telling me how a lady should behave."

In the girl's face was a flash of mocking insolence. Her beauty, Erma thought, tempered by anger like a fine steel blade, had never been more challenging.

Henry threw up his hands in a gesture of annoyed protest. "All I said — "

Joan cut off his explanation. "Do you have to go through it again, Mr. Page, when we already understand each other perfectly?"

He glared at her, started to reply, gave it up, and walked abruptly from the room. He was furious that he had been put in the wrong. Why were women so damned unreasonable?

In the days following the escape of her brother from prison Joan was far from happy. She was worried for fear Jim might be captured. He was so unstable that even if he escaped he might not leave Colorado as he had promised. Rumors came back that he had been seen at Breckenridge, Aspen, and other points. The most persistent one was that he had rejoined the Hayden gang which was operating in the Saguache country rustling horses and driving them to Florence for sale to the Leadville freighters.

Nor was Joan easy on her own account. Her case was coming up for trial at the next term of court and though there was a strong pressure of public opinion in her favor it might not outweigh the fact of her guilt. The sheriff had discovered that the horse on which Jim had left belonged to Cape Wallace and that it had been bought by him the same day, but he had no way of proving it.

Joan was also distressed at the quarrel with Henry Page. There was an appeal about him that stirred in her desires she had never felt before except vaguely. At night, while she lay sleepless in the dark, she flogged herself with her own scorn because the memory of his kisses was so vivid. What kind of girl was she to want a man so volatile and fickle, to be so aware of him when he looked at her that she felt a physical weakness run through her?

He was flying around with other girls, but she never saw him except at a distance. There was gossip that he was engaged or soon would be to Nancy Folsom, one of the catches of the town. Joan held her head up, fiercely proud, but she had a good many bad moments.

The girl's discouragement was reflected in a temporary dislike of the whole Leadville scene. After the first shock at the ugliness and rawness of the place, she had viewed it with the eyes of faith, as most of its inhabitants did. There was in its exuberant vitality an impulse that set the blood strumming with the mere joy of living. But now she saw it in its stark reality. The pocked hillsides scarred with rabbit burrows and gaunt skeleton scaffolds. The smells and filth due to lack of sewage sanitation. The insufficiency of water that made it difficult to keep one's self and clothes immaculate. The human dregs washing into this sink by the greed for gold. Through her swept a nostalgic longing for the clean and pleasant little town from which she had come where she had a score of kindly neighbors who lived like civilized people. She would go home and remember this as a nightmare dream.

But she could not go until she knew her brother was clear of the camp and out of the mining country. Nor could she leave until she had sat pilloried in a courtroom with a hundred pairs of staring eyes fastened on her while the prosecuting attorney excoriated her. And perhaps not then.

In front of Parson Tom Uzzell's tabernacle Joan met Cape Wallace one day. It was the first time she had seen him since the jail break.

"I'm so glad I met you," she said. "I've been worrying about getting you into trouble. I know Mr. Taggart has been bothering you, because he has been at me twice, asking questions about the horse."

Wallace smiled. "The Sheriff is the one worried, not I. It is the style now for men of fashion here to have a horse and buggy or a riding mount. Otherwise you are not in the smart set. Is it my fault a gentleman in a hurry borrowed my horse without permission?"

"I can't ever thank you enough."

"The pleasure was mine. I've enjoyed thinking about the beautiful job you did."

"If I am sent to the penitentiary will you come and see me?"

"I'll have another horse waiting outside for your escape."

"It would be nice if you would invite me to dinner or supper with you today, but of course you can't do that now that I am a criminal."

He laughed at the neat way she had turned the tables on him. "I have to be careful about my reputation, young lady," he told her.

"That's just it. I'm not a young lady now, if I ever was. It would be a boost up for me if a candidate for the Gentlemen's Riding Club took me to the Tontine."

"He would turn out to be a rejected candidate." He shook his head. "I'm still a professional gambler and you are only a make-believe criminal. But I'll remember always that I was invited to invite to dinner the loveliest girl west of the river."

"It's a topsy-turvy world, isn't it? We're both on the wrong side of the tracks. I like you, and you have done so much for me. But there is a silly convention — or you think there is that it would be bad for me to be seen with you. Don't you think we could forget it?"

"No, I don't."

"Perhaps I am just taking it for granted that you like me."

His guard slipped for an instant and his eyes answered her. But his laugh was easy and casual. "Now what can a cornered man say to that except to admit that the sun shines when you are here and the day is dark when you are gone."

"He could say he did like me instead of thinking up a silly compliment."

"Have it your way," he answered lightly. "I do, but my liking must be at a distance. Unless I can be of service to you again."

Joan poked with the ferrule of her parasol at a crack in the sidewalk. "There must be something wrong with me," she murmured.

"You are the only man I ever asked to take me to dinner. Twice I have asked you, and twice you have said, 'No, thank you.' Am I a bold hussy?"

His eyes were no longer cool and mocking. "You are the loveliest thing that ever touched the fringe of my life," he said quietly.

She stared at him, startled at the fire she had stirred up. It was plain to her that he had meant much more than he had said. To find that he was in love with her took Joan's breath. She had known he liked her and had tried to force him to say so as a sop to the vanity of a hurt and jilted woman, but she had not guessed how deep his feeling ran.

"I didn't know," she cried softly.

"You know now — and you can begin forgetting it." He lifted his hat and went on his way.

A queer gladness flooded her. It was good to have someone feel that way about her. But she reproached herself for making him betray his secret. Why had she not let him alone? She knew as well as he did that there would be talk if she went to dinner or supper with him alone in a public restaurant. She had wanted to go with him not only because she found him interesting but also because she wanted to shock Henry Page. If her conduct was not correct enough to suit Henry she would associate with the cousin whose profession barred him from knowing any ladies. A heady scorn was burning in her that demanded satisfaction. Sometimes she was amazed at the change a few months had made in her. What had become of that quiet shy girl filled with conventional inhibitions who had come up timidly from Denver? She did not like the one who had taken her place, a woman passionate, jealous, and contemptuous of the social code which she had always accepted as correct.

Wryly she said as much to Erma that night. The older woman looked across with an understanding smile at her friend who lay relaxed on the bed, the page-boy suit which she had just taken off tossed over the back of a chair.

"I suppose Eve was the first woman who made that discovery about herself," she commented. "After the little episode of the apple in the Garden. And every one of us ever since has wakened up someday to find out that she is a woman. Goodness knows, it isn't the fault of our teaching. From the time we are babies we have it drilled into us that we must be innocent and sugar-sweet. We must never never lead a man on. We must fly — but not too fast — and let him pursue us if we are sure his intentions are honorable. We must not even dream about what marriage involves. If we are good pupils and dumb we go to the altar filled with false ideas, and then life hammers some sense into our heads and we forget all the nonsense we have learned until it comes time to teach the same stuff to our young daughters."

"Dear me, I didn't know you were so advanced," Joan said. "You are such a model of decorum and don't let men step across the line. I suppose you never made a fool of yourself over a man."

"Not more than half a dozen times. We live and we learn. And strange as it may seem to you — for of course you think I'm almost an antique — I still have moments when I have a wild desire for a man."

Joan was genuinely surprised. "A particular man?"

"One I haven't seen in two years." Erma gave a little shrug of her shoulders. "I can take it. So can you. Most women have to accept it once or twice in their lives."

The girl on the bed thought this over. It was a new point of view. She had felt her experience unique, at least in certain phases, as all young girls do, and it appeared to be one common to her sex. It was rather shattering to her ego.

"I met Cape Wallace today," she said after a pause.

"He isn't in any trouble about the horse, is he?"

"I don't think so. There is something rather fascinating about him — something a little dangerous. He is one of the best-dressed men in town and he wears his clothes as if they were a part of him, but of course for good women he is supposed to be an untouchable on account of his business."

"Yes," agreed Erma, looking across at Joan speculatively. "I like him."

"So do I, and I told him so. I asked him to take me to supper with him. He wouldn't do it."

Erma nodded. "No, I would expect him to refuse."

"I kept at him. Why I don't know. Before we parted I made him tell me that he loved me."

"Holy smoke!" Erma exclaimed. "I thought your mind was full of Henry."

"Then he told me I could forget it, and he bowed and walked away." She added thoughtfully, "He's a bigger man than Henry, more generous and kind."

"But you love Henry," Erma suggested.

"Yes, and sometimes I don't even like him."

Erma could understand that too. "We are strange creatures, we women," she said, with a rueful little laugh. "We don't give our kisses to the most deserving but to some scamp who takes our fancy for some trivial reason, such as a handsome face or a good line of gay talk, or maybe just because other women like him and our vanity demands possession of him."

"You make our sex out very silly and light-minded," Joan protested.

"If Henry were baldheaded instead of having that nice curly hair and if he didn't have that charming way with women, would he still be in your thoughts so much?"

"That's not fair," Joan demurred. "He wouldn't be Henry then."

Which was true, Erma agreed.

9

The note came by mail, the address on the envelope and the inside content printed by pen to avoid identification. Cape read the message twice. It was signed a well-wisher. LOOK OUT FOR YOURSELF. THEY KNOW YOU KILLED UKENA AND THEY MEAN TO GET YOU.

Nothing of the paper or the writing told Wallace anything about the sender. The lettering was neat and the paper of average quality. This might be a friendly warning or it might be a threat. He had not enough data to make up his mind which.

He moved to the roulette table over which he was to preside for the next few hours. Customers drifted in and presently he was busy. Mort Heisman was at the bar drinking. Yesterday and the day before he had been in, though prior to that he had not entered the Texas House for a month. Cape had an impression the man was watching him, trying to puzzle out something of which he was not sure. The croupier had felt this yesterday too, until a cross current had completely diverted Heisman's attention. Buck Harrigan had swaggered in for a quick one. He stood with a foot on the rail, hardfaced and grim, the marshal's star on his broad deep chest. As it chanced, Cape was idle at the moment and he observed with interest the attitude of the men toward each other. A rumor was flying about town that their dislike had flared into hatred. The story was that both of them wanted to be chosen sheriff at the coming election. It was a fee office and the intake was large. Neither of the men said a word to the other, but their cold eyes had met in a long challenging look. Heisman ordered his third drink, finished it, and walked swiftly out, his square shoulders and flat back a picture of defiance.

Now he was back again and once more drinking heavily for so early in the day. While Wallace spun the wheel, paid debts, and raked in chips, thoughts below the surface of his mind were active. Heisman was not devoting all this time to him without a very good reason. He must have heard that Wallace was the man who had projected himself into the fight in front of The Little Church, yet evidently there was some lingering doubt in his mind. With Leadville headed for reform he could not afford to kill on suspicion. Moreover, he had to walk a pretty straight line if he hoped to become sheriff. He must not give his opponents a chance to fling the word killer at him. Unless Mort became irresponsibly reckless with drink he would not be likely, Cape thought, to attack him except on a dark deserted street.

It was possible that another factor had entered into the case. If the trouble between Heisman and the marshal had become serious Mort might decide to put aside for the time his anger at Wallace. Harrigan was a dangerous killer with a long record back of him. It would not do to make light of him. He would be enemy enough to watch without taking on another.

Yet Wallace was interested sufficiently in Heisman's movements to check them after his departure from the Texas House. His spy reported that Mort was at Casey's Place drinking steadily. He had a crony or two with him, but since he was in a sullen bitter mood they were taking care not to annoy him.

Cape tried to shrug the worry from his mind, but the picture of the sleepy-eyed, vindictive ruffian waiting in the shadows for him recurred to his thoughts persistently during the day. There was nothing he could do about it. What defense was possible against a murderous impulse born in a brain sodden with drink?

Late in the afternoon Harrigan walked into the Texas House and stopped at Cape's table. "Like to have a word with you," he murmured gruffly.

Wallace turned the wheel over to a relief and moved with the marshal to a vacant poker table.

"You expecting trouble with Heisman?" the officer demanded bluntly.

The impassive face of the gambler registered nothing. His reaction was to go slow until he found out what was back of this. "What makes you think so?" he asked.

The marshal brushed this evasion aside with an impatient gesture. "Don't fool around with me. I want to know. A letter came to me in the mail. It said Heisman was out to get you."

"An anonymous letter?"

"Yes."

"Queer. I got one too." Wallace showed Harrigan the message he had received.

"So you were the guy who rubbed out Ukena."

"Somebody seems to think so."

"He was no good. Heisman doesn't give a damn for that. He's sore because you pistol-whipped him."

"He isn't quite sure I'm the man."

"He's sure enough. The story is all over town. Come clean. You're afraid he will gun you."

"I think he may."

Harrigan rubbed a hand along his beard thoughtfully. "The fool is tanking up at Casey's Place. Something is on his mind. What time does your shift end?"

The croupier told him.

"You're armed of course."

"Yes," Wallace answered.

"You live at Tom Walsh's Grand. Go straight home, but don't hurry. Take it easy. I'll be around."

"I'll be easier in my mind if you are, though the chances are it won't be necessary."

"No way of knowing what an angry man in drink will do." Harrigan turned and went out of the back door.

Wallace knew that the marshal had not enlisted on his side because of his interest in law and order. The man wanted to get something on his rival. But the reason was unimportant. His aid would be invaluable *if he intended to give it*. The point that stood out like a bandaged sore thumb was that Harrigan would be in a better position with the public by going into action after Mort Heisman had shot down a citizen than before. The marshal cared nothing about Wallace. He was intervening for his own benefit entirely. It was all very well for him to say go slow and take it easy, but Cape did not want to be the bait for the marshal's trap. It was the croupier's opinion that this bowlegged barrel-chested man with the cold flinty eyes and lips like a steel trap had no regard at all for human life. He would take any advantage possible, though it had to be admitted that when necessary he would risk his own at the drop of a hat.

Cape made an arrangement with the owner of the Texas House to spend the night in a small room upstairs equipped with a bed for emergency purposes. Dusk was settling over the town when he left by the back door to get supper at the Tontine. He walked along the alley, then cut back between two buildings to the street. The restaurant was not twenty yards from him, just on the other side of the Bon Ton millinery shop.

For an instant the pit of his stomach went icy, then the lean whipcord body tightened and the muscles of his jaw hardened. Mort Heisman and Amos Scudder had just come out of the saloon across the street.

The eyes in Scudder's skeleton face popped out. "Look, Mort," he yelped, and flung a bony finger at Wallace. Instantly he bolted back into the saloon to get out of the line of fire. Cape's gaze did not lift from Heisman, but he was aware of men scurrying here and there for safety, of a wagoner whipping his mules to escape the danger lane, of a woman lifting her skirts and screaming as she ran. For the drunken gunman had his revolver out and was cursing at the pedestrians to clear a way for him.

Heisman's heavy squat body was weaving slightly as he moved to the edge of the sidewalk. His first wild shot struck a buggy wheel in front of Cape. "Quit skulkin' back there an' lemme get at you," he cried.

Cape did not answer. His mind, nerves, and muscles were fused in perfect co-ordination to frustrate the furious gunman. Within a matter of seconds he had to kill or be killed. He side-stepped around the buggy to keep what cover it offered as Heisman stepped down to cross the road. Though all his senses were concentrated on the attacking enemy, he remembered afterward that a drunken voice in an adjoining saloon began to sing "Goodbye, my lover, good-bye" and that the crack of a bullwhacker's whip rocketed down the street canyon. The sidewalks that had flung back the beat of a hundred marching feet were now silent and deserted.

Before the roar of Heisman's second shot had died away Cape's revolver slapped a bullet at him.

"Damn you, come out from where you're hiding," the gunfighter snarled.

The body and wheels of the buggy were between them. Cape crouched warily. In another moment the man's shuffling figure would be outlined against the light that had just gone on in front of the Texas House.

From the doorway of the Tontine a harsh voice whipped an order. "Drop that forty-five, Mort. You can't hurrah this town."

The marshal stood there, a sawed-off shotgun in his hands, breast-high and ready for action.

Heisman whirled, completely taken by surprise. He glared at the officer, made his choice, and fired at him. The crash of the shotgun came almost instantly. Its full charge tore into the body of the drunken man. Mort stood motionless, the life driven out of him, then pitched headlong and went down like a falling tree.

The marshal padded forward, soft-footed

as a panther, his eyes fixed on the dead body of his enemy. Already men were quickly pouring out of buildings, into the street.

"You are witnesses, gentlemen, that I had to do it," Harrigan said, his face set hard as granite. "It was Mort or Mr. Wallace, and Mort was out to get him."

"He sure was," Scudder agreed, throwing in with the winning side. "Mort had been makin' plenty threats. I said to lay off but he wouldn't."

"He was a quarrelsome devil," a bystander said. "No complaints, I reckon."

Wallace at any rate had none. He gave up the idea of supper and returned to the Texas House. As yet he was too keyed up to eat. For hours he had been under a heavy strain and could give no sign of it. Now he felt shaky and unstrung, a reaction from the tension of the long afternoon of self-control.

The news that Mort Heisman's body was lying on a slab at Block's undertaking parlors with thirteen buckshot in it drew a long line of morbid visitors. The general opinion was that he was better dead, with which view the *Chronicle* concurred, giving editorial praise to Marshal Harrigan for his prompt efficient action in saving the life of Wallace. This ought, the newspaper article concluded, to serve as a warning to the lawless fraternity.

Joan Regal was relieved at the man's death. With this violent man gone Henry Page would be safer. Not that Henry meant anything to her now, she told herself, except as a casual acquaintance. Since their quarrel she had seen him only at a distance, but she had heard of his social activities. Someone had mentioned he was the best dancer in town and was a desirable guest at the fashionable houses where they had dinner in the evening instead of at noon. Outwardly the only sign Erma noticed of the girl's unhappiness was her restlessness and a touch of bitterness, but the older woman knew that inside her was a frozen rebellious resentment.

Joan wrote a note to Cape Wallace telling him how glad she was of his escape. He thanked her formally in a letter of three lines. His stiffness did not offend her, since she knew the reason for it. Her heart warmed to him, for his emotion like her own was frustrated.

There had been a small fire on the stage of the theater when the house was empty; for a few days while repairs were being made no performances were given. It was the Indian summer season and the weather was fine, every day warm and sunny. A picnic for the troupe was arranged, to be held at Twin Lakes. Erma was having trouble with her feet and decided to stay at home and rest them, but she urged Joan to get out in the sunshine and enjoy herself.

"With whom?" Joan asked tartly. "Ted Downing is in court trying a case, Cape Wallace would not go with me, and I'm not interested in pairing off with any of the actors for a whole day. Why go and be bored?"

She was so final about it that Erma dropped the subject. An hour later Miss Roberts met Henry Page on Harrison Avenue. He stopped to talk with her and inquired about Joan. Was she going to the picnic? Erma thought not. There wasn't anybody with whom Joan wanted to go.

"Would she let me take her?" Henry asked eagerly.

"I don't know," Erma answered. "Not if she has any sense or pride."

"You know I'm very fond of her."

"I know you are very fond of yourself."

"You don't think much of me, do you, Erma?"

"I think you are selfish, fickle, conceited, and ungrateful. Joan is far and away too good for you."

He managed a laugh, though he did not relish her frankness. "Aren't you a little hard on me? I've been pretty busy at the mine."

"And with the girls on the hill. I hear you are going to marry one of them."

"Don't believe everything you hear." He added, "I think I'll go see Joan."

"How generous and kind of you!" Erma said, and went on her way.

When she returned to their room Joan was looking over her dresses. "Do you think this flowered muslin is too summery for the picnic?" the girl asked.

"You've decided to go."

Joan nodded. Her eyes were bright, her cheeks flushed with color. "Henry wants to take me. He explained how busy he has been."

"I met him," Erma said dryly. "From what he said I gathered he has been busy day and night."

"He was awf'ly sweet — and so kind of humble about not having been around. He isn't engaged to that other girl at all."

It was on the tip of Erma's tongue to ask if he had discovered the girl did not have enough money, but she wisely refrained. Why try to spoil a happy day for Joan? Besides, she was not sure it would be fair to Henry. Even though there was some social snobbery in him he had given no indication that he would marry a girl for money.

Three wagonloads of the picnickers rode gaily out of town across the flats toward the foothills where Twin Lakes lay at the base of Independence Pass. This was the first holiday Joan had found time for since coming to the silver camp. It was a day of warm and pleasant sunshine, and Henry was beside her once more. She was radiant with happiness and looked so lovely that the other men envied Page. He was pleased to know that he stood first with her, this girl who was as lithe and graceful as a young race horse.

They crossed rippling streams and passed through forests of spruce, aspen, and pine. In front of them the ribbed range fenced the rolling land from the higher peaks that looked down on the roof of the continent they guarded.

On a spur jutting out between the lakes the picnickers set out and ate their lunch after the men had cooked steaks and made coffee at a camp fire. A hamper of wine had been brought along and toasts were drunk to the ladies. After a time Henry and Joan wandered down to Lower Lake Creek and disappeared in the willows bordering its banks. They could hear the far faint voices of their companions until at last they died away in the distance.

The hours slipped away and, before they knew the afternoon was spent, the sun slid down into a hollow of the hills. Henry looked at his watch.

"Good gracious, it's five o'clock," he said. "We'll have to be getting back to the others."

She sighed. "Must we? It's been a perfect day. I've loved it. But of course we must."

Before they reached the point of outlet for the creek from the lower lake they came out of the willows. Henry's gaze swept the land spur where they had eaten. No wagons were in sight nor any of the picnickers.

"They've gone," he exclaimed.

"Gone," Joan echoed. "But they wouldn't go and leave us."

Yet that was what they had done. When they were ready to go they had piled into the nearest wagon, regardless of the one in which they had arrived. Since the time of leaving had been announced twice, the natural assumption was that none of the party was missing. There had been no check-up to discover if any absentees had failed to reach the camping ground.

"What shall we do?" Joan asked, dismayed.

"I don't know. We'll have to start walking.

Maybe someone may miss us and send a wagon back."

"If they don't we'll be out all night. Erma won't begin to wonder about me before midnight."

"Are you a good walker?"

"Yes. But I wouldn't know the way in the dark. Would you?"

"I'm not sure. But don't worry, dear. A night in the open won't kill us."

Another angle of the situation occurred to Joan. "They'll think we missed getting back in time on purpose."

He shrugged. "I suppose some cats will say that. We can't help it now. We know it isn't true."

"Yes. We know it." Her eyes lifted to his. There was a worried look in them. She was afraid her reputation would be torn to shreds. "But we ought to have been back in time. How could we have been so foolish?"

"It was a rotten trick to play on us," he said irritably. "Why couldn't they have waited?"

"There were so many of them they thought we were among them. It was our own fault, dear. We had better get going before it is dark."

"I suppose so," he agreed, feeling he was not quite living up to the masculine role. "It's you I'm worried about."

Her smile was a little forlorn. "Oh, I'll be all right. Maybe they will come back for us."

They followed the wagon trail as it wound through the hills. Darkness blanketed the earth and, now the sun was down, a bitter wind whipped from the divide. The cold of a two-mile altitude, usual at this time of year, bit into their flesh sharply.

At the summit of a small hill they stopped for a moment to look for any possible shelter. Joan shivered. "Why didn't I bring a heavy coat?" she asked.

Henry was more worried than he pretended. A night in the open would be an ordeal hard to endure. "If we could find a prospector's cabin, even a deserted one," he said.

She snatched at a fugitive memory. "We passed one coming out. Not far from here. On the edge of a clump of aspens. Close to the road."

"Eureka!" he cried. "Of course we did. There was smoke rising from the chimney. He'll take us in and feed us."

The night had grown black before they reached the aspen grove, but the log cabin bulked vaguely in the darkness. There was no light in it and no answer came to their knock.

Henry pushed open the door and walked

in. He struck a match and lit a candle he found stuck in an empty tomato can. On the table was a note written by a lead pencil, the paper pinned down by a piece of quartz. He moved the candle closer and read it aloud: "Help yourself, Pete, if you come. Gone to town to see the elefant. Back tomorrow unless I get drunk. Grub on the shelves." It was signed Jock.

"Nice of Jock to be so hospitable," Henry said, cheerful once more now that food, warmth, and shelter were in sight. He glanced at Joan, who was shaking with the cold. "Everything will be all right now that we're here," he promised. "I'll have a fire going in a jiffy."

He gathered old newspapers and kindling. Presently the fire was roaring. They stood in front of the hearth and let the heat soak into their chilled bones. From the bed he brought a buffalo robe and stretched it on the floor not too far from the blaze.

"Sit down and warm, while I make supper," he ordered. "What shall it be, roast duckling or a nice juicy steak smothered with onions? And of course all the trimmings."

But Joan would have none of that. She was warm as toast now, she said, and insisted on sharing the fun of making supper. They had known a bad half-hour with fear mounting in them and the reaction flung them into high spirits.

"Let's keep it a happy day," Henry said, slipping an arm around her waist. "Let's play there isn't any tomorrow and we are all alone in a world of joy."

On the shelves they found flour, coffee, molasses, sugar, and half a ham. There was no stove. The furniture was homemade, the dishes of tin. Rough whipsawed planks were fitted together for a floor. A stone fireplace served both to heat the house and to cook the food.

He fried the ham and made the coffee while she mixed the flapjacks. They were very merry over this first meal alone with each other and hoped it might be the forerunner of many. After they had eaten they did the dishes, she washing and he wiping.

"We wouldn't want Jock to think his guests were slovenly," she explained.

He put another log on the fire and they sat on the rug watching it blaze. The wind had come up shrill and strong. They could hear it outside roaring down from the snowy range. To sit there in the pleasant warmth safe from its threat gave them a delightful sense of languid wellbeing. Their mood of gaiety was past. The storm shut them in and drew them closer. Talk died away, except for trifles flung out to bridge silences growing too significant. His hand found hers and their palms clung fast.

She said, her voice low and unsteady. "We'd better go."

"Go where?" he asked. "There's no place to go — except out into the storm to freeze."

He drew her to him. A strange weakness swept over her. She tried to fight against the tide dragging at her anchor.

"We mustn't," she breathed.

Outside the wild night cut them off from all the rest of the world. They were a thousand miles away from all the laws that rule it.

It was close to midnight when Erma walked along the corridor and knocked on the door of the room occupied by the Roubideau sisters, a dancing team. The younger sister Dolly opened to let Erma in. She was in a nightgown, just ready for bed.

"Do you know where Joan is?" Erma asked.

"Hasn't she got home yet? The wagons were in an hour ago."

"Was she in your wagon?"

"No, we went out in the same one, but coming back we just took the wagon that was nearest." Dolly turned to her sister, already in bed. "Molly, was Joan in your wagon?"

Molly thought, and said no. "Joan was with Mr. Page all afternoon. We scattered here and there. I don't remember seeing them again. They must have come home in the other wagon. Maybe they went to a restaurant."

Erma did not think that likely. She made inquiries elsewhere and learned that neither Joan nor Henry had returned in the third wagon. The actress was disturbed. She knew that tenderfeet wandering in the mountains sometimes were lost for days and occasionally were not found until too late. But she did not want to raise a hue and cry unless it was necessary.

She put on a coat and went downstairs to the street, which was as usual roaring with life. A miner she knew, Peter Clancy, came out of the Texas House and stood hesitating whether to turn right or left.

Erma called to him and he joined her. "Will you do me a favor, Peter?" she asked.

"I will that," he replied. "What is it you're wanting?"

She told him where Wallace lived and said it was important she see him at once. Clancy concealed any surprise he might have felt and offered to carry the message. Fifteen minutes later Wallace joined Erma.

He agreed it was better not to send out a search party yet. The chances were that Joan and Henry had been careless about the time to return to the wagon ground and had reached there too late. If so, the fewer people who knew about it the better. Unless the missing two had found a cabin they would be lucky to escape pneumonia, though it was possible Henry might have lit a fire in some spot sheltered from the wind. Cape told Erma to bring down all the heavy blankets and coats she could carry and be waiting for him at the door when he returned with a surrey.

"Don't worry too much," he comforted her. "I'll probably find them in some prospector's cabin."

"I'm going with you, Cape."

"It will be cold," he warned. "Do you think you had better?"

"I'll dress for it. Hurry up. I'll be here ready for you."

Wallace wrapped Erma up in a blanket over her coat. At her feet she had a stone pig filled with hot water. As long as they were on fairly level ground Cape held the horses to a fast trot. The cold wind whipping across the flats bit into Erma's face, though very little more than her eyes was exposed to its fury.

After a long silence Erma said, "If they are only indoors somewhere."

"Yes." Wallace's anxiety for Joan escaped him in anger at Page. "Henry ought to have known better. He must have been told when the wagons would start, but he is always late for everything."

For hours they wound in and out among the hills. To Erma it seemed the night would never end. At last a gray light in the eastern sky announced that day was near. They began to hear the twitter of birds and the scurrying of rabbits. The distant misty hills came out of the darkness.

"We must be near the lakes," Erma guessed hopefully.

"Four or five miles." Wallace drew up the team and pointed with the whip. "Look. A cabin with smoke rising from it. We had better stop and ask the prospector if he has seen anything of them."

They tied at a small pine and walked up to the log cabin. Wallace knocked on the door. Low voices came to them, the sound of a chair being pushed back. Henry opened the door. The look of shocked surprise on his face was startling. Beside the table where they had been eating breakfast Joan stood frozen, one hand gripping the edge of it. Her gaze shifted from Erma to Cape, the color washing out of her cheeks. The eyes of the girl fell, but she forced herself to look up again. What she read in Wallace's face withered her. He knew.

Erma moved forward quickly and took Joan in her arms. "Thank God, you are safe," she said.

Henry laughed uneasily. "We made it here just in time. My fault. I muffed the hour for getting back. We started to walk to town and night came. It was bitterly cold. If we hadn't reached this cabin — " He stopped, letting the rest be imagined.

Erma took the talk up instantly. "But you did get here. That's all that matters. I've been so worried — so desperately afraid. I saw you in the storm — frozen to death — and you are here, snug and safe."

Joan buried her face on Erma's shoulder, sobs racking her body.

Gently Erma petted her. "It's all right. You don't have to remember all you've been through — how afraid you were. Forget all about it, dearie. And Cape and I will have some breakfast, if you'll make it, Henry. We're starved."

"Of course." Henry bustled around, preparing food. He was glad to have something to keep him busy. The surprise of seeing Erma and Cape had been too much for him. He had not put on a very good act, but it was not too late to save face now. "We've been wondering how we would get to town. Sorry to have put you both to so much trouble. Inexcusable of me. We got to gathering flowers and time ran away from us. But I think they might have waited for us a few minutes."

"It would have been better," Erma agreed.

Henry gathered confidence as he talked. "Of course it turned out all right, but it might not have. I fixed a fire and we found food. We were lucky, you bet. All's well that ends well." He slid a look at Joan that asked her to speak up and back his defense. She did not see it. Her eyes were avoiding his as well as those of the others.

Erma caught the ball and tossed it back. "It might have been a lot worse," she agreed cheerfully. "But don't forget that Cape and I lost a night's sleep, young man. Next time you go on a picnic use your head."

On their way back to town Joan sat in the back seat with Erma. She retired into an unhappy silence while the others kept up a rather forced sprightly conversation. The story was bound to spread all over the town and the gossip would be unpleasant.

Alone with Erma in their room, Joan flung

out miserably a question. "I suppose everybody knows already we didn't come back with the others?"

"It will get around that you missed the wagons. I don't know what Henry was thinking of."

"He wasn't any more to blame than I. We didn't realize it was so late. It doesn't matter whose fault it was. The point is that we spent the night alone together in a cabin."

"They may not discover that the miner was not at home."

"They will find out. The miner knows he wasn't there. So do you and Mr. Wallace."

Erma smiled. "Cape and I won't put it in the *Chronicle*."

"No. You will try to hide my shame."

"You must get hold of yourself, dear, and keep your head up. You are not the first girl who has been in an unconventional situation."

"If you are going to be bad you must be tough enough to brazen it out," Joan replied bitterly. "I made a fine start. You and Mr. Wallace knew right off that — that — "

"We don't know anything except that you had to take shelter there."

"I was so terribly ashamed."

"It's not too late yet. Be light and smiling about it."

"You should give lessons to fallen women," Joan suggested. "How to sin and not be found out."

"If I knew a girl who had made a mistake I would tell her to use her common sense," Erma said gently.

"I know — I know." Joan flew into her friend's arms. "I've been bad — and such a fool. What am I going to do about it?"

Erma comforted her, as a mother might. "Do what you are doing, dearie. Have a good cry. After that we'll pick up the pieces and mend them."

"I ought never to have gone to the picnic with Henry," Joan said after a time. "I knew how I felt about him. It was my fault as much as his. There's no use pretending it wasn't."

Erma disagreed about the division of blame. From the day when they had ridden up on the train together, Henry had made love to Joan, at first only with his eyes but after the trial with all the charm of voice and manner he could exert. Yet that was not Erma's chief concern. She was resolved that Joan should suffer as little as possible from her indiscretion. Henry must come forward at once and announce that they were engaged.

10

Joan had been quite right. Over the teacups the town clacked about her adventure. The actress girl had spent a night with Henry Page alone in a cabin after having deliberately missed the wagons going back to town. She was, the gossips admitted, a very pretty girl with nice manners, but you could not expect a variety hall girl to have any morals. Among the patrons of the theater she had many rough admirers who felt she was a victim of circumstances, but the good women of the community would accept no such nonsense as that. This was not the first time she had been imprudent, but now she had gone too far. Everybody knew what young men were. You could not blame Henry too much for falling prey to her wiles.

Downing blamed him, bitterly. He had resigned himself to losing Joan, but he could not bear to see her pride humiliated and her good name dragged in the dust. He walked up to the Sally McGee and found Henry busy superintending the timbering of the shaft.

Page was not very glad to see him. For some time he had felt the weight of Ted's silent disapproval and he did not like it. He was under a deep obligation to the lawyer. They had been friendly and he did not want to lose his regard. Henry had a temperament that sunned itself in popularity.

He waved a hand at Downing as Ted climbed the slope. "Come to see how the other half lives — the working world?" he called out.

Clad in custom made boots, expensive corduroys, and a fine linen shirt, Henry did not look much like the miners who swung a pick underground. He wore no hat and his coppery hair flung out golden glints in the sunlight. The superlative good looks of the man stirred resentment in his visitor. But he had to choke it down, since he had come on a mission that presupposed friendship.

They talked of the prospect of striking ore, each of them aware that this was preliminary verbal maneuvering. Downing found it difficult to come to grips with what he had to say, for Henry might very likely tell him it was none of his business. Strictly speaking, it was not, but he was the only man friend left

Joan now that her brother had deserted. She wouldn't thank him for interfering, if she ever found out. It ought not to be necessary, given any sense of decency in Henry.

Page was talking glibly. "I think we are close to the vein. My guess is we'll strike it within the next twenty feet. One of the big outfits made me a kind of tentative offer, but I don't want to sell out and have the buyer hit a bonanza next week."

Downing brushed this aside bluntly. "You haven't seen Joan since the night of the picnic, have you?" he asked.

"No, I haven't." Henry explained what might seem to be negligence. "Fact is, there has been a little silly talk. I thought it would be better for Joan if I wasn't seen with her for a few days."

Ted thought it would have been better if he had never been seen with her, but he did not say so. "The kind of talk that is going on can poison Joan's life, Henry. To hear some of it you might think she was a bad woman instead of being the lovely girl she is. It's up to her friends to stand by her now."

"Sure. It's a bad break. Just because we were unlucky enough to be late for the wagons. A damn shame, that's what it is. But the talk will die out. The thing is not to let it worry us."

Henry's complacency angered the lawyer, but he was careful not to let his feeling reach the surface. "Before it dies down Joan's reputation will be ruined," he said.

"Oh, I'm sure you are wrong. The gabbling of geese isn't important. Talk without any just foundation will soon be forgotten." Henry added cheerfully, "Tell Joan from me not to worry and that I'll be seeing her again in a few days."

"Don't you think you owe her more than that? Since you are responsible for the talk you ought to stop it."

"My dear fellow, what can I do? If I open my mouth it will just keep the chatter going."

"It depends on what you open it to say," Ted differed. "You can stop the slanderous gossip by drawing its sting."

"Can I? How?"

"By announcing your engagement to her."

Henry flushed angrily. "That's absurd. It would be an admission that the talk is true. Joan would bite my head off if I did."

"Not if it was a fact that you were engaged."

"Did Erma send you to me?" Henry demanded.

"No."

"Or Joan?"

"Sometimes I think you are a complete fool,

Henry. You ought to know that Joan would cut her hand off before she would send me to you."

"Then I don't see where you come into this. Or Erma either. Joan and I can manage our affairs without you two butting in all the time."

"Has Erma spoken to you about this?"

"Spoken to me!" exploded Henry. "She has called me every name in and out of the dictionary. Joan and I can work this out if you'll just quit being a pair of old grandmothers. I'm sick and tired of you both."

"That will be fine with us if you really mean to work it out." Downing flung another suggestion at Page. "Erma and I aren't alone in this. A hundred men in this camp are watching you to see what you will do. This Western country is peculiar in its feeling about women. It doesn't like to see a fine girl compromised by a man and then cast off."

"You are making a mountain out of a molehill," Henry retorted stormily. "Why don't you tell the truth? You're in love with Joan yourself. There is no law against your being a chivalrous gentleman and marrying her."

Downing looked at him contemptuously, teeth clamped, the muscles of his jaw standing out like ropes. Without another word he turned and walked away. Both of them knew that their friendship had come to an end. The ties that had bound them had been weakening for some time and now the last of them had snapped.

Henry's eyes followed Downing as he walked down the hill. He was not happy at the situation and he regretted that last fling. His conscience was not at ease. It distressed him to feel that anybody could think he was a cad. Also, he was fond of Joan. He must do the right thing by her. That thought had nagged him a dozen times a day since the picnic. He was more or less entangled with Nancy Folsom. He had not asked her to marry him, but he knew she was expecting him to do so very soon. Well, there was a law against bigamy. He would have to cut loose from Nancy as tactfully as he could.

That evening he sent Joan a note asking if she would meet him in front of the Congregational Church next morning about eleven o'clock. He had something very important to discuss with her. The messenger brought it back to him with the words, "I'll be there. Joan," written on the bottom of it.

Joan wore a close-fitting leaf-green dress with a hat and parasol to match. As she walked up the hill she was conscious again, as she had been in the days following her arrival, that men's eyes watched her. Though she gave no sign of awareness, the thought was strong in her that now she was under criticism they looked at her with a more predatory gaze, as if she had been brought down to the street level.

The hills were lambent with the many blended colors of fall, but down in this sink the tawdry business of the day was beginning once more to mock the glory of the mountains. The chips were starting to rattle and the fiddles to saw. In Rufe's Cabinet saloon a cracked old soprano voice was singing a tearjerker, one Joan had heard several times in the past months.

> *"Was it from a gray-haired mother, a sister, or a brother?*
> *Had he waited all the weary years in vain?*
> *Yet from early morning light he would watch till dark at night,*
> *But the letter he had longed for never came."*

She saw Henry standing in front of the church, lean and graceful, his forearm resting on the fence. He was looking at a loaded jack train disappearing behind the summit of the hill above him. Indolently he turned and caught sight of her. At once he came to life, waved a hand, and moved lightly to meet her.

The pulse in her throat began to beat. Why was it that a woman lived and died in a man's quick smile, in the turn of his head, in the light of his eyes? It was not fair, unless he loved her.

Henry thought her fragrant youth had never been more lovely, and for the moment he wiped out their indiscretions and their sin by ignoring them completely. He took both her hands and held them tightly, his eager gaze fixed on her.

"I'm just making a discovery," he said. "A woman isn't beautiful only because of her eyes, mouth, color, or the planes of her face, or even by the way they are put together, but more because of the lovely soul expressed by them."

A glow of happiness suffused her. "You say the nicest things," she told him. "I wasn't sure. I thought perhaps you might — despise me now."

"You silly little goose!"

"Of course you know what they are saying. When you didn't come to see me — " she let the sentence die unfinished.

He gave her his reason for not coming, to give the talk a chance to die down.

"I wouldn't blame you if you had never come," she cried. "I've been a fool and it is right I should be punished."

"By marrying me," he said smilingly.

"You want to marry me?" she asked.

"Because of the other night," he answered.

"You mean — to make an honest woman of me?"

They had moved down the path to the covered entry of the church. Sheltered from observation, he put an arm around her shoulders and kissed her. "I can give a better reason than that, little Miss Suspicion."

She had met his kiss warmly, but now she drew back from his embrace. There was not going to be any repetition of ardent lovemaking. She had learned her lesson.

"You had better give it," she said. "You are under no obligation to marry me because I'm a weak character. I wouldn't take a man who offered himself out of pity."

He said the words she wanted to hear.

They walked to the top of the hill and looked across the valley to the white-crested range dominated by Massive and Elbert. The world was washed in sunlight today, a beautiful place for lovers to stroll hand in hand. As they moved down Harrison the panorama Joan saw was no longer one of smoke and filth, an ant heap of raw, turbulent, and meaningless activity. It was a haven where men came to fulfill their dreams and find happiness.

Before they parted at the entrance to the Grand Central a small discordant note was sounded by Henry.

"By the way, sweetheart," he suggested casually, "let's keep this a secret for a little while from all the buzzing gossips."

Joan did not see the need of this. She would have preferred announcing the engagement at once. But she did not say so. It was a small thing after all. If Henry wanted it that way, why not?

"I'll tell only Erma," she said.

Erma did not like the postponing of the announcement. To make public the engagement would be to scotch most of the gossip about Joan. If Ted Downing had been the lucky man he would have wanted to tell the world at once, but it was Henry's way to avoid clearcut issues in the hope that postponing them might make meeting them easier. He would probably shilly-shally and not let his friends on the hill know until his hand was forced.

Miss Roberts had gauged Henry correctly. Within a few hours of his engagement he was invited to a party of socialites going on a grand spree to Denver that was to last several days. They were to hear Adelina Patti at the new Tabor Opera House in the capital city and three nights later were to see Booth and Barrett in *Othello*. They would stay at the Windsor and take part in an exclusive costume ball at the hotel. This was too good to be missed. Henry was glad he had cautioned Joan to secrecy. He knew that if the news had got out he would have found his name marked off the favored list. Since there was no use in hurting Joan he told her that he had been called to Denver for a few days on business connected with the obtaining of mining machinery for the Sally McGee. This, he told himself, was to be his last little fling.

Henry had reckoned without the newspapers. The Denver correspondents to the Leadville journals sent up daily detailed accounts of what the visiting contingent of the Cloud City were doing. Featured in the stories were the names of Henry Page and Nancy Folsom. They were seen together at trotting races, dances and the theater. It was expected that shortly the engagement of this attractive young couple would be officially announced. Mr. Page was a prominent engineer and mining man. Miss Folsom was the daughter of Mr. and Mrs. Roderick K. Folsom, who were among the fortunate ones who had struck it rich in Leadville.

When Erma read the stories she boiled with

indignation. The first one she hid from Joan, then made up her mind she had better know the truth and laid the paper on the table. Joan did not pick up the paper until after the evening performance. Watching her, Erma presently knew that the girl had found the story. All day a spring of life had been bubbling up in her. Two sentences quenched her joy. She sat very still, her back half turned toward Erma, and pretended to be reading another page of the paper. Neither of them made any reference to the article. Not until she had seen the third day's paper did Joan speak to Erma about them.

"Henry seems to be having a good time," she said in a tone icily indifferent.

"Maybe he met them by chance in Denver and they have drawn him into their group," Erma suggested.

"No. He lied to me. When I saw him the morning he had no intention of going to Denver, and when he came to tell me in the afternoon I thought it was queer. The stuff he had ordered for the mine wasn't due for two weeks." She asked, searching her mind for the answer, "Why did he ask me to marry him? He didn't need to."

Erma could have mentioned the pressure put on him, but she thought it better to keep silent about it. "He likes you better than he does Nancy Folsom. But he is weak. He wanted to join the party, so he did."

Joan said quietly, "I'm through with him. I couldn't be happy with a man I can't trust, one who would always lie to me if he found it easier."

"Don't make up your mind till you've seen him. He may have an explanation."

"He'll have one, a nice reasonable story, and I won't believe a word of it." Joan's laugh was bitter. "The man I gave my heart to and played the fool with."

"Why blame yourself because he is weak and fickle?" Erma asked gently.

"I'm not. I blame myself because I threw myself at him, because I'm so dumb I couldn't see he is just window dressing."

Joan turned away abruptly, to close the talk. For three days she had been living with her pent-up unhappiness. Erma was pleased to see that the emotions which tore her held anger as well as despair. She would have a good many bad hours, but she would come out of them with no scars that time would not heal.

When Henry returned to Leadville several acquaintances spoke to him of the high jinks he and his friends had enjoyed in Denver.

"We'll be watching the papers for a certain notice we're expecting any day now," one woman whom he met in front of Daniels & Fisher's store told him archly.

He thought, *Joan is going to be hopping mad, but I can't help that. After all she is not the only girl in the world. She ought to know I have to be nice to others, that it does not mean anything.*

He shirked seeing her the first day and when he did meet her on the forenoon of the second he chose a time when Erma and Pierre were with her on the theater stage arranging a change in the routine of the juggling act. Joan nodded to him coolly and went on with the business of the new lines. He stood around awkwardly till they were through. As they were leaving the set he said, "Like to see you alone for a minute, Joan."

That it was not going to be easy to placate her, he knew. She waited silently, slim and straight, her face aloof and cold.

"The newspapers have got it all wrong," he blurted out. "I met those people and I had to go around with them."

"Of course. But what was wrong with the newspaper stories? They said you were devoted to Miss Folsom, that you took her to the trotting races and the ball, that you gave a little dinner for her and sat beside her in a box at the play and the opera. Isn't that correct?"

"It's not the way you think. I was trying to break off with her."

"Break off from what?"

"Don't act like a frozen iceberg, Joan. I'm trying to explain. I had been sort of attentive to her and I didn't want to hurt her feelings by just dropping her abruptly."

"I can see that would be important." The scornful smile of the girl reflected no mirth. "And did you succeed in not hurting her feelings?"

"Let's not talk about her. She doesn't count." From his vest pocket he drew a small box and opened it. Inside was a ruby ring, the stone set with seed pearls. He handed it to her.

Joan looked at it without taking the ring from its cushion. She raised her eyes to look directly at him. "I've been thinking about a good many things these past days, Henry. One of them is why you asked me to marry you." She lifted a hand to stop the answer on his lips. "No, I don't want that reason. You did not have to ask me. Or did you feel you must?"

"Why wouldn't I feel that way — after that night? I'm not a cad."

"Your conscience said you ought to make

an honest woman of me. So you did what was proper. I'm grateful."

"Don't be so stuffy, Joan. It's expected of a fellow. But why go into that? You know how fond of you I am."

"Yes, I know." Her challenging eyes held fast to his. "Who expected it?"

"I don't want to talk about that. We made a mistake. Do we have to go on fussing about it all the rest of our lives?"

"No. Was it Erma who expected it? And maybe Ted Downing?"

"All right, if you insist. Both of them spoke to me about it."

"I see. All of you concerned to salvage what was left of my lost reputation." She looked down again at the box in her hand. "It's a nice ring, Henry. Miss Folsom will like it. And until you are married better not start a flirtation with another girl. Women are peculiar. They don't like weak drifters. I have to be going. I know you will excuse me now."

"You can't do this to me, Joan. You belong to me. You love me."

He put a hand on her arm and she brushed it aside. "Wrong on all three counts, Henry. I'm saying good-bye. I belong to myself. And I don't love you, though I thought I did."

She put the box on a table, turned, and

walked swiftly from the stage. He did not know how weak her legs were nor that as soon as she was alone in her room she broke into a storm of weeping.

Ted Downing saw a good deal of Joan in the weeks that followed. Her trial was coming up soon and he had to consult with her about the defense. She smiled ruefully when he mentioned the word.

"But I haven't any. You know that. All I ask is that you perform a miracle and persuade the judge and jury that it is all right for me to help prisoners escape."

He did not find it a laughing matter. To get an acquittal would have been easier a few weeks ago than now. There had been too much gossip about her. The escapade with Henry would do her no good. He had expected that when he put her on the stand as a witness, shy and innocent and lovely, a sympathetic jury would decide the public would be better served with this girl free than in prison. But he was no longer sure of the effect she would create in the court room. She had acquired a harder finish. She had a poised steeliness, almost a touch of defiance, that robbed her of the helplessness upon which he had depended. He knew it was a protective cover worn to shield an inner shrinking, but the twelve good men in the jury box might not be aware of this.

Downing realized that she was unhappy and it distressed him. Henry was out of the picture, now openly engaged to Nancy Folsom, but he had left Joan with a feeling that she had cheapened herself in giving her love to one so weak and shallow. She had built barriers around her that excluded everybody but Erma and, strangely enough, Cape Wallace. Perhaps it was because he too was a sinner that she could talk with him so much more freely than with Ted.

"I'm giving up my job at the Texas House," he told her one day when they met on Harrison Avenue. "I've bought the Baxter ranch down the valley." He smiled at her. "You're looking at a reformed character."

She looked around in mock alarm for him. "Do you think you ought to be seen talking with me?" She added, "Considering my reputation."

He said lightly, "Are you referring to the 'affair Henry' or your criminal career?"

"Both. I've made a fine mess of things. Three months ago I was a nice girl, well brought up, who lived inside the proper conventions. And now —" She threw out her hands, palms up. No need to tell him what she was now.

"You were a nice innocent little girl," he agreed. "Lovely to look at, just out of a glass cage. Nobody could tell how you would turn out, but it looked like an even bet you would become a prim simpering nonentity. Instead, you have lived — become tuned to tragedy, a woman not afraid to face fire with her head up. My dear, you can't make an omelet without breaking eggs."

It was heartening to hear his appraisal, even though she knew she had not earned it. "I've certainly broken a basketful," she said. "But the omelet turned out flat and heavy."

"It's still cooking," he reminded her. "Look at Cape Wallace. Yesterday a professional gambler, tomorrow a respectable ranchman."

His grin was sardonic, but she would not leave the subject on that note. "I'm proud of you, Cape. I've always known you are too good to waste your time at a roulette table."

"I've been thinking about your trial. Would it do any good if I said I had worked up the plot to free your brother and led you in to take a hand?"

"No, it wouldn't, and I won't have it," Joan replied emphatically. "Folks would say you were just another of my men. It would ruin my case."

"I was afraid of that angle. What defense does Downing mean to take?"

"There isn't any, except that Jim is my brother."

"That may go a long way if you seem to the jury gentle and sorry and unhappy about your brother. Whatever you do, don't act defiant or indifferent. You have to win the jury's sympathy."

"Yes, I know. Sit with my hands folded and my eyes down — and cry into my handkerchief now and then. Mr. Downing has explained that to me. Since I don't want to go to the penitentiary I'll do my best."

"How does Downing feel about you?" he asked. "Tell me it is none of my business if you like."

"I'm sure he doesn't approve of me." There was the ghost of a twinkle in her eyes. "Would you expect him to?"

"I wasn't thinking about your deplorable conduct." His smile robbed the words of their sting. "He could overlook that if it was important enough to him. Downing is a fine man, with rectitude written all over that craggy Irish face. A woman who married him would have a good life."

"Yes — if she wasn't in the penitentiary. By the way, he is quite an orator. If he wants to he can speak for himself."

That Downing would do that when he felt it was the proper time Wallace had no doubt. He would probably wait until the memory of Henry had ceased to rankle in Joan's heart, and since the girl had plenty of good sense she would then be ready to appreciate the lawyer's devotion and integrity.

When Joan was with Downing she was still mentally in sackcloth and ashes. Ted was gentle and understanding. He had forgiven what she had done but he had not forgotten. She reproached herself that when she met Cape Wallace she escaped from her sense of guilt. To him she was the same Joan Regal he had known before her escapade. He made her lighthearted and happy. Youth bubbled up in her again, and of course that was not right. She must keep remembering that she had been a bad girl.

But thoughts of Wallace stayed with her, his careless competence, his surface mockery, the recklessness that gave him charm. When the call came he could gamble without any flourish for the highest stakes. He cared nothing for formal law, yet he had character. He lived by his code as faithfully as Downing did by his, though very likely he would make a jest of his action. Joan had discovered to her surprise that she was a kindred spirit. There was a good deal of the gambler in her too.

11

After his escape from jail Jim Regal made for the Saguache country where the Hayden gang was nested in a gulch above Saguache Creek. From this mountain sanctuary the outlaws raided the ranches for horses which they ran across the Sangre de Cristo range over Poncha Pass and up into the Bayou Salado. Here the animals were disposed of to freighters willing to accept forged papers of ownership. The depredations of the rustlers became so heavy that stockmen issued blunt announcement that thieves caught with any of their brands would be hanged at once.

This was a hint not to be ignored. The bandits decamped with no delay. They crossed the Arkansas and headed north for Tarryall. Here they bought supplies, loaded a pack horse, and moved into a camp on the wooded bluffs above the great Bayou Salado. Dan Hayden made a deal with a contractor engaged in freighting meat to the silver city. He and his men were to furnish two wagonloads of deer and elk a week. A mule skinner named Wood picked up the game at the camp.

On his second visit he gave Jim Regal a letter which had been handed him at Leadville for delivery. The man who asked him to carry the letter to Jim was a stranger, Wood said.

Your sister is in a bad jam. On account of this scoundrel Page. Better get back here quick. Go to the old Wiggins cabin in California Gulch. It is stocked with provisions and you will be safe there. Will drop in and explain everything. I said it might be this way.

YOU KNOW WHO

Jim felt sure the letter was from Quint Vining. Nobody else knew where he was. He was greatly disturbed. It was his duty to look after Joan and he had neglected to do so after he had been warned. He decided to slip back to Leadville and see for himself how things stood. Vining would not have said it would be safe unless he had arranged it so. This could not be a trap laid by the sheriff. The last sentence in the letter must refer to the warning Quint had given him the night before he left Leadville.

To avoid being recognized he traveled by night. Early in the morning he arrived at a roadhouse kept by a man friendly to the Hayden gang. Regal did not put up at the house but slept in the stable where food was brought to him by the proprietor. After dark he took the road again. Occasionally he passed bull outfits or covered wagons toiling up the pass to avoid the congestion of daylight traffic, but none of them paid any attention to the solitary rider.

Long before dawn he looked down on the garish lights of the town and heard the blare of the bands rocketing up the slope. Avoiding main streets, he followed back alleys and skirted the suburbs, leaving Fryer and Carbonate behind him. He turned up Califorina Gulch, the cabins lining the canyon still dark and silent. It had been a long cry since Abe Lee had raised his mighty shout, "By God, I've got California in my pan." Ten thousand men had poured into the gulch in answer to that jubilant yell, had built huts, cradles, and flumes, roared "Susannah" into the starry sky, found bonanza or *borrasca*, and when the placers were played out scattered to every state in the Union and a dozen countries. Now two decades later as many more had come to dig for the heavy carbonate sands the gold hunters had cursed for interfering with the gold in the rockers.

The Wiggins cabin was far up on a ledge covered with small pines, too far back from the lip of the gulch for mining. Old Wiggins had been a trapper. For twenty-five years it had been falling to decay. The trail leading to it was overgrown with brush. More than once Jim stopped to make sure he had not taken the wrong prong. He came to the shack at last almost hidden in a second growth of small trees.

On the table he found a gunny sack filled with provisions, candles, a newspaper, the *Police Gazette*, two dime novels relating the adventures of Deadwood Dick, a box of matches, and a sack of smoking tobacco. There was also a feed of oats for the horse. After picketing his mount young Regal made breakfast and put out the fire at once. Light was sifting into the sky. He did not want the smoke to be seen by any early riser in the gulch. Breakfast over, he spread his slicker on the rotting old bedstead, lay down, and almost at once fell asleep. The long hours of travel had left him very weary.

It was late afternoon when he awoke hungry as a wolf, but he could not with safety light a fire until after dark. The curiosity of some gulch hermit might lead him to climb the prong and find out who was staying in the old Wiggins cabin. Regal had no capacity for patient waiting. He was at the door of the hut a dozen times looking down for a glimpse of Vining on his way up, though his judgment told him the man would not start until after dark. Seated on a three-legged stool, he glanced over the *Police Gazette* from cover to cover, then tossed it aside and picked up the *Chronicle*. His eyes were drawn to a marked item on the fourth page. He read it twice.

> *One of the gala social events of the season will be the wedding of Henry Page and Miss Nancy Folsom at the Presbyterian Church on Saturday afternoon. The young couple will spend their honeymoon at Colorado Springs. After their return Mr. Page will continue to develop his mine, the Sally McGee, which shows much promise of becoming a bonanza.*

Jim crumpled the newspaper and flung it down angrily. He paced the uneven floor. If Quint Vining had something to tell him why did he not come and get it over with instead of keeping him on the hooks? What business of his was it anyhow to drag him here, probably without any need? This fellow Page could marry anybody he liked and good riddance to him.

The stars were out before Jim heard the sound of a horse's hoofs striking on the loose shale of the prong. To be on the safe side, he drew his revolver. A horseman came out of the shadowy background.

"That you, Jim?" a voice called.

Regal pushed his weapon back into its holster. "Time you were getting here," he growled.

"Did you want a dozen people to see me coming up here in the middle of the day?" Vining asked amiably.

"Well, what's the big news that made you send for me?" Jim demanded.

"Take it easy," the older man suggested. "You're not going to a fire." He grounded the reins of the bridle. "Find everything you needed here to be comfortable?"

"Good enough," the boy said ungraciously. "But no liquor. Did you bring a bottle this time?"

From the saddlebags Vining drew a quart. Regal brought two tin cups from inside. Into one the gambler poured a big shot, into the other a small one. To Regal he passed the larger one.

"Happy days," he said.

From the upper pocket of his vest he drew two good cigars. Both of them lit up. Vining sat down on the step and leaned against the rotting door that sagged from one leather hinge.

"Let's have it," Regal said, after he had gulped down the whisky and replenished his cup.

"You asked me to keep you in touch with any developments about your sister and Page. As soon as I found where you were I sent you the message." The cold level eyes in the white impassive face fastened on Regal. "I understood that was what you wanted."

"All right. It's what I wanted. What's happened?"

Vining told his version of the story at length, that Page had pursued this innocent girl with devilish ardor, eager to win her to his purpose, that he had escorted her to the Twin Lakes picnic and deliberately missed transportation back, that he had taken her to a cabin rented from a miner and had spent the night with her, and that the town had been filled with gossip over the downfall of Joan Regal. Page had then deserted the ruined girl and become engaged to a rich society debutante whom he was going to marry on Saturday.

The voice of the villain droned on flat and cold. His thin lips, cruel as a steel trap, made a straight gash across the face from which all expression was frozen. Patient as a cat at a mouse hole, his bleak narrowed eyes watched the victim to make sure of the effect of his story. There was no pity in him for the boy he was destroying, none for the man who would be the first struck down if his plot did not miscarry. Without stopping his tale he saw that the young outlaw's tin cup was kept full. If he was not inflamed by liquor he might shrink from the job he had to do.

A furious anger boiled in Jim Regal. He would stop the marriage of Page with this society girl and force him to do right by Joan. He would show the fellow she was not defenseless, even if he had to make a shotgun wedding of it.

Vining's talk flowed on smoothly. The sympathy of the whole town was with Miss Regal and its anger hot against her seducer. Any necessary violence would be overlooked if her natural protector was driven to it. This Page was a moral leper who ought to be stamped out. Vining, it appeared, did not ordinarily believe in taking the law into your own hand. But how else could you reach a scoundrel like Page? A libertine deserved no favor. This country out here was raw and hard, but it stood for the protection of good women. It did not feel that a designing rake should ruin a pure young girl and go laughing on his way without paying for it.

Jim pounded on the door jamb with his fist. "By God, you're right," he cried. "He can't do that to *my* sister. This scalawag will marry her or I'll stop his clock."

The older man shook his head doubtfully. "Would it be a kindness to marry a fine girl like Miss Regal to a man bad all the way through, a murderer as well as a wrecker of women's lives? I don't know, Jim. You will have to be the judge of that. If she were my sister I wouldn't dare take such a chance."

"What would you do?"

Vining reached for the boy's cup and poured another drink into it. He said, his low voice icy cold, his hard shallow eyes fixed on Regal, "My way would be final."

In spite of Jim's anger and mounting recklessness he backed away from the thought. "I can't kill a man in cold blood."

"I'm not advising it. You asked me what I would do." There was a touch of contempt in Quint's manner. "Some haven't the nerve to be thorough."

"Easy for you to say that," Regal flared out. "I'm a hunted man already and can't show my face downtown. I don't see how I'm ever going to meet him without being nabbed. And if I did I wouldn't dare touch him. They would string me up sure if I was caught."

Vining shrugged his shoulders. "No trouble to meet him. They are having a big masked ball tonight at the Clarendon Hotel. Page and his fiancée will be there. I brought along with me an old domino and face mask on the chance you might want to use them. You would be absolutely safe."

"Am I supposed to tap every man there on the shoulder and ask him if he is Henry Page?" Jim asked.

"Up to you, my friend. Maybe you had better not meet him — if he has you buffaloed. You might find it safer hunting deer in the Tarryall Mountains."

A hot flush beat up beneath the tan of Jim's cheeks. "I'll see him," he snarled. "Don't worry about that."

He tilted another drink from the bottle into his cup.

"For God's sake, don't make any mistake, Jim," Vining urged. "Remember this fellow kills without warning. If you get him nobody will blame you, though you might as well have your horse handy. But be sure of one thing. If he acts or talks mean, let him have it."

Jim said stiffly, "I ain't scared of him, but I

aim to play this my way."

Vining said he was sure Jim would know how to handle the situation.

"First off, I want to see Joan. I want to find out exactly what happened. Maybe there is some mistake about this." Regal ripped out a sudden furious oath. "If it's as bad as you say I'm not going to let the fellow get away with it."

Vining thought fast. It would not do at all for Regal to talk with his sister. You never could tell about women. She might lie to save face. Or she might tell the story in such a way as to mitigate the guilt of Page.

"I've told you exactly what every gossip in town is saying," he answered. "It would be all right to talk with your sister. But how are you going to work it? Soon as you go near the Grand Central you'll be arrested."

"She could come up here."

"That would be plumb crazy. You might as well advertise in the *Chronicle* that you are roosting up in the Gulch. If she was seen it would be a dead give-away." Vining offered a suggestion. "Tell you what. Write her a note and I'll deliver it. Say you'll meet her on the Ditch Walk near the lower end about nine o'clock. Her act doesn't come on till about ten. That will give her plenty of time to get back and dress. After you have seen her you can drop in at the Clarendon for the masked ball and have it out with Page. How would that do?"

Jim thought it would do very well. It could be dark along the Walk and nobody would be there but an occasional pair of lovers. They could step back into the brush if any of these appeared. He wrote a note to Joan telling her it was urgently important to see her at once and that she must be very careful to make sure she was not followed to the Walk.

Vining promised to give it to her personally as soon as he reached town. On his way down the canyon he tore the note into twenty pieces and scattered them in the scrub growth. He was not entirely satisfied with the situation. One could not predict how Jim would react when his sister failed to appear. His anger might take him either to Joan or to Page. Since he could wear the domino to the Clarendon the chance was he would go there. Quint hoped so. He had baited the trap. Now he must be sure it closed on his victims.

Jim Regal picketed his horse in the willows bordering the Ditch Walk. He was a few minutes ahead of time but he made no allowance of that. The liquor he had drunk so freely had robbed him of judgment. Joan ought to be here waiting for him. A pair of lovers passed and lingered to exchange kisses not a dozen yards from him. His restless stirring in the foliage startled them away.

The minutes dragged. It seemed to him an eternity before he struck a match to find by his watch that it was twenty minutes past nine. Too bad he had not brought the bottle with him instead of leaving it in the cabin. There was not a great deal left in it, but he was needing a drink badly just now. What was the matter with Joan? Did she think she could fob him off and pay no attention to his demand that she come and meet him?

He waited till nearly ten before he left. What he wanted to do was to go down and read the riot act to her. But he could not do it. He would almost certainly be recognized by somebody. After all, Page was the one he had to call to account.

From back of the saddle he took his slicker and unrolled it. The domino and mask were inside. He put them on, mounted, and rode down to the Clarendon. That he was drunk he knew, but not so much so that he was not physically entirely master of himself.

He tied at a hitching post a few doors from the hotel. The ball was being held in the dining room of the Clarendon. To him came the music of a waltz and the sound of shuffling feet. Walking down the street, he turned in at the doorway. The waltz had just ended and the men were taking their partners to the chairs lined against the wall.

Jim touched a masker wearing a baseball suit. "I have an important message for Mr. Henry Page. By any chance do you know which one he is?"

The baseball player did not. A polka was being announced and he hurried away to find the lady upon whose card he had written his name for that number.

Regal studied the men on the floor, trying to make up his mind which was Page. Most of them he could dismiss at once. They were either past their youth or were inexpert dancers. He picked on three most likely to be Page. One was a harlequin with a pierrette for partner. They were probably the most graceful couple present. Another was a devil in red and a third was wearing a Highland costume. The one in kilts he eliminated, since probably the man was one of Tabor's troop. It did not seem to Jim likely that a person with the reputation of Page would come as the devil. That would be to point a finger at himself.

After the polka the harlequin chatted with

the pierrette and fanned her. They were both very gay. Jets of mirth sprinkled their talk. The baseball player claimed the pierrette for a schottische. Her former partner pretended desolation and after she had gone strolled past Regal toward a couple of other men not dancing.

Jim intercepted him. "Are you Mr. Page?" he asked, his voice slurred.

The harlequin realized the domino had been drinking. He did not like the tone of the question. It seemed to carry a challenge.

"Who wants to know?" he asked curtly.

"I do. Got an important message for him."

"What is it? My name is Page."

"Tell you outside where we'll be alone."

Page felt a quick alarm. He had never been fully satisfied that the Vinings were ready to call their account quits. This drunken fool might be dangerous.

"You'll tell me here — if anywhere," he said.

"Do you want everyone in the room to hear us? I'm Jim Regal. You can't brush me off, you damned — "

Henry glanced hurriedly around the room, to make sure nobody was watching them. He lowered his voice. "I'll meet you tomorrow morning — anywhere you say."

"You bet. And bring the sheriff with you." Jim raised his voice, anger riding in it. "You'll see me right damned now."

A man and woman standing near looked at them curiously.

"Don't be foolish," Henry urged. "You're making a scene. I'll talk this over with you later."

Regal caught him by the arm. "We'll settle this now."

Page flung off his hand. "Let me alone. You're drunk." Henry was annoyed and worried. With his wedding only two days ahead he could not afford to have the Twin Lakes scandal dragged publicly into the open again. He turned to walk away.

The young outlaw blocked his path. "No, you don't. I won't let you alone till you've done right by the girl you have ruined."

"Get out of here, you fool, or I'll call the sheriff." Henry reached for a handkerchief to mop his perspiring face.

Into Jim's muddled brain a quick alarm leaped. He thought Page was about to draw a pistol. He remembered the repeated warnings of Vining, not to let this killer beat him to the draw. Sweeping the domino back, he dragged out a revolver and fired. Surprise in the face of Page gave way to agony. His knees sagged and he sank to the floor.

Jim stared at the prone figure, aghast and horrified at what he had done. The music had stopped abruptly and the dancers stood motionless on the floor. A woman screamed. Another fainted. Jim's fear-filled eyes stabbed at the masked faces focused on him. He backed toward the door, the weapon shuttling back and forth to quell any impulse to stop him.

"Don't move," he ordered hoarsely, and felt for the door jamb with a back-stretched hand.

He disappeared into the street and raced along it to reach his horse, discarding the domino as he ran. Abruptly he stopped. The horse was gone. His gaze swept the street without finding it. The pit of his stomach tightened into an icy knot. It swept over him that he was lost. A sickness ran through him. He stood, shaken and trembling, not knowing what to do.

A man in the doorway of the Clarendon shouted, "Stop that murderer!" He was wearing a clown's mask and a white baggy costume to match. The cry whipped Regal into action. He dived into an alley, cut across to State Street, and hurried down it to French Row. Here he pulled up, breathing hard. This would not do. In this sink, housing the dregs of the town, they would be sure to look for him. He must find a refuge in which to hide until the first burst of the hunt had passed. His mind jumped to Joan. Always she had stood between him and trouble. If he could reach her she might save him.

He fought to still the panic rising to his throat. Nobody could know who had killed Page since he had been wearing a domino and mask. He must take it easy and use his head. Above all he must not run or show any excitement. Though he was sober enough now it might be best to act a little drunk. Pulling the hat well down over his face, he moved in the shadows of the back streets towards the heart of the town.

By way of an alley he reached the busy street and turned in at the entrance to the Grand Central and started up the stairway. He heard a voice call, "Which way did the fellow go?" Shuddering, he moved faster. As he took the treads the gay lilting voice of a singer on the stage came to him through the wall. Ten thousand people in this town were laughing, talking, drinking, or making love untouched by fear, happy without being conscious of it. How had he managed to get into this trap, like a wild beast driven by its hunters, his heart beating as fast as that of a young rabbit in a man's hands? Every man in the street below was looking for him. Joan would have to hide him and send for Quint Vining to arrange an escape. If he could go back to live over just this one last hour. Oh God, why had he been such a fool?

He found the door of Joan's room unlocked. Opening it, he slipped in and pushed home the bolt Erma had bought as a protection against some inebriated admirer who might get ideas. Too worried to sit down, he paced the floor anxiously. In fancy he saw again the scene at the Clarendon, his victim sinking to the floor, a hundred eyes from masked faces accusing him.

Steps sounded in the hall. A knock came on the door. The heart died under his ribs. He waited, breathless. His eyes stared at the door knob as it turned.

A man's voice said softly, "Is this Miss Regal's room? I'm Cape Wallace."

Wallace. The man who had bought the horse for his escape last time. But it might be a trick.

"If you are there, Miss Regal, better open. Your brother is in trouble."

After a short wait the steps retreated down the corridor. Jim opened the door a few inches and looked out. He said in a low hoarse voice, "For God's sake, help me, Mr. Wallace."

Wallace turned. "I thought it was you I saw coming up the stairs." He walked into the room and pushed the bolt into place.

"W-what do you mean I'm in trouble?" Jim quavered.

"Don't waste time bluffing, boy. Quint Vining and Amos Scudder recognized you when you threw away the mask. They've roused the town."

"Quint Vining?" Regal turned on Wallace unbelieving eyes. "It couldn't have been Quint. He — he egged me on to do it."

"Quint did?" A gleam of light came to the puzzled brain of the gambler. Somehow Vining had made this boy his cat's-paw to pay the debt of vengeance he owed Page.

The tap of light footsteps came along the hall. The door knob turned.

Cape knew that tread. He said, "It's your sister," and opened the door.

Joan's troubled eyes fastened on him. He guessed she had heard the news. A man had told it to her as she left the stage after her act.

"It's awful, Cape. Whoever did it must have been one of Vining's men." She was still in her page-boy suit. Except where the paint left a splash on her cheeks she was colorless.

Wallace moved aside and she saw her brother. Her gaze did not lift from the cringing figure as the dreadful truth sank into her.

"Not you?" she cried in a low voice, and knew the answer to her question.

His imploring hand stretched out. "I did it for you."

Cape's arm slipped around her waist as she swayed. He thought she was going to faint. Her eyes closed, but opened again almost at once. Cape just caught the murmur of her whispered words, "Oh God, I killed him."

"Save me, Joan," Jim begged. "I didn't mean to do it."

"Quint Vining trapped him into it," Cape explained to Joan.

"What can we do?" she asked.

"Let's get the story first." He turned to her brother. "Tell it."

Jim told it brokenly, shifting the blame from himself as much as he could. They had been killing deer in the Tarryalls when a mule skinner named Chuck Wood brought him a letter from Vining telling him to come back on account of Page and Joan. There would be food waiting for him in the Wiggins cabin back of California Gulch.

"Did you keep that letter?" Wallace asked.

"I guess so." Jim searched his pockets and produced the note.

Cape read it and handed the paper to Joan.

"It isn't signed," he said. "How did you know it was from Vining?"

"Because of what he said in it. Before I left town we had a long talk and he told me that Page meant to seduce Joan. I warned Page to keep away from her."

"You didn't say anything to me about it," Joan interrupted.

"I hadn't time — had to vamoose because of the stage robbery."

"And was there food waiting for you at the Wiggins place?" Cape inquired.

"Yes. Grub and other things. Tonight Quint came up there. He told me if I still had the letter to give it back to him. But he had brought a quart of whisky with him and I had been drinking a lot. I was kind of sore at him, and I didn't want to bother hunting for the letter, so I said I had burnt it."

"Why did he go up to the cabin?"

"To tell me how this Page had ruined Joan. He brought a mask and domino so I could wear it at the ball without being known."

"He told you then about the ball and where it would be."

"That's right. And I gave him the note to Joan asking her to meet me at the Ditch Walk." He glared at Joan, flaring to weak anger. "If you had come as I said this would never have happened."

"I didn't get the note," she said.

Wallace put his finger on the truth. "Vining did not want you to meet Jim for fear that might change his mind. He destroyed the note."

"So that Jim would — would — " Joan did not finish the sentence. She could not bring herself to put the murder into words.

Cape followed Vining's evil plan another step. "His followers are inflaming the mob against Jim now. He doesn't want him to talk after he is captured so that there will be a backfire, one that might involve him."

Joan's eyes reflected her horror. "You mean — not to let him go to prison."

"It looks like it. There is a lot of loose talk going on. What did you do with your horse, Jim?"

"Tied it near the Clarendon. When I came out it was gone."

"Gone?" Joan echoed.

"Probably friend Vining arranged that. The only slip-up he seems to have made so far is that he has lost Jim temporarily."

"I've got to get out of town before he finds me," the boy cried.

Wallace frowned in concentration, working out a plan. "You can't go yet, not until the streets are cleared of the mob. But we had better be ready when the chance comes. I'll see Peterson. He runs a livery stable and can be trusted. I'll arrange it so that we can get a horse at any hour."

He did not let his voice or manner betray the dread he felt. With the town alerted to watch for the assassin he doubted if Jim could escape. As he was coming into the building Marshal Harrigan had been posting armed watchers on the main streets. Nobody would be allowed to pass without inspection. It had occurred to Wallace that the best course might be to send for Harrigan and turn Jim over to him. Since he was a candidate for sheriff he might hold his prisoner against any attack. But there was no certainty he would. Since he was depending on the Vining support to help elect him, he might decide to be conveniently absent at a critical time.

Wallace found the streets more filled with excited men than they had been a half hour earlier. Talk of lynch law was prevalent. He felt sure it was being bolstered by the Vinings. Everybody appeared to know that Regal was the guilty man.

He arranged with Peterson to get a horse at any time he needed one. In order that there might be no loss of time Peterson saddled a fast bay gelding and put it in a stall.

Cape walked back to the Grand Central building. On both Chestnut and Harrison the roadways were filled with groups discussing the murder. In front of the theater the excitement was more keen. From one of the men he learned that Ben Vining and half a dozen others had just gone up the stairway to the rooms above. Word had reached them that Jim Regal had been seen entering the building, evidently on his way to the room of his sister.

Wallace pushed through the crowd and took the stairs two at a time.

12

Joan waited in the room with Jim, desolation in her heart. He had shot down a defenseless man and was himself in great danger. The burden of the consequences of her sin weighed her down. If she had not been a wanton, Henry would still be alive and her brother hunting deer in the Tarryalls.

He paced the floor, talking jerkily, all the manhood stricken out of him, explaining away his dreadful deed, begging for a promise that he would not have to pay for it. It was Page or he. What else could he have done? Joan did not refute his weak defense, though she had learned that Henry was unarmed. What was the use? His guilt had been born of hers. Nothing she could say would comfort him, though she knew he was greatly in need of reassurance.

She was empty of all hope.

The harried man looked down on the crowded street through the window and heard the threats of angry men. He drew back, fear flooding him. There was no room for remorse in him. He could think only of the peril so close and deadly. If they should find out where he was hidden —

"Do something, Joan," he cried. "I never meant to kill him — only to frighten him into marrying you."

"He offered to marry me but I found I did not love him," she said in a lifeless voice. The shouts of the men below beat up to her. They sent a chill through her. "You'll have to wait till morning before you try to escape."

"Maybe Wallace will tell them I'm here."

She answered, scornful both of him and herself, "Cape Wallace is my friend, though heaven knows why."

He walked his beat once more. From the window he saw two men with rifles. A score of others no doubt carried revolvers. They would surely come to his sister's room looking for him. They were hunting him as if he were a wild beast and if they found him they would drag him out with a rope around his neck. There must be some way of escape, if Joan would only think of it. Fear choked his throat. He had seen two men lynched for crimes less than murder.

"Quint stacked the cards against me," he

broke out, weak anger blended with his fear. "Like Wallace said. Listen. Quint kept telling me what a dangerous killer this fellow was and for me to watch him close. He said this town would back up whatever I did. So when Page reached for a gun I let him have it. What else could I do?" Young Regal rammed a fist despairingly into the palm of his other hand. He swallowed a lump in his throat. "My God, what a fool I've been. Quint did it, not me. Tell 'em I wasn't to blame, Joan. I was just defending your honor."

He began to walk again, then pulled up abruptly, listening, his eyes quick with terror. "God, they're coming."

The sound of many feet pounding up the stairs came to them. Somebody beat on a door and demanded, "Which room is Miss Regal's?"

Dolly Roubideau answered. "End of the hall, on the right. What is this — a fire?"

Tramping feet came down the corridor. A heavy fist hammered on the door. "Open up!" The order came sharp as a pistol crack.

From Jim Regal's face the color drained. Tiny beads of sweat broke out on his forehead. With a hand shaking like an aspen leaf he drew the revolver from the holster at his side.

"Don't let them in, sis," he said, teeth chattering.

A hand twisted the door knob and shook it. "Open the door. We know he's there."

Another voice cried with an oath, "We're gonna hang the bastard."

"He isn't here," Joan answered shakily. "Please go away. I'm — not dressed." She was trembling, and her weak legs were buckling.

"Put on a coat and unbolt the door. We're not going to hurt you, miss, but we aim to get the killer." It was the pistol-shot voice again.

"Get Sheriff Taggart and I'll let him in," she begged.

"You'll let us in or we'll smash the door."

"Wait till I dress."

"We're coming in right damned now."

A man flung his weight at the door and a panel splintered. Into the torn wood a boot-heel crashed. Through the hole it made a hairy hand came, groped for the bolt, and slipped it back.

Jim Regal fired. The owner of the hand yelped, "Damn it, he's hit me."

Joan's fingers closed on the barrel of the revolver. "Don't!" she cried. "You'll make it worse." Her other hand fastened on his, struggling for the weapon.

The door burst open to let in a rush of men.

"We've got him," Ben Vining shouted jubilantly.

Crazy with fear, the outlaw jerked his revolver up to free it from the clutch of his sister. The strength of the tug brought the rim of the .45 against his throat. The gun roared. Regal staggered back against the wall. His body hung there for a long moment and then slowly sagged to the floor.

Horrified, Joan looked at the smoking barrel in her hand. She dropped it, ran forward and knelt beside her brother, lifting his head in her arms. He was already dead.

A man pushed through the group to her and put an arm around her shoulders. She turned her head and saw Cape Wallace.

He was never to forget the look on her face. "I killed him too," she said, her voice flat and dead.

Her limp body collapsed into the arms of Wallace. He picked her up and moved toward the door. Ben Vining barred the way.

"Let me pass," Cape ordered.

Vining looked at him sourly but stepped aside. "So you are in this too," he snarled.

Wallace did not answer. He carried Joan along the corridor and kicked at the room door of the Roubideau sisters. Dolly opened and stared big-eyed at the unconscious girl.

She saw blood on the jacket of the suit.

"Did they shoot her?" she asked.

"I don't think so. Her brother is killed." Cape walked in and put Joan on the bed. "She fainted and I didn't want her to come to and see his body."

While the sisters scurried around for cold water and smelling salts he hurried away to get a doctor. When Joan regained consciousness she was wildly hysterical. Over and over she cried that she had killed both Henry and Jim. No words of comfort reached her tortured mind. The fever mounted in her and she grew delirious. The doctor gave her an opiate that put her into troubled sleep.

In the morning she was worse. The days ran on and brought no improvement. Brain fever the doctor called her illness. There were a few days in the weeks of sickness that followed in which it was touch and go whether she would live or die. Erma had dropped her work in the theater and taken charge of the nursing. The unvoiced prayer in her thoughts was, *Dear God, don't let her die.*

Before Jim Regal had been dead two hours Cape Wallace called on Downing. "You and I have a job to do," he said.

"I'll take care of young Regal's funeral,"

the lawyer said. "His sister is too ill."

"That is good, but I wasn't thinking of that. Our mutual enemy, Quint Vining, murdered both Henry Page and Jim Regal. I intend to prove it."

"Have you any evidence?" Downing asked. He was not surprised.

"Yes, and if we move fast we can get more."

Wallace went over the story Jim had told and the added fact that the Vinings were instigating the lynching of Regal.

Downing nodded agreement. "It looks as if you are right. Vining hated Page and used this boy to destroy him and then arranged to have Regal rubbed out before he could do any talking. But a moral certainty won't stand up in court. We have to get evidence to back it. I suggest we start with the Wiggins cabin. If we wait many hours there won't be any signs of occupancy there. Quint will see to that."

The location of the cabin was unknown to Wallace but Downing had once seen it from a distance. He thought he could find the way there, even in the dark. Peterson saddled a second horse and they started for California Gulch. The stars were out and occasionally the moon emerged from behind scudding clouds. As long as they stayed in the trough of the canyon it was easy to follow the trail that had been tramped by fifty thousand feet during the past twenty years, but when they diverged from it near the upper mouth of the gulch they met difficulties. For a long time they wandered, following false leads that ran them into pockets or draws that ended in impasses of sharp rock walls. When they stumbled on the cabin at last it was by sheer luck.

Wallace had brought candles with him and he lit them both. One he left on the decrepit table, the other he carried with him as they made their investigation. They checked and made a note of every item of the provisions. What was left of them they packed into the gunny sack along with the almost empty bottle of whisky. On the table were a cheap tablet of paper and the stub of a pencil. The top sheet of the pad showed the impress of the pencil point where it had made marks of indentation on the second page. Most of these were faint, but they could make out the first two words, *Dear Joan*, and farther down the letters *Mr. Vini* . . . The pressure on the pencil had not been heavy enough to show the last letters of the name.

Downing put the tablet and the copy of the newspaper with the notice of the wedding in his pocket. They had a piece of unexpected luck with the *Police Gazette*. The printed address label on it was Vining Bros., Silver Palace, Leadville, Colorado. This too Downing appropriated.

On the way down they stopped at the cabin of an old miner who was a client of Downing, a man whose claim the lawyer had saved for him. The sky was already announcing a new day and Hi Ragsdale was awake and making his breakfast. Nothing would do him but that they must stay and share it with him. Before they left they had enlisted the tight-mouthed old-timer as an ally. He promised to try to find out if anybody had seen Quint Vining in the Gulch yesterday or the day before and to check up if he rode to the cabin again. He was a cheerful red-faced seventy-year-old with a face that resembled a wrinkled winter pippin.

"I owe Quint Vining a scare for backing the jumpers who tried to steal my claim," he told his guests with a toothless grin. "You're doing me a favor by letting me pay it."

Since Vining would soon find out that they were covering his movements for the past two days they decided it would not be safe to leave the evidence they had collected either at Downing's office or at the room of Wallace. Within five minutes of their return to town they turned it over to Sheriff Taggart and were telling him their reasons for believing Quint

Vining was responsible for the deaths of both Henry Page and Jim Regal.

Taggart agreed that they were probably right. It would be like Quint to drag in somebody else to destroy Page for him. But even if the evidence they *had* stood up in court there was nothing in it to show that Vining had anything to do with the death of Page except the word of a panicky killer who was looking for somebody else upon whom to lay the blame. Neither his message sent to Jim at the Tarryalls nor his visit to the cabin necessarily showed any criminal intent.

"True enough," Downing assented. "But we have a suspicion that smells to high heaven. We're not asking you to take any action yet, John. Put in a safe place the letter, the tablet, and the *Police Gazette*. We'll recheck the provisions now and then try to find out where he bought them. Cape and I have just begun to dig into this. We would like to know, for instance, who took Jim Regal's horse from the place where he left it hitched, and why the Vinings were so eager to have Jim lynched rather than arrested. It isn't logical to think their righteous anger would be at a boiling point because Jim had killed the man they hated. They wanted him dead for fear he would talk."

"I hope you can bring it home to them," Taggart said. "We all know what a bad lot they are."

"Remember too, Sheriff," Wallace said with a grin, "that they are grooming Buck Harrigan for your job."

Taggart laughed. "I'm not likely to forget that. Call on me, boys, when you get far enough along for me to step in. It would suit me fine to discredit them."

It was decided that Wallace should check up on the sale of provisions and Downing would make inquiries about the disappearance of the horse.

Before they left, the sheriff raised a question. "There are several stories afloat as to who fired the shot that killed young Regal. You can hear that he did it himself, either on purpose or by accident. Some say Miss Joan killed him, to save him from being hanged. Another version is that Ben Vining did it. You were there, Cape. How about it?"

"I didn't get there till after Regal had been shot," Wallace answered. "Miss Regal was kneeling, her brother's head in her arms. I don't think Vining shot him. From what those present said it was this way. As they were breaking the door Jim fired and hit Chris Fenner in the hand. His sister caught hold of the pistol and tried to get it from him. In the tussle one of them pulled the trigger. Probably Jim, since he had fired the gun only a moment before."

"Yes, but the gun was in Miss Regal's hand when the boy fell," the sheriff objected.

"Of course. When the bullet slammed into Jim's throat he let loose of the forty-five. He was dead almost before he hit the floor. Whether he meant to kill himself I don't know. He had gone panicky."

"I'm told Miss Joan said then and kept saying in her delirium that she had killed him," Taggart said. "It might have been that way."

"She meant that she blamed herself because her brother had killed Page on her account," Downing explained.

"Does it matter who jarred the trigger?" Wallace asked. "Miss Joan was trying to keep Jim from making things worse. Can you blame her? After all it was the best way out for her brother."

"I don't think you ought to suggest that she may have done it," protested the lawyer. "Undoubtedly young Regal did it himself."

"Probably. In any case it makes no difference, except to Miss Joan. She is as innocent of her brother's death as you are. Crime is in the intent."

Downing did not entirely agree with Wallace that it made no difference. Regardless of intent, if Joan had shot her brother it would be always an unhappy memory.

Wallace made the round of the leading grocery stores in the town. With him he had a list of the groceries they had found in the Wiggins cabin. His story was that he expected to go hunting in a few days and would like a price on the supplies needed. It was not until he was in the third store that he struck pay ore. The grocer ran his eyes over the list, jotted down prices, and added them for the total.

"Funny," he said. "I filled an order for Quint Vining day before yesterday that was a dead ringer for yours. He was going hunting too."

That was, Cape agreed, quite a coincidence. But he did not stress the point. He had the information he wanted and it could wait till he needed it.

Later in the day he dropped into Downing's office. The lawyer had been on the street for hours chatting with any loungers he met. Since the main subject of discussion in the town was the killing of Page and the developments arising from it, he had found it easy to pick up the rumors floating around. The man wearing the domino had tied his horse in front of Kirby's Keg and from there had gone straight into the Clarendon. So half a dozen men had told Downing, but none of them had actually seen him do it. One of them said that Donald MacRob, who worked a shift in the Robert E. Lee, had come out of the Keg just as the masked man arrived.

Cape offered to follow the lead and after nightfall contacted MacRob at his boardinghouse. In answer to a question he replied that he had been standing in front of the Keg at that time talking with Dan Simmons. After tying, the rider disappeared at once into the Clarendon. Not more than a minute or two later Amos Scudder had crossed the street, untied the horse, and ridden it away. Wallace found Simmons, who confirmed the story. From Peterson they learned later that Scudder had brought a horse to his stable and left it there. He had, he said, found the animal wandering down Chestnut Street and brought it in to be cared for until the owner claimed it.

Toward evening old Hi Ragsdale came in from California Gulch to report that Quint Vining had ridden up to the Wiggins cabin during the afternoon. He had dropped work for the day and was lying in the brush above the cabin when Quint showed up. That Vining had been disturbed to find somebody had been there before him was apparent. He did not stay in the hut five minutes, but after he came out he lashed at his mount with a quirt because its foot had been caught in the bridle rein.

The sheriff had Scudder brought in for questioning. Taggart's first question startled the man. The shifty eyes in the fleshless skull face narrowed defensively. Scudder played for time.

"I dunno as I quite got yore point, Sheriff," he parried.

"I asked you why you unhitched another man's horse last night from in front of Kirby's bar and rode off on it."

"Don't you reckon mebbe you're thinkin' of some other fellow?"

"I'm thinking of you," Taggart told him bluntly. "There were witnesses — plenty of them. Don't stall."

"Oh!" Scudder showed sudden enlightenment. "You mean that roan Jim Regal was ridin'. That's right. I took it. You bet. I figured he stole it, so I thought the best thing to do was to take it to a stable and leave it there till I could talk with you about it."

"How did you know the rider was Jim, since he was wearing a mask and a domino?"

For a moment Amos was stumped, but he

twisted out of the trap glibly. "Why, he lifted his mask for a second to mop the sweat off'n his face."

"Not according to what others present told me. They were surprised to see a man come to the ball on horseback and they watched him, trying to guess who he was. That won't do, Amos. How came you to recognize Regal?"

Scudder looked at Taggart sulkily. "What's this all about? Are you claimin' I stole that horse?"

"As sheriff of this county I'm investigating a murder that took place last night," Taggart said, his voice low and hard. "What made you recognize Regal?"

The man shrugged his shoulders. "I jes' thought it was Regal. Don't ask me why. You don't need to see a fellow's face to know who he is."

Wallace was sitting on an edge of the sheriff's desk, one leg dangling. He said gently, "Perhaps you knew Jim was in town."

Scudder's wary eyes met those of Wallace, anger smoldering in them. When the man had come into the room he had ignored the presence of Cape and the lawyer. He said now insolently, "Have you got any chips in the pot, Mr. Wallace?"

"Perhaps you knew he would be wearing a

domino and what he had come to do," Cape suggested, his voice still pleasantly conversational.

"I won't stand for that," Scudder cried. "No honest man would." He jumped up, ready to go.

"I'm not quite through with you," Taggart said. "After you had taken the horse to a livery stable you hurried back. You did a lot of treating at the Keg — and a lot of talking too. The point of your talk was that Jim Regal ought to be hanged as soon as he was caught."

"So he ought. It was cold-blooded murder."

"Of a man you tried to lie to the gallows not three months ago," Downing said curtly.

"That's yore story," Scudder snapped. "It's not mine."

"I reckon not," Wallace agreed. "Any more than it would be your story that with Heisman and Ukena you lay in wait to murder him in front of the Little Church."

"Prove it," snarled the worried Vining henchman. "Who saw me there?"

"Quint Vining's friends don't seem to have any better luck than his enemies, do they, Amos? Sam Ukena and Mort Heisman blasted off the map, and you in trouble up to your neck."

"Don't you worry about any trouble I'm

in." Scudder turned to Taggart, his fleshless face set stubbornly. "If it's yore play to arrest me, say so, damn it."

"No need to get on the prod, Amos," the sheriff told him. "I got you here to ask about that horse and you try to feed me lies. No, I'm not arresting you. Any time you like you can walk out of that door."

"I'm walking now," Scudder said and went.

"He's on his way to Quint," remarked Taggart.

"Yes," Downing nodded. "A frightened man. He won't forget that five men have died because Quint tried to jump the Sally McGee. He knows that Quint's power is slipping and that he'll be sacrificed if it is necessary."

"The question is, what will Vining do," Taggart said, his finger tips drumming on the deck. "This is in the open now. It's his move. He must know it wouldn't be safe to make any gun play now."

Downing made a guess. "He'll be a fine citizen shocked at the tragedy which has occurred while he was doing his best to save Jim from committing the crime on which he was intent."

They agreed that they must find evidence tying him closely to the murder of Page. It would not take much of a push to frighten Scudder into becoming a state's witness.

13

From the moment that Quint Vining walked into the Wiggins cabin the day after Jim Regal's death he knew that he must be on guard. Somebody was gunning for him. His mind fixed on Cape Wallace. He had found out that the man was a cousin of Henry Page. The fellow's testimony at the trial had won an acquittal in spite of the piled-up false evidence of the prosecution. Later in the day he had saved Downing and his client from the ambush set for them. With the aid of Mort Heisman's own blundering he had managed to have that gunman rubbed out. He was Johnny-on-the-spot again when Ben broke into the room of the actress. It could not be by chance that the man was always on hand to make him trouble.

When Scudder reported to him the tale of his visit to the sheriff's office, Vining's unease quickened. Taggart was honest, efficient, and fearless. It was to his political advantage to weaken Quint's influence. Both Downing and

Wallace were dangerous enemies likely to make trouble if they could get enough on him. The attorney would not go outside the law, but from experience Quint knew the man was likely to strike at his vulnerable spots within it. Wallace on the other hand cared nothing about formal law. He went his way, a man quiet and self-contained, no trouble seeker, not even a gunfighter in the common acceptance of the word, but with a banked force back of the reckless eyes and sardonic face that might explode violently.

Vining realized that if his connection with young Regal came out it would look bad. But his visit to the cabin did not necessarily tie up with the murder of Page, unless his enemies could prove that the domino was his. Jim Regal must have implicated him of course. Otherwise the cabin would not have been searched. But Jim was dead and anything he had said could be discredited as the effort of a guilty man trying to shift to another the burden of his crime. The weak link in Vining's chain of defense was Scudder. The man knew too much, and he was frightened. If enough pressure was put on him he would break. The best thing to do would be to send him to Montana or to California where he could live under another name. With a few hundred dollars put in his pocket Scudder would be glad to get away.

Scudder was — very glad indeed. He did not like the way things were shaping. On one side was the chance of going to the penitentiary, on the other the danger he would risk in betraying the Vinings. He settled his boardinghouse bill, packed his valise, and started for the stage office. In front of the new Tabor Opera House a man tapped him on the shoulder. Startled, he looked around.

"Taking a little trip, Scudder?" Cape Wallace drawled. His hand was in the bulging pocket of his coat. What was in his hand the other man could guess. He would have been wrong. There was nothing in it.

"I got to go to Denver for a couple of days," the traveler explained. "Be right back."

"Let's talk that over," Wallace suggested. He tucked his left arm under the other's elbow and moved him into an alley. "While we take a little walk."

"I only got a few minutes. The stage is about ready to leave."

"It will roll right along without you. Why go to Denver and blow your money? Patronize home industry."

Scudder flared to weak anger. "You got no right to keep me here," he sputtered.

"That's so," Cape agreed. "You can sue me later. Or have me thrown in the calaboose. But now act nice and friendly while we stroll."

"Where you taking me?" Scudder set his feet to resist the steady pressure of the arm propelling him forward.

"To a place where you'll be safe as a baby in its mother's arms. Nobody will hurt you, Amos." Wallace added, very gently: "Unless you fool around asking for trouble."

They walked down the alley, across the next street, and into another lane. They did not hurry, but ambled along at an easy gait. Two men who met them noticed nothing out of the way in this rather affectionate companionship.

"I've a mind to holler," the captive said.

"Oh, I wouldn't do that," Wallace told him lightly. "I wouldn't want to have to decimate you."

"Do what to me?" Scudder did not know what the word meant, but it sounded awful.

"Decimate you. There's probably nothing more painful in the world. What say we mosey up Fryer Hill? You look kind of washed out. What you need is more exercise."

They took the slope up the hill to the Sally McGee. A man with a sawed-off shotgun on his lap was sitting on the dump. Apparently he was a guard employed to prevent jumpers from getting the mine. Nobody was working on it. The miners mucking for Henry Page had been let out after his death.

Wallace said to him, "I've brought you a boarder, Hi. Be sure to look after him nice."

"I'll treat him good as a scalawag like him deserves," Ragsdale promised with a chuckle.

"You can't do this to me," Scudder protested. "It's kidnaping. You can get ten years for it."

"Hard to prove if you can't find the kidnapee, Mr. Scudder," Hi piped in a high voice gleefully. "We aim to take you down and to the breast of the tunnel. I've got a shot all ready to be fired. If we got in a tight spot I'd let her go and you would be buried in a couple of tons of loose rock."

"I'm hoping that won't be necessary," Wallace said cheerfully. "I brought him here because I didn't want his friends to put him out of business before he could talk. We've got the Vinings right at the end of their last crooked mile. Let me tell you where we stand, Amos. This is your last chance to tell the truth and save yourself."

"Maybe you two had better go downstairs first," Hi suggested. "Some eyeballer might drift along and see our guest."

Cape thought that a good idea. Despite Scudder's earnest objections Ragsdale lowered them down the shaft. At the bottom Wallace escorted his prisoner to the end of the tunnel. With a wave of the hand he indicated a flat slab of rock in the rubble that covered the floor.

"Take a chair, Amos. We're going to have quite a pow-wow."

Wallace told in detail all the evidence they had gathered against Quint Vining, reciting as facts what as yet were only suspicions, such as the ownership of the domino.

"It wasn't Quint's masquerade costume," Scudder cut in.

"Whose was it?"

The man had spoken too quickly. He tried to cover his mistake by a general denial. "Why, I dunno, but I don't think Quint has got one."

Cape flung out a guess confidently. "But Ben has. He wore it when the girls on the line gave their ball."

"I ain't got a word to say," replied Scudder obstinately.

For an hour Wallace hammered at him. The man made admissions, tried to explain them away, became entangled in his own verbosity, but he made no confession.

Wallace left him there, after tying him hand and foot and warning him that if he cried out Ragsdale would fire the charge planted in the wall beside him. It was Cape's opinion that a night spent underground in darkness without food would loosen the fellow's tongue. The only reason he did not talk now was because of his fear of the Vining vengeance.

Cape left the prisoner in the custody of Hi Ragsdale and went down the hill to keep an appointment with Downing. He did not tell the lawyer of his meeting with Scudder, since he did not know how the attorney would react to his lawless arrest of the man. But he did mention rather casually that he might soon have favorable news to report.

Downing started to ask him about it and changed his mind. When Wallace wanted him to know what it was he would tell him. He had been up to the Grand Central building to inquire about Miss Regal, he said. Erma had met him at the door of the room and told him Joan was a very sick girl. The doctor's order was that no visitors at all were to be allowed to see her.

They decided that if she did not improve in the next day or two they would bring a doctor from Denver for consultation. It might be better to send her down to the Mile High city on account of the altitude as was done with pneumonia patients. No doubt Erma would be glad to go there with Joan to look after her.

Cape Wallace was a self-contained man with few friends. He had learned to be sufficient to himself, to live alone without loneliness. Debarred on account of his occupation from the society of his equals, he had never let himself establish contact with the parasites who infested the silver camp but had gone his own way, a lone wolf. The inner restlessness that had never found expression except in the reckless eyes had become more urgent since he had met Joan Regal. She was in his thoughts continually and the unhappy fate that had overwhelmed her depressed him. He saw her, as he always had, a lovely young thing, fine and loyal and gallant, caught in a web of evil that was none of her weaving. She must get away from here, out of this raw wild town to begin life again in a gentle law-abiding atmosphere. Edward Downing was in love with her. If he had any sense he would fling up his practice and take her with him to another state. Cape's mind was on the girl's future as he walked up the hill to the Sally McGee to find out what effect a solitary night in the bowels of the earth had had on Amos Scudder.

He found the prisoner subdued but full of complaints. This was no way to treat a man who had done no wrong. To Wallace it became clear that Scudder was willing to tell all he knew if he could be assured of protection against punishment from the Vinings. Confidently Wallace promised him that he would be guarded day and night and that when the law was through with the Vinings they would be put where they could not harm anybody for a long time.

Scudder made a full confession, beginning with the attack on the Sally McGee, the death of young Vining, and the false testimony at the trial. He told of the ambushing of Page and Downing and of the meeting next day at the Silver Palace at which Quint had told the others to stand aside and let him take care of the killing of Page. To accomplish this he had taken advantage of young Regal's anger and had played on his vanity to induce the boy to destroy his enemy. He, Scudder, had unwittingly helped Quint to get rid of the killer by removing his horse. At the time he had not known the death of either Page or Regal was intended.

After dark Wallace and Ragsdale took the kidnaped man to the sheriff's office, where Downing and half a dozen of the leading men of Leadville were gathered by appointment. Under a pledge of immunity Scudder repeated his story. He was questioned for hours and told all he knew. That Quint Vining was responsible for the death of the two young men was clear. All the evidence gathered dovetailed to confirm this opinion.

The group remained to discuss a plan of procedure after Scudder had been taken to the jail for safe keeping. Downing pointed out that it would be very difficult to convict Vining of murder. He would have the best defense attorneys that could be procured and they would slant Quint's interest in Jim Regal's return to an entirely creditable motive, his desire to see justice done a wronged and deserted girl. Even if it were proved that he supplied the mask and domino they would claim he had done so only to give Jim a chance to plead his sister's cause with Page. The testimony of Scudder would be partly discredited, since he was admittedly a fellow criminal who had been promised immunity. Some of his story could be used to bolster Vining's case. The defense would show that Quint had no prior knowledge of the attack on Page and Downing the night after the trial and that he had ordered his followers to desist from such action in future.

Taggart agreed that Scudder would be a very shaky witness and that probably the Vining faction would counter by having Wallace and Ragsdale arrested for kidnaping. He backed the advice of Downing, to serve notice on the Vinings that they must get out of town within twenty-four hours or stand trial for murder. Quint would not dare face the chances of a trial for fear of other defaulters among his followers who might drag out crimes of his that had been covered up. Nobody knew better than he did how quick rats were to leave a sinking ship.

A messenger was sent to the Silver Palace to ask the Vinings to come at once to the office of the sheriff. They arrived half an hour later bringing with them Seth Mabry, the prosecuting attorney for the district, a man who owed his election to the Vinings. He had been aroused from bed and had dressed hurriedly. His fine silky hair and his urbanity were a little rumpled.

Quint looked around the room, his white face impassive and his eyes bleak. He took the offensive at once. "I see this is a meeting inspired by my enemies," he said.

The sheriff offered him a chair. "I'll stand," he snapped. "What is this all about?"

"It's about murder," Downing answered

bluntly. "The murder of Henry Page and Jim Regal — and your share in both."

Quint let his gaze rest coldly on the lawyer. "You've always hated me, Downing. I don't know why, unless it is because I would not have you as my lawyer. What you say is ridiculous. Regal shot Page and then committed suicide. I did my best to talk Jim out of his madness but he was inflamed with liquor and went hog-wild."

"Liquor you took to him at his hiding place," Wallace said.

The sheriff interrupted. "Let's get down to business, gentlemen. Downing, suppose you give a summary of what you and Wallace have found out."

Downing put the case concisely and forcibly. When he came to the confession of Scudder the bravado of Ben Vining was visibly shaken.

Quint said, "Where is Amos? Confront him with us and let us hear this alleged confession."

"He isn't here," Ben blurted out. "He left yesterday on the stage."

"No, he changed his mind," Wallace corrected blandly. "In spite of the five hundred Quint gave him for a getaway."

Quint flung a question at the sheriff. "Are

you arresting us, Taggart?"

"Well, put it this way, Quint," the sheriff drawled. "We've gathered a lot of evidence that shows you are in this deep, but I haven't arrested you yet. I expect I'll have to soon."

"You haven't a scintilla of proof," Mabry protested. "Gentlemen, this is an outrage. I wouldn't take such a case into court."

"You wouldn't get a chance, Mabry," Downing told him dryly. "We would ask for and get a special prosecutor."

"That is an insult," Mabry shouted.

"If you are holding Scudder somewhere bring him here and let him face Ben and me." Quint swung round on a heavyset man smoking a black cigar. "I'm surprised at you, Willett, letting yourself — the mayor of the town — be dragged in by my enemies to support charges so vile as these."

Willett had come across the plains in a covered wagon many years before and he was as tough as one of the bulls he had driven. He took the cigar from his mouth. His voice was colder than the wind blowing over a frozen lake. "I'll give it to you straight, Quint. You are through in this town. You and Ben both. In my opinion you are guilty as hell, but we are giving you a choice. Either get out of here lock, stock, and barrel or face a murder charge. Take your choice. You have twenty-four hours to *vamos*. Somebody else can close out yore affairs for you."

"If you can get a conviction why give me an option?" jeered Quint. "Aren't you too generous?"

"We can get evidence a-plenty," the mayor retorted. "Don't fool yoreself about that. Scudder isn't the only rat who will squeal."

"If he has," Ben snarled angrily. "I don't believe he's within a hundred miles of here."

Quint's arrogant eyes raked the faces focused on him. "We're being framed, Ben, by a bunch of scoundrels. All right, Willett. Inside of half an hour we'll give you an answer." At the door he turned, hate-filled eyes shuttling from Wallace to Downing and back again. "I'm going to remember you two."

Mabry brought back their decision — to leave Leadville.

14

The newspaper reports of the showdown that had driven the Vining group from the silver city had the effect of building up a strong sympathy for Joan. It was felt that her brother had been trapped into shooting Page. She had tried to save him and was very ill from the shock of his death. The papers published daily bulletins as to her condition. Ladies who did not know her sent in dainties to tempt her appetite. A doctor was brought from Denver to consult with the local physician in charge. She had become the darling of the town. In an attempt to regain his lost popularity Mabry had written *nolle pros* on the record of the indictment against her. The case would never come to trial.

None of this mattered to Joan. Even after her temperature dropped to normal she lay listlessly in bed and failed to gather strength.

"She doesn't care whether she gets well or not," Erma told Downing. "She blames herself for the deaths of both Henry and Jim. If I try to set her right she won't listen, just lies there looking at something far away. It might do good if you would talk to her."

Downing thought he had never seen anybody as lovely as this frail girl. She smiled wanly when he came in and gave him her thin hand.

"We've been worried to death for weeks," he said. "I never saw anything like the way the whole town has watched the bulletins about you. There have been public prayers for you in the churches."

"Everybody has been very good," she told him. "I don't deserve it." She thought but did not say, *It would have been better if I had died too*.

"Of course the case against you for helping Jim escape has been dropped. Nobody objected to that."

She thanked him, but he knew she did not care. She had no will to encounter a drab future. The live spring in her that had bubbled so eagerly had gone dead. When he told her they were going to take her down to Denver to recuperate as soon as she was able she only sighed and wished she was not so much trouble. He left, distressed that he had not reached her.

Once she asked Erma if she had seen Cape Wallace lately.

"He was here every day while you were in danger," Erma said. "Would you like to see him next time he comes in from the ranch?"

"I don't know. It doesn't matter much." Joan turned her face to the wall and cried a little.

When Wallace came next day to inquire how the patient was Erma took him in to see Joan. He walked into the room without any sick-bedside manner, sailed his broad-brimmed hat ten feet across the room to a perfect landing on a marble-topped table, and drew up a chair beside her. He took her small white hand between his two big brown ones and said, "I've missed you." The whimsical smile on his strong tanned face did more for her than good news.

Erma saw for the first time a gleam of interest in Joan's eyes. The actress thought, *There is kinship between these two. She will talk to Cape if I leave them alone.*

"I have to go to the drugstore to fill a prescription," she said. "Will you look after Joan while I'm gone, Cape?"

"*Till a' the seas gang dry, my dear,
And the rocks melt wi' the sun,*"

he promised Erma gaily.

After she had gone the two looked at each other for a long moment before he said gently, "How goes it, little partner?"

"How am I to go on living?" she cried. "Everything that touches me is damned."

He said: "A thousand people in this town have prayed for you since you fell ill. A hundred feet have tiptoed up these stairs each day to ask how you were getting along. Your presence has blessed this camp. Anyone will tell you so."

"I killed two men who were dear to me," she whispered, and her throat choked. "I couldn't talk about it to anybody else. At night I lie awake and think of it."

"A great deal has happened since you fell sick," he said. "The Vinings and their gang have been driven out of town because of their crimes. One of their hangers-on confessed. When Henry stayed on after his trial he was already doomed. The gang discussed it, and Quint insisted he be left to do it his way. He chose Jim as his instrument in order to escape responsibility. He primed the boy with liquor — pointed out how to do it — warned him Henry was a killer and he must strike first."

"But if Jim had not come back here on account of me — "

"It would not have saved him. There is a long story in this morning's paper about the destruction of the Hayden gang. They robbed another stage, were followed and trapped. The posse killed five of them and captured the other. Jim had taken the wrong turn in life. When you helped him to escape you begged him to go home, but he headed straight for his bandit companions. That hour he turned his back on his last chance. If he had not died here he would have been shot down with his friends. It was his choice, not yours."

She began to cry. He knelt beside the bed and put an arm around her. It would do her good to break down and get rid of that cold icy lump in her bosom. Presently her hand reached for a kerchief and he gave her his.

"When Jim was little — he was the dearest boy," she murmured.

For years she had worried about him, Cape knew. The boy had caused her a great deal of needless suffering because he was so wild and undisciplined. But his death had wiped out all his faults. She thought of him now as the boy she had loved and shielded.

"No sister was ever more loyal," he said.

"You can't do wrong and not pay for it," she said drearily.

"I've found that out. The consequences go on and on."

He smiled. "You are hard on poor Cape Wallace. He was a gambler — a man nice young women must not know. Nothing he can do will redeem him."

"You know I didn't mean that."

"No. But you think there is another law for you. There is forgiveness for you just as there is for me. Every day is a new day. The sun shines and the flowers bloom. We can start life over again if we will. You go to church and you join in singing that the vilest sinner may return. Don't you believe it?"

His grin was infectious. A wisp of a smile touched her face.

"I guess I think too much about myself."

"You don't like to face the truth, that what has happened is for the best. You wanted to change Jim and you couldn't. But he is all right now. He is at peace. Nothing can hurt him." There flashed to his mind a verse from the Bible his mother had made him learn when he was a small boy. "There the wicked cease from troubling; and there the weary be at rest."

She repeated the words and they went to her heart like water to the roots of thirsty plants. "I'll remember them all my life," she said gratefully.

They talked of lighter things. Erma was going to take her to Denver for a week or two. Then she was going home. She would teach school, one of the lower grades where she could have little children. That is, unless her record followed her there and she was not thought worthy. Cape could see that the thought of expiation was still in her mind. Yet there was newborn hope in her.

When Erma returned she was delighted to find a light in the invalid's eyes and vibrancy in her voice.

Downing went to Denver with Erma and Joan. His excuse was that he had a client there he wanted to see about an impending suit. A good many were down at the stage office to see them off, some of them because Erma's engagement at the Grand Central was over and she was leaving for Oregon. Cape Wallace was there, but in the press of well-wishers Joan found time for only one word with him.

"You promised to see me in Denver before I go," she whispered. "I don't know where we'll be staying but I'll send word up by Ted Downing."

"I'll be there," he told her.

Downing had made arrangements for them to put up at the American House, since Joan insisted on paying her own way and her purse was depleted. The women found him useful. He fended off the reporters from the *Tribune* and the *News* who hung around trying to get an interview with Joan. He sent grapes and pears to their room. On the second day he rented a buggy and drove them in the warm sunny afternoon across the Platte to the suburban town of Highland from the upper edge of which they looked across the valley, splashed with the gold of the aspen and cottonwood foliage, to the long range in the west, extending from Pikes Peak, seventy miles south, to Long's, far to the north, looking down on Dunraven Park.

After he had returned the buggy to the livery stable Downing reported to them a piece of news. He had caught a glimpse of the Vining brothers going into Ed Chase's gambling house, the Palace. Fortunately they had not seen him. From a *News* reporter he had learned that they were staying in Denver until they had sold all their Leadville holdings. There was a rumor that they had made Chase an offer for his place.

"I'm glad you are leaving tomorrow morning," Erma said. "I don't suppose they would dare hurt you, but you never can tell."

Before he left Erma gave Ted Downing a

chance to see Joan alone. It was her opinion that he wanted to propose to her. What Joan needed was a strong responsible man like Downing for a husband, one who would shield her from blows such as had been hammering her down. So Erma went on a shopping jaunt, to see if the Denver stores were superior to the Leadville ones, she said.

Downing did not quite know why he was out of step with Joan of late, unless it was because she sensed the deep shock he had felt at the relation between her and Henry Page and his disturbance later when she arranged the escape of her brother. He did not know much about women's ways, but ingrained in him was a demand for goodness in the old-fashioned meaning. They ought to be inviolate, living in a world remote from the sins and passions of men. What had first attracted him in Joan was her shy innocence. He saw her walking in this raw bawdy town a lovely creature untouched by its grossness. To discover that she was less than an angel had been a blow. In Joan's case he could forgive because he loved her. His explanation was that her youth and innocence had been betrayed.

Joan was writing a letter in the small upstairs parlor of the hotel when he found her. It was a plain room furnished without charm.

The sofa and chairs were upholstered with shiny horsehair material and the wall pictures were cheap prints of Lincoln and Grant.

The girl stopped writing. "I'm glad you came," she said. "I'll never be able to thank you enough for all you have done for me, but I want you to know how grateful I am."

"I wish to God I could have done more," he answered, and took her hand in his. "You know I love you, Joan. Maybe you are not ready to hear it yet, but since you are leaving I have to speak. Will you marry me?"

She said gently, "I wish I could. You would be such a good husband for any woman — so safe and kind. You're the best man I know — far too good for me. But I can't marry you. I don't think I shall ever marry. I'm . . . not good for men."

"That is nonsense, dear. I would try to make you happy."

"I know you would and I'm proud that you care for me." She shook her head slowly. "But it wouldn't do. There is a nicer girl than I am waiting for you somewhere, Ted."

"It's you I want."

"You're sorry for me, and your heart is tender," she explained. "I've had a bad time, and you pity me. Yes, I know you love me — but you have to make allowances for me. I wouldn't like that, and after a while you would be tired of it."

"What it comes to is that you don't love me, Joan."

"I'm confused dear. I have been so unhappy. For a time I wanted to die." She smiled wanly. "You see, I don't know what I want, except to go away and forget."

"Is it still Henry?"

"No — except that I was such a fool. I wouldn't be any good to you, Ted. I haven't spirit enough to try. It's going to be all right with me someday. I know that now. But I have to wait and make my life over. Maybe that doesn't make sense. But it's the way I feel."

He knew her decision was final. There was no use trying to change it. Even if he could wear her down to consent he would not get what he wanted, the knowledge that her sweet and eager spirit was meeting his with joy and spontaneity. Before he left the room he knew that she was going out of his life.

15

Wallace knew something of farm life, since, though his father lived in town, he had owned a farm in the neighborhood and as a boy Cape had spent a good deal of his summer vacations there. Life on a Colorado cattle ranch was more exciting. The freedom of the open range, long hours in the saddle with white-clad mountains at the horizon's edge, the sense of personal ownership, all brought a new interest to his existence. But in the days following Joan's departure he had no zest for the work. He could not escape a feeling of restless emptiness.

It flashed into his mind that it would be a world wonderful if he could ride these hills with Joan beside him, or if he could know that when he came home at night she would be waiting eagerly to share the day's experiences. He put such dreams behind him. To marry him would be too great a hazard for any woman. It was in his horoscope to gamble with life and he had made a sorry job of it. He realized that all the Western pioneers were in a sense gamblers. They bet their youth and strength that they could make a home by subduing a country that never before had been made to serve the needs of man. But he had gambled out of trivial reasons, because of a resentment at an atmosphere hypocritically smug and a way of living too humdrum. His restlessness had made of him a parasite. He had wasted years before he had been willing to acknowledge the truth that a man has to saw wood for his breakfast, that unless he does he can find no happiness.

From Downing he learned that at the end of the week Erma and Joan were leaving Denver, one to go to her theatrical engagement in Oregon and the other to entrain for the East. Next day he was in Denver, for the first time in a year. He found the town greatly changed. It was a railroad center and the supply point for the silver boom camps. The Cherry Creek village had become the "Queen City of the Plains." Dean Hart of St. John's Cathedral was conducting a vigorous campaign against gambling and for the Sunday closing of saloons and theaters. The ladies were forming societies to encourage art and literature. At the new Tabor Grand Opera House the most famous singers and actors in the world were being booked. In all ways the young city was trying to escape from the reputation of its wild ramshackle youth and was bulging with civic consciousness. The city administration frowned on lawlessness.

Yet Cape Wallace walked the streets with an eye alert for danger. He had enemies here who would destroy him if they thought it could be done safely. His train had arrived after dark and he had registered at the St. James. Later he had strolled around to the American House and found that Erma and Joan were out. To pass the evening he dropped into the Tabor and saw a rising young dramatic star, Minnie Maddern, in *Fogg's Folly*. The play he voted trash but the girl in the lead both capable and charming.

In front of his hotel he met a tinhorn gambler named Charles Russ who had been driven out of Leadville with the Vinings in the cleanup. A dull flush of anger suffused the man's lean face.

"So you're here," he said bitterly.

"In person, Charley," Wallace admitted. He watched the fellow closely, uncertain how far his rage would take him.

"Maybe you have come to run us outa this town too."

"I don't throw that long a shadow." Cape spoke amiably, no edge to his words. He did not want any trouble if he could help it. "Whatever game you are playing I'm taking no chips in it."

"How do I know that? You're one of those meddlers who can't mind their own business." Russ finished with a string of scurrilous epithets.

Wallace waited silently till the man had ended, the eyes in his strongjawed face cold and hard. "Quite through?" he asked evenly.

Russ opened his mouth to begin again and closed it without saying a word. The anger faded out of his face. He was remembering the nights when Ukena and Heisman had died. Fear fluttered in his stomach.

"If so, get out of here — quick." Wallace snapped the last word out like the crack of a whip.

Russ turned and left hurriedly.

As soon as Wallace reached his room he took from a valise the revolver lying there beneath his shirts. He thought, *I'd better carry a pistol while I'm here. He'll run to the Vinings.*

The sun was shining brightly through the window when Cape awoke. After he had bathed and shaved he dressed with care. He did not call on Joan until it was nearly eleven o'clock.

Erma came into the parlor. "Joan will be down in a minute," she said. "You just got under the wire. We're leaving tomorrow."

He wished her a good run in Oregon, then asked her what Joan's plans were.

"She talks of teaching school," Erma told him. "I think she will make a good teacher. She likes children."

"Any news about her and Downing?" he asked. "I thought that might come to something."

She shook her head. "I hoped so, but she thought not. He asked her to marry him. Joan still isn't very happy. I wish I didn't have to leave her. I wanted her to come to Oregon with me, but she did not care to go."

"She will pick up an interest in life after a time," Cape said, not very confidently.

Erma slanted a long penetrating look at him. "I suppose you know she takes more interest in you than in anybody else."

"She has a sense of guilt and thinks I ought to have one too," he explained. "So she can talk with me freely."

"I believe you are in love with her," Erma said. "If so, let her know."

"She knows."

"Have you proposed to her?" the actress asked quickly.

"No." A wry whimsical smile touched his lips. "And I'm not going to, dear lady. She can do better than me."

Light footsteps sounded in the hall and Joan came into the room. She hesitated a moment at the door, shyly, then moved forward to shake hands with their guest. "I'm so glad you came," she said. "I was afraid you — wouldn't find it convenient to leave your ranch."

He held her hand, looking down into the girl's lovely face. He thought that illness had refined her beauty, given it a new spirituality, and his heart ached that it should be so, for it was born of pain and grief, and she was too young to have the bubbling gaiety in her quenched. The round full throat, the flat back, the slim perfectly poised figure she still had, but the unconscious cleancut pride had been chastened to a gentle humility.

They talked of trivial things and passing interests, her journey, his ranch, whether Erma would find the Oregon towns as friendly as the mining camps. But beneath the surface of their thoughts the wasted minutes held a deep significance. They were letting their chances of happiness slip away from them. A wild clamor of the blood stirred in her, but she repressed sternly any sign of it. She had forfeited her right to reach for joy.

Erma wanted to leave them alone, but she had promised Joan to stay. She did her best to bridge the conversational gaps with chatter. Cape asked them to join him for midday dinner at the Windsor and she accepted for Joan and herself. While they were in their room getting ready Joan reproached her.

"I don't want to go, dear," she protested. "I'm tired, and we don't seem to have anything to say to each other. Let me stay here while you go."

Very firmly Erma declined. "You're going too. He came to see you, not me. If you want my opinion you are both acting very silly. Apparently neither of you have a lick of sense. He thinks he isn't good enough for you because he has been a professional gambler and you think you aren't good enough for him because you got into trouble."

"Earlier in the week you were trying to marry me to Ted Downing," Joan answered with a flicker of spirit. "I suppose any man will do."

"I was wrong then, but I think this is the right one."

"Once you told me he was a gambler and I

ought to be careful about being seen with him, but now you feel I'm damaged goods and had better take what I can get."

"You know that isn't true," Erma protested indignantly. "It's only that I know Cape better now. He's a man to be proud of, and he has done a lot for you."

Repentant, Joan turned from the glass in front of which she was brushing her hair. "You make me say things I don't mean. He's fine. I like him — a lot. And I'm awf'ly grateful to him. It's just that I don't want ever to get married. Please understand, Erma."

"I understand that you are whipping yourself because you have made a mistake many other girls have made too. Some of them were strong enough to put it behind them and live full useful lives. Some crumpled up. I thought you had character."

Erma led the way to the parlor. She was glad she had lashed out at Joan. It was time somebody talked plainly to her.

Wallace had never been more unsure than he was while walking across town with Joan and Erma. He had felt strongly that she ought to return to the quiet staid life of her home town and blot out as much as she could the tragedy of her Leadville experience. But as he moved beside her, the enchantment of her gracious youth stirring in him, he wondered if he had made too much of the barrier his way of life had put between them. What she needed was someone who could bring summer back into her heart. Maybe Erma was right in thinking he was the one who could do it.

They were going into the Windsor when Cape caught a glimpse of a man ducking into a doorway. The man was Charles Russ. A chill ran up and down the spine of Wallace. He had no doubt the man was watching him for the Vinings. If so, it might be only a defensive move, to make sure he had not come to Denver with the intent of making trouble for them. Knowing that they were here on a not-too-firm probation, Quint would not be likely to start any fireworks. But there was a chance he would.

At dinner the talk dragged in spite of Erma's attempt to keep it going. Cape rallied to her, but Joan was too depressed to talk. In a few hours she would be homeward bound, carrying with her nothing but unhappy memories. They had reached the dessert before Erma decided to toss out a bomb and see what the effect of it would be.

"I knew two young people once who were in love with each other," she said. "They could have married and been happy except for a silly false pride. She had made a slip and built it up into a monument of sin. He kept silent because he had been in an unsavory business and did not want it to reflect on her. She needed him very much and I feel sure he wanted her. But since they were a pair of fools they went different ways. She withered and became a sour old maid and he an embittered bachelor. By the thinnest margin they missed a lovely life on account of their own stuffiness. Now if you'll excuse me I'll go back to the hotel and let you figure out who are these ninnies I am prophesying about."

Before Erma could rise a waiter stopped beside Cape. "Mr. Wallace?" he asked.

"Correct," replied Cape.

"Mr. Saul Willett from Leadville is in the bar and would like to speak with you, sir."

"Tell him I'll be there in a minute." After the waiter had gone Cape turned to Erma, a warm smile on his face. "I'm obliged, lady. You're absolutely right about one of us. I am going to call for a showdown. I'll be back after a word with the mayor. Don't either of you leave, please. When I return I promise not to be stuffy."

He rose, his gaze shifting to Joan. Into her pale cheeks the color was beating. Her eyes fell as he stood beside her for an instant, his hand resting on her shoulder with a gentle pressure of the fingers. Then he walked out of the room, straightbacked and strong.

Joan's eyes followed him. They were soft and shining. She said, almost in a murmur, "Oh Erma, how could you?"

Cape strolled into the bar, still filled with the elation of new hope flowing in him. He would not let her go home alone. He would make her see that whatever road she took it must be with him.

Abruptly he pulled up. Even before his swift glance swept the room he knew the pattern of the set-up as a familiar one. This was a trap. Ben Vining stood at the bar, his back to it, flushed with drink, eyes hot and angry. Charley Russ was in an opposite corner, so placed that Cape could not watch both of them at once. The bartender and the other two men in the room were not in the play. They did not know yet that there was going to be trouble.

Vining said harshly, "I hear you've come to drive us out of town — or maybe to murder us the way you did Ukena and Heisman."

"You've heard wrong." Wallace kept his voice low and even. "I'm here on strictly private business of my own."

Ben Vining slammed a fist down on the bar. "By God, that's something new. You're the worst meddler I ever knew."

Russ laughed. The gaze of Wallace shuttled to him.

"Don't be so unfriendly, Charley. Come over and join us."

"I'm all right where I'm at," Russ answered sulkily.

Cape did not raise his voice, but there was a hard edge to it. "I said come over here and stand by Vining."

"Now looky here, you got no right — "

The words of the tinhorn died away. He was staring at Wallace and he saw a faint rippling of the lithe body's muscles. He was not sure there had been the slightest movement, yet a warning had been flashed to him.

"All right," he added hastily. "Whatever you say." He shambled to the bar and joined his companion.

Through the open doorway leading to the pool room came a man in his shirt sleeves carrying a cue. Unaware of impending trouble he moved to the bar close to Vining.

"I'll take a rye straight," he said.

The bartender paid no attention to the order. His fascinated eyes were on the three men who had taken the center of the stage.

One of the other customers was vanishing into the hotel lobby. His drinking mate still sat at the table they had occupied. This little flare up, he guessed, would not run to shooting.

"I mentioned a rye," the man with the cue suggested.

Vining said, "We ought to have bumped you off long ago."

"You can't blame yourself for not trying," Wallace retorted. "It's too late now."

"So you think."

The coatless man said, "Say, what's this anyhow?" There was alarm in his voice. His anxious glance shifted from one to another, then to the doorway through which he had just walked so carelessly. It was not more than eight or nine yards away but it looked as far as Chicago, for to reach it he would have to pass through a line of fire if trouble was as near as he feared. It was plain to him that Vining was in an uncontrollable rage. His right hand was hovering close to the butt of the gun hanging in the holster under his coat.

"Take it easy, Ben," drawled Cape. "Quint won't like it if you start anything in broad daylight. You know the Vining rule — shots in the dark from an alley."

That he had never been in greater danger in his gusty lifetime Cape knew. Ben was beyond thinking of consequences. For him the hour had struck. The clock pendulum back of the bar would not swing a dozen times before his gun would be blazing. Cape had moved forward and was not three steps from him. He could not miss.

"You pack a gun, fellow," Ben taunted. "Don't you ever use it?"

Cape read his mind. He wanted to drive his victim to reach for a weapon. By the time it was in the open it would be too late. There was no sign in the impassive face of Wallace that invisible fingers were clawing his stomach muscles into a tight icy knot.

He said quietly. "Forget that gun talk, Ben."

"You're huntin' trouble and you've found it," Vining cried.

His weapon swept out. The pool player fell back and flung up his arm to protect himself. The end of the cue struck Vining's wrist as his finger crooked and knocked the barrel up. Cape was already diving at his enemy when the bullet slapped his shoulder. It did not stop him. The weight of his driving body slammed Vining against the bar. His hand closed on the hairy wrist a few inches above the revolver. A second bullet crashed into the face of the clock. The closely locked figures slid along the mahogany and went down together. Vining's hand scraped hard against the metal foot rail and the gun went skittering across the shiny floor. The bodies of the struggling men tossed and heaved, rolling over and over as each fought to get astride of the other and pin him down. Vining was the heavier and the more powerful. In his favor Wallace had youth, agility, and a stamina not depleted by dissipation. Ben found a throat hold, but Cape whirled him over and hammered his head against a brass spittoon. A groping thumb jabbed savagely at Cape's eye. Their threshing limbs moved so fast and so violently that neither one could gain a hold. It came to Cape that this could not last long. The loss of blood from the shoulder wound was sapping his strength.

Russ had his revolver out, waiting for a chance at Wallace as the lurching bodies writhed to and fro. The bartender was an old-timer who had quelled a dozen brawls and knew exactly what to do. He leaned across the bar and brought a bottle down hard on the head of Russ. The man's knees sagged and he went to the floor. With the bottle still in his hand the barkeeper ran around the corner, picked up the two weapons that had been dropped, and pushed them into the hands of the pool player who stood frozen in his tracks. A moment later the bottle descended with a thud on Vining's skull. The fellow's arms released their hold on Wallace. His body relaxed and he rolled over against the foot rail. Though dazed by the blow, he tried to scramble to his feet. The bottle hit him again and he went out.

A passing policeman, drawn by the sound of the shots, came running into the room. He saw three men on the floor, one of them bleeding from a gunshot wound. His glance shot to the bartender.

"Who's to blame for the massacre, Mickey?" he demanded.

Mickey told him what had occurred.

"So the Vining crowd are starting to hurrah this town too," the officer said. "We've got our orders about these birds. They'll have a sweet time explaining this."

The sound of two shots in quick succession startled Joan. She rose and looked at Erma, the color washing from her cheeks. The firing was inside the hotel.

Erma had heard too many casual shots boom down Chestnut Street to be much alarmed. "Somebody loaded with too much tanglefoot celebrating," she suggested.

A waiter disappeared into the lobby. He

came back presently with news he could not keep to himself.

"Two fellows have shot your friend in the barroom," he told Erma.

Joan caught at the back of the chair to steady herself. Her heart was pounding like a hammer. She ran into the lobby and across it to the barroom. A man tried to stop her from entering but she tore her arm from his grasp and dodged forward in and out among the crowding men. Two men handcuffed together were being taken away by a policeman. Her glance fell on Cape Wallace standing by the bar, his forearm resting on it. His waistcoat was soggy with blood.

He waved a hand to her and grinned. "Everything all right. Nothing but a scratch. No need to worry." But he clung to the bar for support.

She put an arm around his waist and gave sharp orders. "Somebody get a doctor. And carry him to the billiard table." Her worried eyes fell on Erma coming toward them. "Arrange at the desk to get him a room, dear."

"It's only a little pill in the shoulder, honey," Cape protested. "Nothing to make a fuss about."

He walked into the billiard room without any help and sat down in a chair. A doctor came and dressed the wound. Cape wanted to go back to his own hotel but Joan would not have it that way. Erma had secured a room for him here and he could get to bed at once.

Cape's grin was a little sly. "But I'm not going to bed," he said. "It isn't night yet."

"The young lady is right," the doctor snapped. "Bed is where you belong for a day or two."

"Of course it is," Joan agreed sharply.

"How about letting me and this young lady talk it over alone, doctor?" Cape suggested.

"We can do that after you are in bed," Joan urged.

He answered her with one decisive word. "Now."

Erma laughed. "I know a stubborn man when I see one. Better give him his way this time, Joan."

As soon as they were alone Cape said with mock sternness, "What right have you to start bossing me, young lady?"

Color streamed into her cheeks. "It's just common sense when you are wounded —"

He interrupted. "You haven't answered my question. Why?"

Joan's breath came faster. She felt a disturbing weakness stealing through her. "Be good, Cape," she begged. "The room is full of people watching us. Later we can talk."

"We won't have time later. You'll have to start packing for your journey. We'll talk while we have a chance." He leaned back lazily, the smile on his sardonic face tender and derisive. "There's warm color in that lovely face. You look almost like a girl in love and not like a plaster saint with wings sprouting."

"Cape," she said, almost in a whisper. "Everybody is looking at us."

"Can you blame them? It isn't often they see the most beautiful girl west of the river proposing to a man."

"Please," she implored, "I'm — embarrassed."

"She either fears her fate too much," he misquoted.

"You're taking advantage of me," she charged.

"Of course I am. A man desperately wounded has his privileges. You either have a right to boss me or you haven't. Which is it?"

His eyes, challenging and eager, held hers during the long moment of decision. He was offering her a life gay and exciting, the gambling chance in it minimized by her assurance that there was a core of hard fine decency in him. A heat of gladness flooded her. She knew he was the one man in the world she wanted.

A lovely smile lit her face. "I'll not go home tomorrow," she told him. "I'll stay with you —- if you want me."

"I want you," he said. "Seal the bargain before witnesses."

Disregarding the group at the far end of the room, she leaned forward and kissed his lips.

THORNDIKE PRESS HOPES you have enjoyed this Large Print book. All our Large Print titles are designed for the easiest reading, and all our books are made to last. Other Thorndike Press Large Print books are available at your library, through selected bookstores, or directly from the publisher. For more information about current and upcoming titles, please call us, toll free, at 1-800-223-6121, or mail your name and address to:

THORNDIKE PRESS
P. O. BOX 159
THORNDIKE, MAINE 04986

There is no obligation, of course.